When Love Passes By

A Ayisha Sultana

ISBN 979-8-89026-435-0

Secrets make the relationship apart if the person knows about it or make it closer if it is a good one. I never kept any secrets from my beloved ones, I always disclosed them.

I dislike people who keep hiding it from me, doesn't mean I hate them. I will understand it if they are honest with me, even if the words are harsh to handle for me. At least I will know they are not forged in loving me or hating me, I will consider it as being realistic. I have always been frank with everybody even with someone who went against me.

But this time, I have to keep furtive to save my relationship with my husband. Secret that he had hidden from me, now I know about it. He would be devastated that I know his past even when he doesn't want me to. My head is aching to think about the event, his face filled with shock and pain; I don't know what he will think about me.

Keeping apart the event, I should never reveal anything about it to anybody. Now I know why people carry on secrets, it makes you keep other people safe, especially loved ones. If I was in his shoes, I would have taken time to bare it or not at all.

Contents

Chapter 1

The Argument

It was a rainy day in the month of September, I was working at my desk doing paperwork and looking at the watch I was wearing, it was quarter to 6 pm. I was waiting to strike 6, to relieve myself from work and reach home early as possible. It is hard in the rainy season to catch an auto or bus in the city of Chennai, auto people always hike the price for a ride and buses come later than the usual time. The hard part is that you are drenched in water even when you have an umbrella that covers only the head and a foul smell comes from your body.

I left the Office at 6.05 pm even though it was still raining. I took an auto to reach home. It is 5 km away from my office. When I reached home, I saw my father is watching T.V. as usual in the entrance hall giving me a quick look as if he didn't care and my mother was cooking in the kitchen.

I said to her, "Ma, Please stop cooking. I told you I'll come home and cook every day."

She replied with a smile, “I know. But it is raining outside and you will be coming home with wet clothes and a tired look on your face. You work so hard in the office and I don’t want you to look weary after cooking.”

I gesture my hand towards her to hand over the ladle to me and begin the work of her but she pushed me slightly with her elbow and said, “I finished cooking, this is the last one. Now, go and freshen up.”

As mother said, she had cooked rice, papad, and shallow fried cauliflower side dish except for the gravy.

“I told you not to cook, last week you did the cooking even when I begged not to,” I said sternly.

“Cooking doesn’t make me tired at all, dear. Besides, cooking is not even a tough job.” She said.

“I know that cooking is not a hard job for you. The oil you put in the gravy and side dish is too much compared to my way of cooking. Can’t you understand that oily food is not good for your health?” I reminded her.

“I know, I know. The Doctor said to me to avoid fast food and food soaked in oil doesn’t mean I cannot eat once in a while. Don’t try to be my doctor, Leena. Go and call your father, food is ready,” I heard the irritation in her voice when she said those words.

“Do you know what, it is tough to convince you? Do whatever you want to do.” I said wryly leaving the Kitchen, “And by the way, Hi! Good Evening.”

“I have never seen a girl arguing first then wishing me later. It works the other way,” She replied and grinned at me.

“Maybe I was born different,” I winked at her while standing at the kitchen entrance.

Dinner was always alike, Father watching the news on television, Mother asking how my day was in the office. And I repeat the boring work stuff that happened in the office. I wonder if there are any other questions Mother asked besides this. I requested Father to change the television channel, he replied without looking at me that he would give me the remote after a few minutes until his dinner is over.

We live in One thousand one hundred square feet house that includes two bedrooms with an attached bathroom, a rectangle-shaped hall with a balcony, and a kitchen. The second floor was built the same as we are living on the first floor and the Ground floor is intended for Commercial warehouse for rent. My father bought the plot and built this house when I was 8. Mother helped him build this house by lending him half of the jewels. That makes her half of the Property Owner, but Father was cunning. He became the sole owner of the house by Registration without sharing it with my Mother.

I detested my father for not being impartial with his wife. He was not only unfair in house matters, but in other things too. I thought about how mother was trapped with this man in marriage. Maybe she didn't see it coming. If I was in her position, I would have divorced him early.

I constantly asked her why she didn't leave him. She told me she lived in a time when divorce was treated as taboo in society; even if she was divorced other men would approach her. She was most concerned about me. It could have affected my future as well.

Setting aside these thoughts, I finished dinner and started clearing the dining table. I gave her the medicine prescribed by the doctor.

Mother looked like me, apart from the light wheatish color and body features; broad shoulders and hip, long hands, few wrinkles on her face, and a little curvy due to eating oily fat food. Her height is about 5 feet 6 inches.

I always envied my mother's height. Though mother told me my height is 5 feet 3 inches which are enough but I considered myself below average. My body is lean, which will lead to men's admiring comments; not athletic.

Nothing new was on the channel; the same Saas-Bahu serial, the repetitive movies. I used to like the serial when I was 10 years younger than now. They are repeating the same shit again and again. I shut off the television and went to my room to browse the internet.

My room is small compared to my parents with a queen size bed next to the window facing east, a mahogany two-tier bookshelf with a bottom cabinet next to a computer desk, an attached wardrobe, and a dressing table with a mirror on it.

After a few moments, mother knocked on the door, "Leena, Please open the door."

I sauntered towards the door and opened it, "what is it, Ma?" I asked.

"Are you busy?" she inquired.

"No," I replied.

"Umm, I have come here to talk about the Matrimony Alliance," She hesitated a bit.

"What? For whom," I questioned her while sitting on the computer desk chair and mother sat on the bed.

"For you, who else is there in this house?" She replied with delight.

Before she could say anything, I Interrupted, "Ma, I told you I don't want to get married. Marriage is not my cup of tea."

"See, I know that you don't want to get married. Listen to the Groom's Profile at least. It is a good one," She pleaded to me as a child begging for a toy in a shop.

"Please don't persuade me to change my mind about this. I have seen many Grooms and their Parents. Their biases, arrogance, and shameless approach have made me cringe towards them. And I know from that very moment, men are not like they used to be before the 21st century. Men are not loving, Funny; indulge in selfless acts these days without expecting anything in return," I said it with a breath.

"All men are not like that. Look at your father," She stopped.

"What?" I gave her a "are you kidding me" look.

"Sorry, look at your Father's brother. Isn't he a good man? All time caring and thoughtful about his family and others around him," she said to convince me.

"Yeah, like I said he was born before the 21st century. I am talking about this today's century," I said, rolling my eyes.

"Hmm," she stopped for a minute to think and I was thinking about what was in her head to divert me from the opinion.

"Listen," She coughed and commented, "Don't blame men only; even girls are competing with men in bad things."

"Like what?" I inquired.

"I mean like hanging out with men without their parent's awareness, going out and working at the time of curfew, etc," She replied firmly.

"Ma, don't hold women to blame. Every woman has a right to live and choose their partner. Do men tell their parents that they are hanging out with their girlfriends? Women work at night to provide shelter and sustenance for their families. They are fighting for their rights, doesn't mean they are terrible. Do you think I am a bad girl, if you think I am a terrible person then you should never let me marry a good boy?" I said with fake glee on my face. I never thought she as a woman would express these things.

"No, you are not. I don't have any intention to argue with you. I just wish for you to settle down with a man and have children. If you have any thoughts of being with a woman than a man, then," She said with hesitation.

"What do you mean?" I asked without looking at her.

She cleared her throat as if she was ready to give her speech, "I mean if you have any intention to live with a woman than with a man, you can tell me."

I am stunned to hear this from her, all I could say was, "Wow," I have no idea for how long she has wanted to ask me this question, maybe because my constant rejection of marrying a man made her want to know about it.

I always liked girl companionship, doesn't mean I am sexually attracted to them.

My astonishment turned to amusement and I was curious about what would be her reaction when I tease her that I am interested in other girls, though it is just for entertainment to see her face.

"Leena, What are you thinking?" She interrupted my thought.

"Okay, umm what will you do if I am like that kind of girl you are considering?" I told her pretending that I am lesbian. However, I couldn't hide my smile.

"Are you serious about what you are saying?" She asked hesitatingly and expecting me to say 'no' about the topic.

I nodded spontaneously at her for response and gauging over the things she had not anticipated. She was silent for a few minutes and said, "I think it is just a phase and you will get over it when you see a therapist. It has been caused due to work stress resulting in mental stability to choose such kind of Orientation or hanging out with girls all the time made you choose that companionship.

I don't understand what got into you for being like this. Have you given any thought to what people might say about you and your family? They will always question the parent's upbringing and your father will blame me only for turning you..."

I have to interrupt her before she can go on and on about me, “Ma, Don’t be so dramatic. I am just pulling your leg. I would like to see the consequences of what you might think.”

“What? Are you sure?” She is not convinced about it, ensuring I was meaning it.

“Yes. I was kidding with you,” I beamed at her. She reciprocated the same for a few seconds; and then her face turned to an angry bird and yelled at me, “It’s not good to irritate your mother like that. I will get a second heart stroke because of your Idiotic fun.”

“I am sorry for playing a game with you. I didn’t mean to cause any pain,” I assured her. She widens her smile by apologizing to her; she immediately forgives the person who asks for sorry. She is a broad-minded woman, though she doesn’t adapt to changes regarding sexuality. I don’t blame her as she has lived in Orthodox society.

Thus it is clear enough to make her realize that I am straight. She inhaled a huge breath and I noticed her relief.

She said feebly, “I can tell that you don’t desire marriage as other people do. Your father will not be bothered nor take care of you if anything happens to me. After your father is dead, you will be all alone in this house without a family of your own. Don’t you need children to spend your life with? As I am aware, you love children.”

I was looking sideways to get rid of this topic, and I can make out that she will not leave me alone in my room unless I say yes; which I am not willing to do.

She never troubles me except for the marriage proposal, perhaps she believes that I have reached the point of age to get married or no one will accept me if it extends beyond that age.

That was obvious for people who live in this country. She was waiting for me to respond. Before I could say anything, I have to make up my brain to elude this matter.

"I know you worry about me, but this is not the life I wanted. Besides children, I had made some plans to adopt them, perhaps one child is enough," I mumbled without thinking.

Words were ringing through my head, did I say this? The idea about the adoption came a few months before, though I never realized that I would be saying it to her.

Before I can delve into my mind, I have to look at mother's face. Her look didn't reveal anything away, it was quite blank.

"Are you crazy to think about adoption? You simply can't go into the Child Welfare trust and adopt the child as if buying things in a shopping mall. There are some rules to be followed by a person to be fit Physically, mentally, and financially stable. You need a partner even if you are planning on it," She explained hastily as if she is thorough about it.

"Really," I questioned her, "But I heard single parent is enough to take care of a child."

"Look Leena, Adopting and nurturing a child by a single parent is not a child's game. You need a partner to go with it. By the way, why did you consider adoption? Is it due to not finding a husband?" She was searching my eyes to get an answer from it.

However, when I get away from this husband thing it turns around to annoy me. Anger was rising in my blood for this unceasing situation.

This time I will not at all tolerate this issue, "Ma, why I considered adoption because I don't want a husband. I never want to turn out like you, being stuck in your marriage. Tell me one thing, what benefit have you got from marrying Father or what profit is there in marrying? It is a social norm to pressurize men and women to get wed and stay in neglectful adversity." I almost yelled at her.

Her face became shocked; she had not anticipated something coming from my mouth while I was the one who put balm on her grief and misfortune. Her tears are about to come out but she forces them back.

We rarely bicker over things only if the matter is so extreme. It made me uncomfortable to influence such pain on her by telling her about her failed marriage and living in it.

"Ma, I never meant it. I said it in a careless state, don't take me wrong. I am sorry," I pleaded slowly.

"It is fine. I expect that you will understand me. I am finding a way to make you help in establishing yourself without my fear that you end up alone," She said.

Her face became extremely vulnerable for a moment. She was about to say something before she rose; moved slowly towards the door and stood on the threshold, turned to look at me.

"I think I am done convincing you. Do whatever you want," Her words were dry but her face was hurt. She left me alone in the room and I took a few minutes to shut the door.

As I was trying to push away the guilt, I could feel tiny tears coming out of my eyes. I was so mad at her that I couldn't control the emotions.

There is a problem with me, I cry after I show anger towards people as if I have committed a fault. I have seen many people when getting angry, they don't even reveal any remorse for hurting anybody.

I am not interested in browsing the internet. So, I shut down the computer, went to bed early, and tucked myself with a blanket. The room was giving me an empty buzz; I could hear clearly outside the drizzling water hitting the ground from the clouds. This night didn't go well; maybe tomorrow will be a good day.

I got up at half past one; I heard the hard banging on the door and it was father calling out my name to open the door. I rose immediately; switched on the light and went to open it.

“Are you awake? Your Mother is not feeling good. I think it is the Heart attack again," He told me hastily.

“What?” I quickly went to the parent’s room; I could see that mother was whimpering over the pain, clasping hardly any pillow in her left hand and holding middle chest in her right hand. I panicked and I told her to lie down on her right side as it puts less pressure on her heart. I immediately called the Ambulance.

It was 3 pm and I was waiting outside the Emergency room. I was yawning again and again because of a lack of sleep. I could feel my skin become rough due to crying, and the tears dried out. Father went to buy some medicine prescribed by the Doctor. The hall in the Hospital was quiet; I could see a few people sleeping in the visitor’s long chair side by side across the corner. I felt comfortable seeing people in this hall alone.

The Doctor came out from the Emergency room along with two nurses. I got up from the chair to ask, “Hello, Doctor! How is the Mother now? Is she alright?”

“It is nothing to worry about for now. It is another attack like last time but mild. Has she been sleeping on the left side of her body?” the Doctor inquired.

“Yes... Sometimes,” I said sheepishly.

“Well, you have to advise her to sleep on the right side to avoid such complications in the future. Sleeping on the left side puts pressure on the heart and chest. What did she have for dinner yesterday?” The Doctor questioned me again sternly.

“She had rice, vegetable gravy, papad, and fried cauliflower,” I replied in a hoarse tone. The doctor raised one eyebrow making me feel regretful.

“You have to suggest that she stop eating fried food too. She has to follow the diet summary to maintain her health. Have you got the summary before?” He reminded me.

"Yes, Doctor. You gave us while leaving the hospital last time," I was feeling guilty for utter nonsense to allow her to eat oily food even when I read her summary which has the perfect diet plan.

"Excuse Me, Miss," The doctor interrupted my thought.

"Yes, Doctor," I asked anxiously.

"As I was saying that about the diet plan which is not enough. Most of all, A Patient with heart disease must not be bothered by pressure, stress, and rigidness in moving around. She has to feel light, make her do some exercise, or recommend joining the happy club." The Doctor gave me some hints to keep away from such an attack.

"Okay Doctor, I'll make sure that she starts doing exercises. When should I discharge her?" I asked hesitantly.

"First, we have to shift her from the Emergency room to the Patient room within a few hours. We will see for a day how her health will be. If she does not feel any kind of pain again, then you can discharge her from the hospital," His voice became gentle when he is telling me these instructions.

"Thank you. Doctor Ravi," I beamed at him for a second and asked him politely, "Shall I see her now?"

"Of course, you may. But don't interrupt her sleep," He said cautiously and stopped me, "Keep in mind. Don't stress her for any reason; she might hyperventilate which is not good for her."

"Okay Doctor, I'll keep it in mind," I assured him.

The Doctor left the corridor along with one nurse. As I was about to enter the Emergency room to meet my Mother, another Nurse called out, "Miss, have you bought the medical items prescribed by the doctor?"

"No, Sister. But my Father went to buy it. He might be on the way," I replied her.

"Okay! Please meet me in the Nurse's ward when you have the items. It is next to the Reception," Her face was stiff and gloomy when I noticed her; probably working a night shift made her look like that.

"I will," I assured her.

She left the corridor gracefully and after a few seconds, I could see Father was returning with the medical supply.

"Is the doctor left? How is your Mother now?" He asked in an anxious tone.

I told him what the Doctor said and I could see father was tired as well undergoing all the duties to bring his wife here. He is a man with a few responsibilities to undertake, if we pour more tasks; he becomes sulkier. It is not that he is getting old; I have seen him my entire childhood till now how he used to put household and outside errands upon his wife. Apart from this, she worked in a beauty parlor as a beautician for 18-19 years. Though I am grateful to him for helping me today; that is enough for now.

"Papa, I think you are sleepy. You can go and lie down in a visitor's chair," I advised him with a sense of care.

"Okay. I will lie down for a few hours. Wake me up if you need anything," He said wryly, handing me the bag full of syringes and chemical bottles. He directly went towards the empty visitor's chair.

I get furious about his behavior that he doesn't have any urges to meet his wife for a minute. When I entered the Emergency room, a room with four beds separated by long curtains; saw a middle-aged nurse dumping the used medical bottles and syringes in the basket. She smiled at me and asked, "Are you her daughter?"

"Yes, I am. How is she doing now?" I asked her in a low voice while I was standing near my mother's bed. Her breath was harmonious to hear, and I think she is dreaming of something pleasant.

"She is good and sleeping. We never allow people in here apart from Doctors and Nurses. Since there is no other patient in this room, I will allow you for a few minutes only. Are those the medicines prescribed by the Doctor?" She questioned me eyeing the bag.

"Yes, It is. The other nurse told me to remind her when it is bought. I'll go and bring her after a few minutes," I guaranteed her.

"No need to worry about that, I'll call her from here," She smiled and dialed the extension number of the Nurse Wardroom and requested her to come to the Emergency room.

While she was doing her work, I concentrated on mother; thinking about the situation that happened a few hours before and how she was going through pain. Last time, she had to use an Oxygen mask to breathe and I am glad that she is sleeping now blissfully without it. I have to be thorough about something that must not cause any stress leading to an attack. I know in my heart that she is the only person I have ever loved so dearly.

"Excuse Me, Miss! I think you should leave her now to rest," She broke up the thought, alarming me to leave the room. Another Nurse has already entered the room to do her job. I have no intention to leave the room but I have to follow the rules.

"We will call you when it is necessary," She convinced me to leave the room.

"Okay! By the way, thank you," I told her while I am departing; the corridor was unusually silent, apart from the breathing and snoring of the people.

I sat in a long empty visitors chair next to father; I could feel my head aching and my body shivering due to the cold weather caused by the rain. I am longing for some tea or coffee to relax; probably I need some rest. It is better if I close my eyes for a few hours.

Chapter 2

Reviving

I slept for a few hours which made me feel better but still, there is some tiredness in my body. When I woke up staring out the window; the rain had stopped and the clouds started clearing away, letting the sunshine. The Cold was still there to give me shivers which reminded me to have some Tea or Coffee. Before I depart to the cafeteria, I went to the Nurse's room; there was one Nurse available who was sitting on a chair leaning on the table doing her paperwork. I asked her about my mother's health, to which she replied she is sleeping and will shift the room once she woke up.

I went to the Hospital Canteen and asked the Attendant to give me two cups of hot coffee. The Attendant informed me that beverages are not yet prepared; after fifteen minutes it will be ready. I saw my watch, it was 6.40 AM. I thought I cannot wait here long; gone to check if Father woke up or not. Else I must drink two cups of coffee all by myself which is not good for the stomach.

I went towards father's visitor's chair, trying to wake him up, and asked about the coffee and whether he wanted it or not. Father obviously said he really needed coffee, why would I even ask him? It is a habit of his to drink tea or coffee in the early morning. It is just that I am very much dwelled on mother's health; seemed to forget about other things.

Father and I had breakfast together in the canteen at 8.08 AM, Mother's breakfast will be provided by the nurse according to the Doctor's suggestion until the patient is shifted. Mother woke up around 8.30 AM; I hope she feels better now.

I asked her worriedly, "Hi Mom. How are you feeling now?"

She gave me a quick smile, "I am fine." She tried to get up from her bed. Before she strains herself more, I told her to lie in bed for a few hours. She obeyed me without any question. I told her how sorry I am for behaving yesterday; for which she has forgiven me already.

One of the Nurses called me to go to the Reception area to talk about moving the patient to which ward; I went towards the Reception. The Receptionist handed me the laminated paper of the bedroom price list. I asked the Receptionist for shared bedroom availability; for which she said it is vacant.

The procedure of shifting has been completed and the Nurse instructed her staff to bring breakfast for the Patient. The room with the attached bathroom was located in the middle of the corridor on the first floor much near the elevator; this room was painted with light cream and dark crimson windows border as were the long curtains and bed sheet which has hospital logo on it. There were two separate beds in between long curtains along with two small beds for Patient attendants or relative beds as I can say; next to Patient beds were two medical instrument tables and I.V stands. The other patient's bed is empty which is good that there will be no disturbance. The Staff brought the food tray, placed it on the table, and left.

I could see that she was not satisfied with the food she was having for breakfast; everything was boiled. She was giving me a criticizing look at the food.

“Can I have some Pickles?” she asked me cautiously.

“Ma, are you out of your mind? You know that you can’t have oily food. Besides, this food doesn’t look bad,” I ordered her.

“You eat it if you find this food delicious. I will not eat boiled food,” She scowled.

“Please eat it,” I told her politely. She reluctantly took one bite of green vegetables to which she gave me a sickening expression.

“Yuck! There is no salt in it,” She criticized the food.

“What? Let me check,” I took one small piece of the vegetable, and nibbled slowly.

“Food is perfectly good; the taste changes in your mouth because of medical drips. It will get better later,” I insisted.

She knows that she has no choice but to compellingly surrender; she was eating every spoon slowly. Her way of eating reminded me of children scowling at the vegetables; to which I cannot hide the smile.

Mother noticed my smile and raised her eyebrows, “Why are you smiling?”

“Nothing, it's just you made me remind of children who hate vegetables,” I told her conveniently. She smirked at me taking another bite.

I stared at the clock, it showed 9.40 AM. It is time for me to call the office and inform them about taking leave today. I quickly dialed the office landline through my mobile.

“Hello! Is this Ridhima?” I asked.

"Yes, who am I talking to?" Ridhima said.

"I am Leena. Can you transfer the line to the HR Manager?" I requested.

"Yes sure." I was enjoying the Piano tune of the landline while the Receptionist of the office transferred the call.

"Who are you talking to?" Mother interrupted.

"I have called my office," I informed her. I showed her stop hand gesture before she could disturb me further and the line has been connected to HR Manager, Mr. Vivek.

"Good Morning, I am Leena speaking. I called you regarding that I won't attend the office today," I said.

"What is the reason, Ms. Leena?" He questioned me firmly.

"Well, my Mother is admitted to the hospital due to heart pain," I told him slowly.

"Oh! Is it serious?" His voice changed from sternness to a concerned tone, I could hear his voice shaking a bit.

"No, she is fine now. Can you hand over the work schedule for today to Mrs. Raheela, she will take care of it on my behalf," I informed him.

"Ok, is there anything else?" His voice became stern again, probably after I told him the matter was clear.

"No, just tell her to call me for any information," I said. He disconnected the call; Mr. Vivek has always been tough with his Colleagues especially me, Mrs. Raheela & a few others; though the news made him slightly worried, which I never expected from him. It may be due to a situation like a hospital thing that happened a second time with Mother this year.

"Why did you call the office? You should have gone today. See, I am alright now. Why are you taking leave unnecessarily?" Mother intruded my thoughts.

"Yes, I can see that. But why take risks? When I am gone to the office, you will eat Pickle or some other heavy food behind my back," I teased her.

"Don't talk rubbish! How can I eat such food surrounded by Doctors and Nurses?" She reminded me that I am ridiculous to say it.

"I know about you; you will always find a way to eat while I am gone," I was accurate that she would not keep away from oily food. Last time, she ate Bread Pakoda while I was not in the hospital on the third day. I don't quite understand why she craves such things which are not healthy for her.

Father entered the room relieved to see his wife having breakfast and sat down beside me. I am happy to see that he cares for his wife sometimes, though he is not a Poignant person. I know that he takes other people's physical condition seriously when it is extremely dangerous.

"How are you now?" He asked mother, astounding me.

"I am fine," she replied back while taking food.

"Good. This room looks nice; last time the room was better. Why have you not booked there?" He asked me narrowly.

"You mean to say 'the General ward'?" I questioned him.

"Yes," He replied.

"No I think this is best for Mother," I told him, literally avoiding his stare.

I preferred Mother to stay in a shared bedroom, which is safe according to the mother's health.

If the mother comes to know about the charges, she would insist me to shift to the General ward, which is not good for her condition. There will be many patients in one big room and their visitors will not stop talking. Obviously, I cannot shut everybody's mouth to keep her calm. I still remember my last experience in General Ward which made her restless.

"How much is the cost of this room," He asked me in a low voice.

"Why do you want to know?" I inquired him.

"I am just curious," He shrugged.

"Ok don't tell mother. It cost Rs.3900 per day," I told him unthinkingly.

"What are you saying this room cost Rs.3900?" he shouted at me, making me jump.

Mother heard this giving me a shocked look; this makes me feel how stupidly I told my Father the truth. I thought at this moment I can trust him but he is always ready to stomp on a ray of hope.

"What are you saying, Leena? Is it true?" she asked me, still her face looks terrible.

"Yes," I said slowly, regretting the moment I told father about it.

"Are you stupid to spend money on hospital bills? You know I am ready to stay in the General ward. Please call the Nurse to change the room," she requested.

"Ma, Please I want you to stay here which is good for you," I pleaded with her.

"No dear, it is out of our budget. If we spend so much money on this room; think about the other bills like doctor fees, and medical charges," she reminded me.

"Ma, we can afford this and it comes under our budget only," I interrupted her and turned toward father furiously, "Are you happy now? I told you not to tell her. She is getting hyper now because of you. Do you have any concern at all about her?" I scolded him.

"Why are you angry at me? We should be angry at you for taking decisions without informing us," he yelled back as if I have done an inappropriate thing.

I exhaled myself and turned toward her, "Ma, all the cost of the beds has been increased. So, I thought it is better to put you in a shared bedroom."

"Really, how much is the cost of the General ward now," she eagerly asked me.

"It is Rs.2500 per day," I told her the exact amount I had seen in the bedroom price list.

"It was Rs.1700 per day last time. How could they increase so much within a few months?" she asked me. Mother always becomes tense when something unusual happens. For me, it is not a big deal to worry about it.

"Shared bedroom rate has not increased, that's why I selected this bedroom instead of the wardroom. Ma, now leave this topic and concentrate on your health first," I advised her to stay calm for her benefit.

"Oh!" she said "Ok! Then there is no problem for me. It's just 1400 rupees difference," I love her when she calms all by herself. I know that she has the strength to make herself change from edgy to relax.

"No. It is still costly. I think if we change it to the wardroom before they start charging us for this room," Father as usual always find some flaws in every decision we make.

"It is better if we stay here and I don't want to drag her from one place to another," I told him without looking.

"I don't think it is a good idea about staying here. We don't know how much will it cost for the other bills," he again interrupted me flaunting his stupid idea.

"Papa, Will you come outside for a minute?" I could not handle his repeated argument about the money; I left the room and realized that he might be following me but still he was inside the room. I know that he will not come outside to get scolded by me; I went into the room and gave him a reproached look to come outside.

Finally, he came outside and I began, "What is wrong with you? Do you have any fear that she might go into pain again? All you think about is money and expenses," I told him angrily.

"You are saying this now. When the last days of the month end, you and your mother are always whining about the money," he was stiff with his words when he expressed it.

"You know why we whine about it. It is because of you, because of your stupid, no-use extravagant expenses," I told him without gasping for air.

"You always take that topic to make me shut up. I am advising you as a father, to make it less expensive by changing the room," he pleaded but still his voice was firm.

"It is not costly according to me; we will handle it if you just support me and mother," My voice became smooth when I said the last sentence expecting some goodness from him.

"You are saying because you have a job; you will start caring about the money when you don't have it. You will regret it when it is too late," I knew what his answer would be; it is foolish to think that I might be wrong.

"No, I won't regret it. I am aware of how to take care of the money even when I don't have a job," I rebelled against him.

"Tell me, how?" I could hear his words both tormenting me and pleasure in him; he never stopped bullying me through his comment.

"I am not in a mood to tell the person who has no regard for people when he had a job," I know how to hurt him but this won't affect him at all. He will and as usual stick to his own point.

"Women always turn out to be egoistic when they earn money," he commented again.

"No, Papa. I just have a glimpse of ego from you; you are the head of the ego. Proud and stubbornness run through your veins; so is mine," I revealed what he wanted to hear from me; I had no interest in what he thought about me. I stared at him for a few moments and left the corridor to be with mother.

As I recall his face turned angry and shocked as I said those words to hurt him but it haunts me back more to treat Father like that. Not every child wants to disrespect or hurt their Parents this way. I heard him leaving the corridor straight to the stairs and I sat on the edge of Mother's bed.

"What is it? Where is your father?" she asked me.

"He left, I think. Maybe he went to the canteen to drink more tea," I told her about the argument that happened between me and father in the corridor. She never gave me an irritated reaction on the subject of my behavior toward him.

"Do you think I was overreacting toward him?" I asked her for advice about why I felt guilty about my actions.

"No dear. You treated him well; I know how he gets on our nerves. He didn't even ask me how I was feeling; though his word was only to commence conversation to find the cost for the room from you," She reminded me about the scenario that just happened a few quarters ago; I have never thought about that though mother was clever and knew what he wanted. She spent 29 years with him and she has more experience than me regarding his habit.

"I thought for a moment that he started caring for you when he said those kind words," my heart was sobbing to think his manners have not changed even when his wife was in this situation the second time.

"Don't think about him. He will never change nor regret his actions," She suggested it to me when she saw the pain on my face. I couldn't hide my feelings in which both eyes revealed tears.

"Don't cry for him. I have cried and begged to which he has not even cared. And I don't want you to cry and expect him to change. He will always be a cold-hearted man," She was right about him and I should put the thoughts about something else other than his action.

The Nurse came into the room after half an hour and checked all tubes attached to the mother; the pain relief medical drug bottle hanging on the IV stand which has ended replacing with the new one. She informed me that the Doctor will be around at 11.30 am to check on the Patient and left.

As minutes passed, we were joking about the situation that happened in the office, about the colleagues, about the embarrassing moments, etc. Mother was laughing hysterically through the continuous jokes which we are feeling good about; to relax her which she rarely does it.

As the Nurse said that the Doctor will be visiting our room was not true, it has been a quarter past 12 pm. We waited though we were not in a hurry to go somewhere else.

I heard the knock on the door which was half open. I saw the doctor standing on the threshold alerting us to enter along with two more nurses following him.

He checked her with his stethoscope and instructed his Nurses to give more painkillers and antibiotic drips till evening. His nurses left the room following his order; the Doctor advised me not to be concerned about her health, to discharge tomorrow morning, and to have a regular check-up with him once a month. I agreed with him, that routine will make her healthier.

The pain medication made her sleep all afternoon; she got up at 3.30 pm. The lunch that was served to her was worse than the breakfast I tasted. It is for her good and the hospital staff knows what to feed to the Patient. After lunch, she slept more which I believe the pill drugs made her drowsy. I left the room and wandered the whole corridor taking a peek at the hospital Patient room; looking at paintings attached to the wall of the corridor. I hate hospitals; good for Patients but dreadful for people when they have nothing to do in the Hospital. Maybe, if I could talk to somebody to pass time except everybody is busy with their relatives or Patients I guess. Father came in between to check on me and Mother; asked whether I want lunch or not to which I said I already had. He left the room after our small talk. I called my Colleague Mrs. Raheela to know about the work environment in the office; I am sure she will not be busy at this time of work.

She asked me about what happened to my Mother and I told her everything. I asked her if there was any cause for me to take leave today; to which she said that it is not an issue at all that I must be more anxious about my mother than the job. I informed her that I will come to the office tomorrow afternoon once I finish discharging her, making her settled comfortably in our home. The Nurses came in between to check the medical IV drips.

At last, Mother woke up at 8.04 pm while I was playing Candy crush game. I am really the worst player of mobile games compared with other online players. I kept aside the mobile and watched her gloomy eyes. Her eyes were drowsy and awake at the same time; I think the medicine is still in her head to make her woozy.

She mumbled something which I could not hear; I told her to close eyes for a few minutes more so she could talk clearly. She obeyed as

I told her; after a little moment, she was awake and asking for water. I immediately gave her a few mouths of water; stopped when it was dripping from her mouth.

I helped her to sit, allowing her back to lie on two fluffy pillows and she asked, "What time is it?"

When I looked at the watch, it was 8.30 pm. I updated her about the time. Something made mother's eyes widen in disbelief; she looked at the clock hanging on the wall.

"What is it?" I asked her.

"I don't believe I slept that long. I thought it was 5 or 6 pm. What were you doing here? Have you slept?" she asked me cautiously.

"No, I haven't. I was playing games," I informed her.

"You should have taken a nap, look at your eyes, it's very dull," she gave me an odd look as if she was angry with me.

"I am fine. How are you now?" I asked straight away to distract her from the subject.

"Dizzy," She told me bluntly.

"I should call the nurse now," it is better to inform the Nurse that the Patient has woken up from her sleep.

"Wait," she stopped me.

"What?" I asked her.

"Where is your Father?" she asked me narrowly.

"He came here a few times for a few minutes and left the room," I informed her as if I don't care.

"Did he leave you here all by yourself to manage?" she asked astoundingly.

"What do you expect of him? He is what he is that cannot be changed. Do you want me to call him?" I asked her.

She sighed, "Yes" was her answer.

I called him through mobile, I dialed him first, the second still no response. I dialed the third time, he picked up the call.

"What is it?" He asked in a careful tone.

"Where are you? Ma needs you to come here," I asked him calmly. I want to snap at him but I have gotten used to his behavioral nature.

"I am in the canteen, drinking tea," his voice sounded as if he was yelling at me. He always has a loud tone while speaking on the phone.

"Please come here once you finish it," I cut the call and waited for him to come; sometimes he listens to me when I request him. Keeping aside my sense, I wonder why Mother wanted me to call father. Every job is done now here for her, all the medicines, doctors, and nurses' checkups.

Oh! I know now how stupid I am to call my Father to get him scolded by Mother and he will consider that I deliberately called to get yelled at him. I don't and never cared what he thinks about me; it might affect Mother being stressed by his unkind characteristics.

"Ma, Please don't make a scene here and be calm toward father," I requested her.

"Don't worry I will ask him politely about his whereabouts," She convinced me but I am not sure that her reaction will be quiet.

"Really, tell me you will not get angry at him," I asked her again to ensure her stability and she smiled at me vigorously.

After a few minutes, I heard Father approaching us slowly and sitting next to me. His face was stricken with weariness as I could see that tea he had; has not boosted him at all.

“Where were you the whole day?” mother asked him curiously.

“I was wandering in the hospital and the canteen many times,” He replied modestly.

“Why were you roaming some other place rather than staying with your daughter in the room of the hospital, she might need something,” She asked him in a sensitive manner about the matter.

“I came here in between to check on you and Leena, didn’t I?” he looked at me to support him.

“How long have you stayed here in the room?” She asked him firmly.

“I think it is two hours,” He lied.

“Don’t lie to me. Leena, tell me the truth,” She was angry at his lying.

“Ma, please just leave it for now,” she gestured to stop, interrupting me.

“Leena, please,” She compelled me.

“Only ten or twelve minutes,” I honestly told her. Father was helpless and silent now because of his lies being caught.

“Why do you always lie to me? Why can’t you stay here with your daughter?” She yelled at him, disappointing me at last.

“Why are you shouting at me? What else do you want me to do? I brought you here safely, isn't it enough for you?” he exclaimed back.

“I know you will tell me these words, making me feel grateful towards you. Have you asked the Doctor about my condition? Tell me,” father couldn’t reply to her question. He was staring at me continuously and asked me, “What Doctor said about her?”

“See, you don’t even know what is going on here and you are desperately seeking an answer from Leena,” she literally argues with father knowing that his attitude will not change, but still she expects a change in him. It appears to me that she will never let go of him this time.

“Ma Please. Just leave him. Pa, please leave the room, if you stay here more she won’t stop arguing with you,” I requested him for which he obeyed me immediately leaving the room. I knew he would search for a way to get out of the argument, and I rescued him this time only for mother’s sake.

“Why are you saving him? If you always do this, he will become more careless,” She reminded me of the thousand moments he has shown recklessness towards us.

“I know. What important to me now is you, not him. It is better to make a good person in a state of peace of mind than arguing with the person who obliges us to fight with him,” mother lingered in thought after I said those words.

“You are right. Sometimes I become stupid to argue with him,” she shook her head for disappointing me.

“Sometime?” I teased her.

“Are you teasing me?” she narrowed her eyes.

“Yes. I am teasing you,” I smiled at her and she returned the smile.

“I have no objection of your teasing at all. You can tease me how much you can. As you are not my daughter, you are a friend,” I could see in her eyes the anger and pain has gone from it, and emotions took place.

“You know I am always your friend,” there was a long pause and I looked at my watch which reminded me to call the nurse, “I’ll better call the nurse and arrange the dinner for you as well,” I left the room after informing her.

My mind delved into the matter of the parent’s fighting, and if I have not stopped it could have gone worse for her. It is always another episode of argument between Mother and Father. It constantly happens twice or thrice a week and I am used to it. But I should not take it lightly these fights; I should end it then and there or perhaps conflict arises.

After informing the nurse, I went for looking for father. I could not see him anywhere, not in the Reception, not in the visitor's chair. Maybe he left the Hospital wandering alone in the Canteen; either there I could not find him. I called him many times but he never picked up the call. I know his attitude toward us and making us guilty for accusing him. He has done this several times in order us to please him that we are the devil and he is an Angel.

Mother and I have not taken any effort to coax him after the fight in which he is the one who should be blamed. When Mother was young, she could not understand his egoistic narcissistic treatment towards her; always she apologies to him. When time passed on, she gave up regretting him and took a stand against his vanity.

He tried to treat me with his behavior as well as I was the new target. But he failed at it with me, as I never cared for his silent treatment. I had many things to do at that time, my school, my friends, my homework, spending time with my cousins and relatives etc.

I gave up looking for him and went back to mother parceling the dinner for me in the canteen. She and I ate dinner heartily when we talked about our previous encounters of blissful days. We talked until the Nurse came to warn me to allow the Patient to rest. As I saw the time on my watch, it struck 10:15 pm.

I don't want to make her awake any further, so I commenced to make a small bed hastily to sleep on it. Mother asked about where the father is; to which I gave her the details of searching whole hospital grounds for him.

"I think he went home," was her reply.

"Yes. I think he is," I half-heartedly told her. He did not abandon us here alone for the first time; he did it many times if I recall it. Whenever I and my mother argue, we never leave each other whatever may happen; though we might be angry at each other for a few moments or hours.

We confronted each other or other relatives whatever the topic is found offensive to us. Like the argument, we had before the Heart attack. It is in his nature to abandon people who ever he found not up to his expectation or scolding him. All this was torture to him, although he cannot understand that he is the one torturing us clearly. I am aware that he pretends he is not the blamer, but deep down in his heart knows who the blamer is. He has no longing for reconciliation with us by saying sorry.

He very well knows how to take care of himself, and probably had his dinner before we had. I tried to put away all the thoughts before I go to sleep; as I am tired.

Chapter 3

The Proposal

I woke up at 7 am in the bright sunny morning shining across the Window, though it displayed toward mother's bed. I will better close the Window before the sunshine rays wake her up. I busied myself doing chores by packing all the necessary items before discharging from the hospital except a set of two churidar kept on the bed for me and Mother to change it.

I will call Father after we have breakfast, and I would not think of his yesterday behavior. The Nurse entered the room with medicines tray in their hands to check the patient.

The Nurse informs me to wake the Patient and I did as she told me. I try to wake her up but she doesn't. I shook her more this time at last she opens her eyes blindly and yawns. She scrutinizes me and the room as she doesn't remember where she is now. Maybe it will take time to recall where she is. I request the Nurse to give her some time and she left the room informing me to call her when she is awake entirely.

Mother was silent and I asked her what is it. She was crying as I watched her. I requested her to stop weeping and wiped her tears.

She said, "I just make myself a burden to you. I am a selfish mother eating carelessly, getting hyper; I am not doing anything for you."

I reminded her, "Don't say it. You have done so much for me that I cannot repay you."

"I know but dragging you into this position makes me feel like the problematic woman in your life. I couldn't give you peace even though you took care of me; I am a bad parent," sobbing lightly.

"Father is a bad parent, not you. When a person gets old, he or she has to go through health issues as you do. Every parent has the right to expect care from their children and I will take care of you even if you like it or not," I calmed her.

"Not every parent gets sick or hospitalized. They still are healthy as horses and I feel that their children are lucky," she snorts after she said.

"Well, I am lucky to have you," I said beaming at her.

"Hmm, well. You will not say lucky when I keep on dragging you to the hospital three or more times," she teased me.

"So you are planning on getting hospitalized in the future? I will never let that happen to you because I will keep an eye on you always," I replied firmly.

"Don't Worry. I will not take the risk again; I won't make you feel regret about me," She affirms me.

"That is good. Now! Do you want to get discharged or not from the Hospital rather than chit-chatting with me the whole day," I told her attentively.

"Oh, I think you must go and make the preparation to discharge me soon. I don't want to stay here any longer," she said with a pang of regret in her voice.

"But First I have to call the Nurse back to check on you. I'll be right back," I left the room to call the Nurse.

Minutes passed and the discharge procedure took us longer than we expected. The thing is the hospital staff doesn't want us to leave as they think it runs according to the Patient and I agree with it. The point is they immediately take the Patient in but when it comes to discharging, they take hours to process.

As the day progressed, I arranged everything for her to be comfortable in bed with water, and medicines and set out from home at 1.10 pm to go to the Office.

I had a hectic workload in the office. A few colleagues stared at me in between, pitying me. I just ignored it but one thing I hated about it a pity. It made me uncomfortable. I don't understand people won't help but pity is the thing that makes them believe that problem goes away.

I arranged and rearranged all papers before leaving the office. I reached home too soon exhausted. I gave a quick check on mother's room, she was browsing the phone.

She gestured for me to come inside and sat down beside her. She said in a humble tone, "You have to listen to me seriously about your future. You will regret it when you get older. So, please never stop seeing until you find the Groom."

"Haven't you grieved marrying father? Do you want me to take the same step as you took? It isn't obvious enough for you?" I asked in a humble tone.

"I was not given any choice as you got. If my parents asked me, I would have definitely said no to him. I am giving you chances to select," She said in a pressing tone.

"I don't have a heart in it," I said negligently.

"See, you and your father will always fight like this even when I am gone. Do you want to stick with your father for the rest of your life?" She gave me a stern look.

"I have planned for him, no need to worry about it. I will bring him a second wife to irritate him ten times more than him," I could not hide my smile. Mother paused for a moment and said "Do you think this is a joke?"

"No Ma, I am completely serious about it," her expression became smooth and she laughed aloud along with me.

"I don't think there is a chance to irritate your father, he is born to irritate others. Even a bad woman will not survive and leave him because of his behavior or she will kick him out for sure," she replied with a fact.

"I honestly agree with you," I said with a smirk.

"I want you to try until you find a compatible and generous man. Just try," she tries to convince me.

"What should I do if I marry a ruthless man who pretended to be kind at first?" I questioned her thinking about the future.

"You know what to do. You can divorce him and come to me. I will always open my arms for you," she confidently said.

I thought for a few minutes and said, "Deal."

"Deal, it is then; I hope the divorce issue should never come to you," she prayed.

I live in a free country and India has offered many benefits for women even when it comes to divorce their husbands without being annoyed except if she marries a psycho. I hope the person I marry is not a psycho.

She handed me her mobile and showed me the Groom's picture. He looked like a sports model with a slight smile on his face. Well, you cannot judge him by looking at a half-body picture. His face is new and I have not seen him in any of the Matrimony sites.

I asked her, “Who is he?”

“He is Ranjan Rao’s brother-in-law, Samarth Karthik,” She said excitedly.

“Who is Ranjan Rao?” I inquired.

“We met him at your cousin sister’s wedding. Your uncle introduced us to him, remember?” she reminded me.

“Oh, yes. He is Uncle Rakesh's School or College friend. He owns the hotel in Ooty, right? He is a funny person. His jokes were hilarious,” I said recalling every moment at the wedding.

“Mr. Rao was looking for his wife’s brother a bride and got impressed after meeting you. So, he decided to arrange the marriage proposal. He asked your Uncle about you. After that, your Uncle told me all the information about him. Look at his Profile,” she swiped the mobile screen.

I was scanning the details

Marriage Bio-data

Full Name: Samarth Karthik
Date of Birth: 16-01-1986
Complexion: Fair
Height: 6.0
Weight: 75 kg
Blood Group: B Positive
Education: MSc in Botany, MBA in Business Management
Occupation: Managing Director in Family Tea Factory
Father’s Name: Sundar Karthik
Occupation: Managing Director of Sundar RO Plant

Mother's Name: Bhavana Karthik

Siblings: Madhavi Karthik Rao, Elder sister of the Groom

Sibling Spouse: Ranjan Rao, Husband of Madhavi Karthik Rao

Residential Place: Ooty

--------------x--------------

The Bio-data was plain and simple, with no fancy text or designs as I did to mine. As I saw the last word, I was shocked. I had a terrible experience vacationing in Ooty as I couldn't enjoy the weather, especially during November. All I could feel was icy cold. I am not blaming the beautiful scenery and exotic chocolates. The time we had a vacation was the worst month or you could say the starting month of severe cold.

"The residential place says Ooty. Do you want me to go there? You know I never liked cold places," I complained.

"It is not that bad. You will love it when you settle down there," she remarked.

"Really, you were the one who was cursing the weather more than Tejaswini Aunt. Remember?" I reminded her.

"Yes. It was not cold; it was raining heavily as well. It was spoiling our vacation. Tejaswini on the other hand was not happy with our company. I would have not complained about it if I lived there two more days without Tejaswini," she told me annoyingly.

The Vacation was 4 days in duration. My family and Uncle Rakesh planned a joint trip. I, father, and mother never liked Aunt Tejaswini, wife of Uncle Rakesh. She is an obnoxious, harsh, fighting cock woman. She thought her husband is paying all the money for the trip. In fact, we paid equally. Unlike, Uncle Rakesh was determined to pay for everything. Mother was stubborn and insisted on equal share. We have missed many visiting spots due to rain. We whole lot regretted going during November month for vacation.

"So, you are saying I should get married to him? You know I don't want to go far away from you," I asked.

"I know, I know. Just meet him. It doesn't like you are getting married tomorrow. We will decide after you meet him," she interrupted me.

"What do mean by meet him? Is he not coming with his family?" I questioned her.

"Well, the boy insisted to meet you personally outside. Mr. Ranjan informed your Uncle and me clearly. And I said yes when I talked to him," she said.

"You said 'yes' without consulting with me? You knew what happened last time when I met a Groom alone," I nearly shouted at her.

"He was a rascal trying to test you whether you are a calm girl or bold. It is indecent to approach women like that," She said sternly.

I still kept in mind the man who asked whether I am a virgin or not. I felt a cringe like never before in my entire life. He was a handsome, charming man at first. His tone went serious later. I don't want to make matter worse; so I replied calmly. I asked him the same question but he never said anything. What a Scoundrel!

I knew he was not a virgin; I left and rejected him on the spot. I believe in equality, I wanted a celibate person because it is who I am. If a person wanted an untouched person for marriage; then he or she must be chaste too. It is not like different rules for men or women. I might accept him even if he was not a virgin; I hated his audacity to ask me such a question.

"What do you think?" she asked me interrupting my thoughts.

I had no choice so I unwillingly said "Ok."

I detested her when she emotionally blackmails me and we women always give up because of our parent's strategy. God has been unfair to create only women to be bounded by their surrendering nature, yet men have no root to succumb to emotions.

I searched for him and his company through internet which represented a fine reputation in Ooty and is considered a good brand among the 130 tea factories. This shows the severe competition to undertake. I am sure he will reject me instantly as I don't have anything to give compared to his background.

Chapter 4

The Meeting

It was Sunday morning; I could see it was drizzling outside and the climate was a beautiful light breeze. We fixed a meeting on weekend for both of us. It is 9 am now and I was getting ready to meet him around 11 am. It is not like I am going alone; father accompanied me. Mr. Samarth is accompanying his brother-in-law, Mr. Ranjan.

Mother insisted to wear Sari; I declined it. I wore half sleeve white Kurta, black jeans and a small hanging earring. It made me comfortable with whatever I like to wear. I applied glow makeup on the skin to match the Kurta. I took a green mini sling bag to wear across the body. I did an easy-open hairstyle with fancy clips.

Many people gain confidence and experience in meeting new people again and again. I still suffer from such encounters; I feel nervous as it is the first time. It is the same topic but I lack in it. Possibly, it is due to a person's behavior and vibes. Now, it stopped raining when we left home but I feel a little droplet of water, a cool breeze blowing on my face while father was driving the motorbike.

It took half an hour to reach our destination to find a space to park the bike; it was crowded. However, we managed it. They have informed us to meet outside the designated Café in Besant Nagar. The place was rich in style, with palm trees across the road. There are many cafes, bookstores, and shopping complexes built here now than before I visited this area; the view is dazzling today. It is perfect for romantic couples.

It is 10.50 am, I expected to see our party as soon as we arrived; however, we waited a few minutes on the platform. Father took out his mobile dialing the phone. I told him to wait for a few more minutes before dialing; he didn't listen. He said they are around here.

Finally, as I began to see clearly; we saw Mr. Ranjan striding toward us on the platform. He looked the same as I met him 6 months before; no changes. He waved at us and I couldn't see his brother-in-law with him. As he came near us breathing heavily, apologizing for the delay.

He said laying eyes upon father and me, "We couldn't find the spot to park our car; it is crowded."

"It is Sunday today. Many families and couples gather together to have fun," father replied smilingly. Father is always good at charming for the first few meetings; then he becomes evil later showing his true color.

"True. My brother-in-law left me here to meet you first. He will be here once receiving the parking ticket. How are you?" he asked Father cheerfully and shook their hands.

"I am fine," Father reciprocated the same.

"And you dear?" He glanced toward me.

“Fine and how was the journey?” I asked him as they have arrived yesterday from Ooty.

“Good. I never expected the climate would be so good today. Leena, you look more beautiful than last time,” He praised me.

“Thank You, Mr. Ranjan,” I replied.

“And you Mr. Rajesh look fit than before we met,” He teased him, and both laughed hysterically.

They both talked about their work, especially Mr. Ranjan; he is more talkative than him. Father was getting impatient and asked him to call Mr. Samarth. Before he could do so, he said, “Ah! Look, here he is.”

He was walking slowly toward us. I can see he is neither excited nor indifferent. He is dressed in a light blue shirt rolled up his sleeves with faded black Jeans. His feature was not too big or too small, but strong and tall as I think he is going to the gym. He had dark brown hair that was trimmed slightly side by side. His face is typically handsome. He looks more attractive in person than in the photo. He stopped a step back looking at his brother-in-law and glancing toward me and father. He smiled but only for the shortest second.

Mr. Ranjan followed my glance, “Yes, let me make the introductions. My brother-in-law, Samarth Karthik and this is Mr. Rajesh Kumar, his daughter Leena Kumar.”

He shook his hand first with father. He said, “Hello” and then looking at me said ‘hi’ and I said ‘hi’ back.

“Any problems getting here?” father asked him.

“Just a parking problem,” he answered quickly.

“Can we go inside this Café?” father said pointing toward the direction where we are standing.

Mr. Ranjan interrupted, "I think we should let your daughter and Samarth alone in this Café shop."

Father questioned, "Where will we go?"

"We can go to some other snack shop. Once they were done talking, they will call us and we can meet exactly here. We have informed your wife about this, right?" Mr. Ranjan explained.

"Oh, yes. I forgot," Father replied. Father glanced at me to ensure and I mouthed yes. Mother advised both of us on every detail of it. Well, he is not a good listener.

"Is it ok for you, dear?" Mr. Ranjan asked me for reassurance.

"Yes," I replied.

"Ok. Call us when you need anything. Samarth, go with Leena," He said sternly.

We both saw them leaving us; I let him sense the nervousness occurring in me and he asked, "Are you okay?"

I said, "I am fine."

"Shall we go inside?" He reminded me.

"Yes," I answered. I walked my way inside the café, looking for a good spot to sit. The place was filled with couples and friends. Only some tables were empty. He looked over me and pointed toward the glass window. I could see the road view and it was perfect. He sat down across from me at a square table.

I have visited too many snack shops and restaurant that is filled with dim light and sound ambience and covered rooftop; this is my first best-sight snack bar. It raises an extraordinary scene due to the atmosphere; I could even see the rainbow.

The waiter comes over to our side to place an order, handing us the menu. I am gonna make a simple order.

"What would you like to have?" asked Mr. Samarth as a polite gentleman.

"Ah, I would like to have a cappuccino," I said. Mr. Samarth observes my every move as if he is reading me.

"Anything else besides coffee like cupcakes, cookies, etc," He asked again.

"Some cookies, Please," I said to the waiter. I could see indirectly that Mr. Samarth was smiling at me as if I said something amusing. I have to confront it.

"And you, Sir?" The waiter turned towards Mr. Samarth for his order.

"Please bring me the same," he said. The waiter left us and I am amazed by his choice of food. My face revealed everything to him.

"What is it?" He asked me.

"What?" I said hiding his question.

"I can see in your face that surprised look," he confronted.

"It's nothing," I replied.

"You can say anything to me. I won't mind," he said politely.

"I could ask you the same thing that you were smiling when I ordered cookies," I questioned him.

"Oh, you noticed. I thought my observation is good. I have biscuits or cookies with hot beverages all the time; not cakes, pastries, and other snack food. I see you have the same taste," he explained. That's true; I never like it, especially with Mixture Snack. It creates acidity.

"I thought I got something on my face," I said releasing the doubt.

"Your face is fine. Now, it's your turn to tell me," he questioned me sternly.

"I thought that the man who is running the Tea factory may order tea; you preferred to drink coffee instead. Why?" I explained to him. Some People follow stiff rules to consume what business they do.

"I like coffee too. It's not like I have to drink tea if I am organizing it, the taste will change according to mood. I do deal in coffee too. I love tea, it is my business passion but there are a few varieties in it which I don't like to drink," I can see shine in his eyes when he talks about his business and as I looked deeply he has bright brown eyes.

"What is that?" I asked.

"Lemon Tea," He said shyly.

"Is it in your company?" I was curious.

"No. Every brand I dislike. People with different tastes consume differently. Lemon tea is giving me profits and I am glad about it," he said.

"I considered that you are making an impression by ordering the same," I teased him. He laughed gently.

"It is not like that. I have come here before many times, they serve the best coffee here. I think you have made up your mind that I will drink only tea and I can see, there is more to tell," he caught me.

"No. I guessed it," I lied to him. My repeated head shake gave away the lie.

"I know there is more. You can tell me," he said sternly.

I better lie or tell him about the previous experience I had. I believed in telling the truth, "There are many people who impose their taste and likeness upon others to follow."

"You assumed that I will force you to drink tea or reject you for not drinking tea. Why did you imagine like that?" he commented.

"I know. It is absurd. I met a guy for Alliance a few years before. He has a Gold Jewelry Showroom. I was wearing artificial earrings that day. He made a sarcastic comment when I said it is fake earrings," I looked at him and stopped for a moment appreciating his face.

"Go on," He said.

"He said that I should stop misusing money on buying things that are not worth it. He even told me that I must wear only gold and silver after marriage," I said quickly.

"What? Is he out of his mind; it is up to you what you want to wear," he said as he couldn't believe it.

"You are right. I like gold; but some things look good on me and I buy them," I clarified.

"What did you say to him after that incident?" he inquired.

"I rejected him not only for that reason but also for some serious purpose," I told him quietly.

"Oh, ok." He replied. I hope he does not ask me to explain the purpose, that a guy's family asked for a huge dowry from my parents.

"Now, I understand. So, do you like tea?" He teased me.

"I drink it when I have a headache or while socializing," I said shyly.

"Which teas do you like the most?" He asked coolly.

"Ginger tea," I said.

"Good choice," he replied.

The waiter came and placed all on the table and asked, "Is there anything else to order, Sir?"

"No, thanks. Leena, do you want to order anything else," he said. I said no.

The waiter left us. I was constantly looking at the food and him; Chocó-chip cookies were looking mouthwatering. I poured one sachet of sugar into the cup, mixing it with a spoon. He was not taking sugar and drank his first sip. He looked at me and waited for me to drink. So, he could ask more about me. I looked at him; he turned his face away from me concentrating on his coffee. I could feel he is shy or uncomfortable.

He was patient until I finished half cup of coffee and a few cookies. I got serious and cleared my throat before he could ask me, "Mr. Samarth."

He looked at me closely, "Please call me Samarth."

"Ok, Samarth. Why do you want to marry?" I asked him straight away.

He looked at me as if I have asked about his bank balance. Maybe, the question is silly to ask but I had to know his intention and plan. Many men marry because of various reasons.

I began again, "Is it something wrong with the question?"

"No. Nobody asked me this question before," he has not gotten out of his dense thought. He looks confused.

"Not even a single person asked you," I inquired again.

"No," he replied.

"What did girls ask you then?" I was curious to know the questions of past tried rejected brides.

"Only hobbies, interests, lifestyle, do I want kids, etc," he said with a smile. Well, I have gone through that phase of inquiry.

"So, tell me why are you marrying?" I asked him firmly. I had to know that anybody imposed some kind of pressure on him.

He cleared his throat, "I am content with life, my sister's family around, and my job. One day, I kind of felt lonely at my place when I saw others with their companion. I thought I should settle down."

His Parent are living in London for the past few years; obviously, he would find himself lonely. Mother said that he is living in Ooty his entire life and never wanted to shift. Even his sister's family is in Ooty but living apart from each other; around a few kilometers.

"When did you think about that?" I inquired.

"A few years ago," he said calmly.

"What were you doing before those years," I asked.

"I was concentrating on the business, traveling with friends," he replied.

"Why arrange marriage and not love marriage? Have you not found anyone in college or other places?" I asked him carefully. It is hard to believe he is single.

"Unfortunately no," he shyly smiled at me.

How a handsome man like him could be so bashful? These days, women approach men to date. Maybe because of his introverted behavior, women find it boring. He might not have approached women as other men do. I have met a few self-conscious men that are good-looking; they gained the confidence to draw near the girl they like. They were successful. Perhaps, he has not met his type.

"Why do you want to marry, Leena?" it was his turn to ask me.

"It's just that," I paused and found an accurate word to say, "Mother used to say that marriage is like a sweet, if you do not have it; then you will regret it your entire life. If you eat it, then you have to accept the fat of the sweet."

He laughed for a moment and said, "You have a good sense of humor."

"Thank you," I said smilingly.

"You believe spouses are like the fat of the sweet. Do you want to eat it?" He asked.

"Maybe," I replied.

"What are your hobbies, Leena?" he asked a simple question unlike me that hit with the tough one. I know where he will go in the end as every man does while meeting.

"Reading, watching movies, Playing cards, Cooking, etc.," I said in one breath.

"Cooking is not a hobby, it is a chore," he said with a stern gaze.

"For me, it is both. I love cooking," I ensured him. "Do you cook, Samarth?" I said to him in a low tone. The man who has been living alone surely knew how to cook.

"Not much. Do you watch serials?" He inquired.

"Serials are contagious. I stopped watching it when I was nineteen," I said. He slightly smiled and got back to his usual firm behavior. As I thought I was the same as him; firm, not giving any excitement or neglect.

"What do you want from your spouse?" he asked.

"I don't have a list. He must not be immature and too strict," I gazed at him and I am serious about it.

"That's all. Are you sure?" He demanded.

"Well, I appreciate a caring person, supportive, not judgmental. And most importantly, he must not be a pervert," I said confidently.

"Your answer is plain, I thought you will have lots of lists," He scoffed as if I told him a joke.

"Did I say something amusing?" I ordered.

“No. Actually, I am amazed,” his eyes were welcoming.

“How is that?” I raised an eyebrow.

“Don’t get me wrong. Whomever I met, their answers were romantic, sense of humor, non-drinkers and non-smokers, good physiques. I understand women have priorities and fix up a list in choosing a husband; your expectation refers to a moral code. Don’t you have any other expectation apart from that?” he explained.

“It is a lot to ask from men. Having too much expectation leads to disappointment,” I told him.

“You are right. But women should not be too choosy. I got rejected for being non-vegetarian,” he slightly grinned. What happened to women these days, are they turning themselves to eat only vegetables?

“Some women could not stand the smell or don’t want to cook for their spouse,” I replied.

“I don’t want her to cook, I would have eaten outside. I rarely eat chicken and egg in a week. Was it not enough?” he complained.

“Have you explained all this to her?” I asked him.

“Yes,” he annoyingly told me.

“It is her loss for not being modest. Do you drink or smoke?” I questioned.

“I don’t smoke, I rarely drink,” he answered quickly.

“Why do you drink? It is not good for health,” I was curious.

“Sometimes it is hard to sleep during cold days. I just take one or two small pegs. Are you alright with that?” he informed.

“Yes,” I said. I am sure he is honest with his answers, unlike my father who drinks constantly. I have to ask him one more thing about drinking, “Do you whine or blabber after drinking?”

"No. I just go to bed to sleep. It keeps you warm," he confirmed. Thank God, he is a sleeper.

"Do you mind if I drink?" I dropped a bomb in his lap to check what he will say.

"Have you drunk alcohol before?" He asked.

"No," I replied.

"Then, Why do you want to do it if you have not done anything before?" he inquired.

"I am curious. I want to taste it," I said carefully.

"It depends upon you. I will advise you to consume a small amount of it, it will be better for you. If it is too much, then it will affect your health," he explained to me as if I were a student. It is better that I tell him the truth. Maybe, later before he rejects me.

"So, do you mind if I drink alcohol?" I looked at him straight into his eyes.

"No," he smiled and assured me.

"What do you want from your spouse?" I strike him with the same question.

He peeked into my eyes and intensely told me, "I want her to understand me."

And I waited for him to say more, to say the list but he stopped. He has not brought any file about this question or he forgot to elaborate. I should press him to tell me more.

"That's all. Will you explain how to understand you?" I sarcastically asked him.

"It is difficult to understand me. For you, I will tell you in short. I want her to be loyal, caring, and honest. Mostly, I want her to be patient as I disclose slowly," he described.

Disclose slowly; is he giving me the vibe of an introverted guy or is he hiding something? I hope he is not a psycho or a wife-beater. I would ask him by what he means patience; but how?

"What do you mean by patience? Is it anything to worry about?" I am curious now.

"It is nothing bad. I am not a talkative person but I do respond. If she wants something from me; I could not provide or give information immediately. It takes time. I will do according to her comfort. It's just that I don't want her to nag me to explain everything at once," he said.

"So, you mean to say that you are like an onion and it takes time to peel every layer? Am I right?" I asked him.

"Exactly," he confirmed.

"Well, I can live with that," I told him. He smiled at me closely; it is making me blush. I have to be strong; there are lots of questions to be answered. I was staring at my phone to see the time. It shows 11.40 am. When I looked up, he was constantly glancing at me. This makes me uncomfortable. What is he thinking? Has he made up his mind about me to ask further or quit it? This silence is creepy. I'll interrogate to kill the silence.

"What are your hobbies?" I asked him. People say that hobbies are the revealing features of a person's nature.

He lightened up his stare and said, "I like reading especially non-fiction, Outdoor games in summer, indoor games during winter, traveling by driving, and playing with nephews and niece."

"Are you close to your sister's family?" I asked about his sister.

"I am extremely close to them," his face cheered and I am aware that he is devoted to them.

"What about your parents?" I asked. His face gloomed suddenly as If I reminded him about the terrible person.

"I am not..," he hesitantly said, "I am not in touch with them for a while. However, I am fine with them."

I could see some sort of pain in his eyes. Maybe, he had a big fight with them. Later, I am sure that he will become close. I never talk to my parents for a few days. When I calm down, I mingle with them. Every child never stays angry with their parents for long. And I know; it is not the time to ask the reason about his family issue.

"Do you like music?" I asked him to lighten up the mood.

"Yes, especially melody," he said coming nearer to me and asking, "Are you ready to leave your job and live in Ooty?"

Now, he dropped a bomb on my lap. This is the hardest question to answer; leave my mother, my past life, my city, my freedom, and my job. Though I am not concerned about the job, I will get it anywhere. Will he allow me to work if I wanted to? I decided to expose the intention.

"I have no problem leaving the job, but I look forward to working in the future. Is it ok for you to allow me?" I asked him in a low tone.

"You will not find any time to do a job. It is a big burden to take care of the house," he explained. Does he want me to be a housewife? I am not ready for that. Seriously, I want to give an opinion about the job.

"What if I manage the house efficiently and still have time, what should I do then?" I questioned him. Now, I excitedly waited for his answer.

He thought for a moment and said, "You can come to the factory to work, to know the business. Let me clear you, I will not allow her to work in another company."

Is he kidding? I would rather be a housewife than work professionally with a spouse. In my opinion, it is hard to be a husband and wife to each other; it is tougher for spouses to work together professionally. They will surely blame each other if there is a financial loss that will lead to a major fight and divorce.

"Hmm! It is unbearable to leave mother here and to live in a place that is far from her," I told him sadly.

"You don't need to be bothered, your mother has your father and I heard that your uncle ensures to keep an eye on your family. I visit here often for business meetings. So, we both can stay with your parents. In case of emergency, it will take a maximum of 4 hours through flight to reach here," he convinced me.

He gave me a perfect idea. Was it because he likes me? Has he approved me to be his wife? I must wait till the end. I don't have any inquiries left.

"Okay," I said.

"Ok, what?" he inquired.

"You are right. It is a good idea and I am done inquiring. Do you want to ask anything else?" I asked.

He raised his eyebrows, "Done already. Are you sure?"

"Yes, I am sure," I told him. He stared at me for seconds to ensure that I am not jesting.

"Well, I am done too," he replied. He drank the rest of the coffee in one sip and called the waiter for the bill. He was browsing the phone until the bill comes.

What? That's it? Is he not gonna ask me whether I have any previous relationships? Is there any medical condition? Do I have any qualities? Do you want kids? Am I a shopaholic? Etc. I better ask myself for him.

"Will you not ask me whether I have had a boyfriend before or not?" I asked him.

"Do you have a boyfriend?" he questioned.

"No," I said.

"I am not interested in your previous relationship. If you have now, then you can tell me why you have come to meet me," he cautiously asked me.

"I am sorry. Let me explain, I don't have time for a boyfriend and don't have the intention to keep one. Many guys repeatedly asked me this question. I thought you will ask me the same. If I have one, then I would have said no to you," I described him.

He came closer to me, "I am happy with your answers. Is there anything else that I need to know before we leave this place? You don't have to hide or lie to me. I am a broad-minded person."

Now, I feel kind of guilty about the alcohol thing. I said, "I sort of lied to you about drinking. I never want to come near or taste the alcohol. I despise the smell of it."

He smiled at me broadly and asked, "Well, I promise you that I will never come near you when I am drunk. But, my brother-in-law is a social drinker. I always visit my sister's family often and want my wife to accompany me. Are you ready to deal with it?"

"We will see that later," I informed. I don't want to get carried away; there are many steps to pass between myself and him. Even if we say 'yes' to each other, we must pass the test of our family's opinion. I have no problem on my side, Father is ready to get rid of me and mother would say yes to whomever I marry; inside the religion. What is important is what the Groom's family wants from us. How much dowry we will provide? When and where the wedding should occur? Etc.

Chapter 5

The Conclusion of the Meeting

The Waiter brought the bill to us. Mr. Samarth took out the fancy wallet from his jeans. I did ask him to share the bill; he replied that he is the one who invited me here, not me. So, it is his right to pay the bill. His response was genuine, unlike other men who might feel emasculated. I don't understand why some men feel shame or egoist for sharing the bill. They never show shame in asking for a huge dowry; such double standards.

As I recall one of the meetings, a guy told me to pay the whole bill when I talked about sharing it. It felt awesome that I found the perfect guy who won't bring up his ego when it comes to money. The whole process of the meeting went splendidly. Obviously, he gave me a shock by rejecting me.

Throwing away my thoughts, I dialed the father's number to come over to the restaurant and he waited till I shut the call. He suddenly asked me, "Are you sure, do you want to leave? We four can have lunch together."

Is he suggesting me to stay with him more? I could see his intense stare for the response. Did he like me? Perhaps he wants to know more about me or is he asking me out of courtesy?

"Thank you. Maybe later," I hesitated.

"Okay," he said. There is a disappointment in his tone. He raised from his seat at the exact time I did. He gestured for me to lead the way and followed.

Mr. Ranjan was waiting outside their Restaurant along with Father. As I came near them, Mr. Ranjan asked me, "Have the conversation gone well, dear?"

I politely replied, "Yes."

He stared at Mr. Samarth for his approval, "And you?"

"It was good so far," Mr. Samarth said calmly.

Father interrupted, "I think we should leave now. We will be expecting your call."

"Yes. Father is right, we should leave," I supported him.

"Why don't you both have lunch with us?" Mr. Ranjan looked at his brother-in-law for approval.

"Yes. That's a great idea and we will drop you at your house," Mr. Samarth said in agreement. Mr. Ranjan raised his eyebrows and closely looked at Mr. Samarth as he said something shocking. At first, I considered it the best idea. But, I have no further questions to ask him.

"Thank you. Father has work awaiting him," I lied. "And we have our bike," I hesitated.

"Okay. Let your father go to do his work. You can come with us, dear. We will drop you," Mr. Ranjan insisted and I could see his face revealed something amusing but controlled his grip.

"Sorry. I do have some work too," I lied again.

"Today is Sunday," Mr. Samarth reminded.

"Yes. I brought the paperwork to complete it today," Father looked at me for why I am lying.

"At least come with us, we will drop you off before your father reaches home. Do you mind if we give a lift to her, Mr. Rajesh?" Mr. Ranjan asked the father.

"No. Please take her," he said frankly.

Mr. Ranjan turned to me for my consent. I have a few rules that never travel with someone whom you have first met. I know Mr. Ranjan is not a stranger; still, I have doubts about so many things.

"I appreciate your offer, though I would like to leave with Pa," I replied.

"Okay, as the lady says. We will leave now and call you by end of today or tomorrow," Mr. Ranjan said and shook his hand with Father.

We all said bye to each other and left the premises. Father started his bike and asked, "Do you like him?"

"Yes," I said.

"Why didn't you take a ride with them?" he asked while driving.

"I was uncomfortable going with them. That's why," I said.

He shook his head side by side, I know what it means. He probably is angry with me for denying their offer. He wants me to be a girl who is desperate for getting married. I am what I am. I like to take things slowly and steadily, just like a turtle.

We reached home at 1.30 pm and saw mother watching Television in the hall. She turned off the flat screen and inquired, "How was it? How was the meeting?"

"Good," I replied ignoring her anxious stare.

"How is the man? Was he good?" She asked.

"He is a gentleman," I said truthfully. She released her heavy breath and I could see she is relieved to hear it.

"Do you like him?" she inquired again.

"Yes," I confirmed her and she flashed me a smile.

Before she can ask more, father entered the hall and complained, "Mr. Ranjan is an excellent person offering us to have lunch with them and your daughter declined him."

"He did?" mother questioned me.

"Yes," I replied calmly. Father sat down on the couch across from me listening to our discussion.

"Why didn't you go with them?" She asked.

"I find it is not decent to say 'yes' right away for lunch. I was not excited. I had enough of knowing Mr. Samarth and we should wait for the result from his side," I told her.

"Nobody offers lunch casually unless they like you. You must have gone with them to understand more about him through Mr. Ranjan. He is a talkative person," she said. She is right. Why I have not considered that strategy. Perhaps, my ultimate confidence has not been agreed upon.

"Leave it, Ma. It is over now," I said tiredly.

"Ok! Did the Groom ask you first for lunch?" she was eager this time.

"Yes. He did," I said.

"Oh. It means he likes you," she said jumping and clapping like a girl who is excited to visit an Amusement theme park.

"Probably," I replied.

"I am gonna call them right now," She picked up the phone to dial the number.

"Who are you dialing?" I inquired her.

"Mr. Ranjan. Who else?" She said casually.

"Don't. Please don't call him. He said that he would call us by end of today or tomorrow," I sort of yelled at her.

"Did he say that?" She asked father. I feel betrayed when she asked her husband instead of me.

"Yes," he replied.

"Alright, we will wait," at last she said.

It was half past 7 pm. Father was resting in his bedroom and Mother was watching the television screen fidgeting with the remote continuously. Her eyes roamed from the flat screen to the mobile. Her desperation to wait for the result is a common thing and I tried to concentrate on cooking dinner.

I woke up father from his sleep to have dinner and we sat down together to eat, we heard an incoming call from her mobile. The mobile screen shows it is Mr. Ranjan.

She picked up the call, her face gave away nothing. She listened to him like a Robot, adding 'ok' 'yes', and 'sure' in between the conversation creating a suspenseful mood.

I focused on eating the food, and so as the father. The chat took more than 5 minutes and I had to look away from her. Finally, she hangs up the call.

I was curious, "what did he say?"

"The boy said yes and he wants to know more about you. So, Mr. Ranjan told me that they will visit us on the third Sunday of this month to discuss further," she explained excitedly.

"Who are all coming?" Father asked her.

"Samarth, Mr. Ranjan, his wife, and their children will visit. He informed me to bring your brother to accompany us from our side. You know, to complete the topic of marriage," she elaborated.

Of course, Uncle Rakesh is a close friend of Mr. Ranjan. They met in a College when Uncle Rakesh was in last year and Mr. Ranjan was in the first year of Semester, same department different year. Uncle Rakesh will ensure to keep the communication light; if there is any argument occurs. I entrust him above father. He is a man of sound mind, a soft heart, and optimism in nature. I had wondered how this gentleman has been a good Elder Brother to my irresponsible Father. Sometimes, I envied his children.

"What about his Parents? Aren't they coming?" I asked her.

"I don't know. Maybe, their Parents allow their children to take decisions. The boy's sister is 39 years old and has three children and it is enough for her to take matters into her hand," she explained.

"That's true," I approved her. I hope she is mature.

"I cannot wait for three weeks but I had to," She said sadly distracting me from consideration.

"It is good news," father said smilingly.

"Yes, it is," Mother replied looking at me. "Are you not happy, dear?" she inquired reading the gloomy face.

"I am happy, Ma. I don't want you to get carried away about the Marriage proposal. You remember that we always end up getting disappointed," I reminded her.

"You are right. We shall wait and see," she approved.

Chapter 6

The Gathering

Three weeks gone, today is the third Sunday; the second week of October. Today is the day that our fate will be decided. I hope this goes well. Mother insisted to wear a silk Sari, but I end up wearing a parrot green silk Churidar. The color suits me. I put a fancy purple dupatta on one side. I started wearing a Gold Jhumka set and applied make-up slightly. Mother bought me three gold Jewelry set for the wedding; I am wearing one of them. She claims me to wear more jewels to show off that we are not under grade; obviously, I refused. It is a weird way to show status in society. They are visiting us to meet the girl, not the jewelry-adorned Bride that is meant to wear at the wedding.

We fixed to gather at a similar time around 11 am. Now, it is 10.20 am. We cleaned the house more than before it was. We bought Samosas, milk peda sweets, Mysore pak sweets, and other snacks. Hot beverages will be prepared by me to serve them after they enter the house. This is the test to prove my cooking skills if they stay for lunch.

As I was getting ready, I could hear Uncle Rakesh's voice from the hall; revealing his punctual habit. If you want any work to be done, you can rely on him. They commenced discussing what to ask. How to ask them? Every Parent does this training before the meeting. I have seen it many times this process.

I got ready and I waited and waited. I checked the mobile to spend the time. It got past 11.10 am. I hope not they changed their mind to meet us or got stuck in the traffic.

Eventually, I heard their voices buzzing continuously. I could not hear Samarth voice. Perhaps, I should take a peek through the door.

No, I will wait for the Mother to come inside and there she is, “Are you ready?” she asked.

“Yes. Has all come?” I questioned her.

“Yes. The boy is handsome just like a hero in movies,” she said excitedly. She compared him with the actors.

“Okay. Should I go to the kitchen to prepare tea?” I asked doubtfully.

“No, no. I’ll do that. You stay here until I come to pick you up,” She told me clearly.

She left me and I tried to hear every conversation. Their voice is so low; I could hear a few things only. Like, how long was the journey to reach here? Any problem faced on the way? I could hear my family constantly battling to feed the guest in case they hesitate or refuse to take any snacks. Typical hosting!

I was nervous as usual. What if his sister rejects me? Will mutual understanding occur about the dowry or not? There is a lot of question playing in my mind.

Then there is a hush and Mother has come inside the room to pick me up, “Come, dear. It’s time,” she said.

I took a long deep breath, leaving the room to enter the hall. All eyes were set on me and mine on them. I sat down on a space on the couch next to Mother.

Samarth's sister Madhavi appeared alike but with different cheekbones and hair; she has higher cheekbones than her brother. Her hair is curlier while Samarth's is straight and silky though they have the exact shade. She has broad shoulders and wide hips but she looks slim in front of his stout husband Mr. Ranjan. She wore a plain red kurta and white palazzo pant. I changed the glance from her to her children; all were smiling. Her teenage daughter seems to be leaner and more beautiful than all of us; her facial features are like her mother's. Her second child is a boy around 10 or 12 years old resembled his father and the third is cuter than his elder brother.

She introduced herself and her children's names are Rashmika-Daughter, Siddharth-Son, and Vinay, a younger Son. Rashmika is 16 years old, and wore a dark blue gown-type churidar; Siddharth looks 12 but he is 9 years old due to his Father's Genes I guess. Vinay resembled his sister and father and is 7 years old. Three children carry a similar fair shade as their Mother and Uncle.

She asked me a basic question about education, work experience, and how many recipes I know to which I replied that I have completed MCA, DCA in computer, worked as an Admin for 6 years- first job for 2 years and the second that I am working for more than 4 years. I informed her that I know 36 recipes thoroughly. She was astonished and told me that she knew only 15-20 recipes by hard. Mother asked a few questions to Samarth about his background, his education, and his business. Uncle Rakesh interrogated his bank balance and has any previous girlfriend. Father was silent gawking at sweets and I think he is hungry.

Gladly, she was happy to ask further basic questions, and I answered without any problem. She interrogated me on a deep matter of whether I want children, and whether I am ready to settle down in Ooty and live far away from family. Yes, I love children I said. In my mind, I am marrying for that matter only.

I explained all that Samarth suggested before meeting each other families. She looked toward her brother and smiled, satisfied with the answers. I feel he told her those details. She asked her children to ask me to which they shyly declined. I expected Rashmika will ask me though she is shy like the rest of her brothers.

Madhavi shifted her body to sit more comfortably and said, "We are pleased with your daughter's reply. I want to ask her and my brother directly whether they are comfortable with each other's answers. Leena, is your answer Yes or No to him?"

I said, "Yes," to her.

She turned toward her brother asking the exact question and he said smilingly yes too. All applauded with happiness. I became shy at that moment.

She continued, gazing at Mother, "So, when are you coming to visit us in Ooty and talk about engagement?"

"We will come soon. There is one thing you have not questioned?" Mother asked her hesitatingly.

"What is that?" she replied calmly.

"What is your expectation during the Wedding and for your brother?" Mother asked her.

"We don't want anything from you. It is up to you what you want to give your daughter. We just want a good Wedding," she replied.

"Are you sure, son?" Uncle Rakesh asked Samarth to confirm.

"We are sure. We want nothing from you," he said confidently. I am shocked right now; why his family is not demanding any dowry from me. Uncle Rakesh obviously had given information about our status to him. I live in a two-story building owned by my Father; after his death, it will belong to me as I have no siblings to share. I will give credit to them if they are calculative.

Probably, he has his own house; own factory, and car which is why he refused to accept anything. The man who has everything will not ask from his spouse but something different. What is it I shall know in the future?

"We shall have a grand wedding then," Father suggested.

"Why not?" Uncle Rakesh replied.

"Yes. It is a good idea," Mother told.

"Yes, Yes. It should be a grand Wedding and Reception. What do you recommend, Samarth?" Madhavi asked.

"I have no problem," he said.

I suddenly opened the mouth, "I do have a problem." All gaze shockingly set in my direction. It makes me nervous about their intense stare, especially Samarth.

"What is it, dear?" asked Mr. Ranjan comforting me.

I took the courage to say "I would like to talk to Samarth for a few minutes alone."

"About what, Leena?" asked Uncle Rakesh. Mother and Father angrily looked at me thinking about what more I wanted to say.

"You don't have to be scared. You can tell us," asked Mr. Ranjan.

"I want to tell Samarth alone," I insisted.

Madhavi felt the agitation creeping over me and said, "We should let them clear their doubts before discussing further. Please take them to a room."

"Balcony is enough," I said immediately. Surely, Mother will take us to the room I live; it is messy right now.

Uncle Rakesh and Father got up and took each plastic chair and placed it near a balcony. Samarth sternly looked at me now and then. He raised from the couch as I did the same leading him to the balcony. We sat across each other surrounded by flower pots.

I could feel their gaze on our side and I narrowly looked at them to confirm. They turned away after meeting my eyes.

Samarth started, "What do you want to ask?"

"Please don't get me wrong. I just want to say that I want a simple wedding," I said.

He raised one eyebrow sarcastically and said, "Are you kidding me? You could have said this in front of all."

"I know but Elders won't approve of it. They surely compel me to listen to them," I said.

"Every girl's dream is having a big fat wedding. Why are you opposing it?" he questioned confusingly.

"I have no intention to get dolled up for the whole week. Weddings should get over in one day or less. I would recommend Court Marriages," I explained.

"Court Marriage? Are you sure? You are ready to do that?" he questioned me with doubt on his face.

"Yes. Of course," I stated. He listened to me carefully.

"Is this the reason or if you have any financial problems to conduct the wedding?" he interrogated.

"No, it is not about money. Well, Mother had a heart attack twice and I don't want her to get a third time or you know," I gulped hard when I thought about death.

"You don't have to sacrifice your dream wedding if you have any? We will ensure that she will be healthy as she is now," he insisted.

"I never had any 'Dream wedding'. I simply want to get married around a few people to witness," I explained theoretically.

"I understand. If you want Court Marriage, so be it," he said, at last.

"I am glad you understood. Unless you have any suggestions from your side. Do you have something in your mind about Marriage? Do you want a grand Wedding?" I had to know his intention.

"If it is big, small, or simple; my intention is to get married," he replied calmly.

"It is not a big thing for you. It might affect your sister's purpose for having only a brother; I am sure she has some plan," I warily said.

"You don't worry. Madhavi listens to every decision I make and won't mind at all," he replied comfortingly.

"Are you sure?" I insisted.

"Positive," he said smilingly.

"Please stick with me if they did not approve. They will change our mind," I pleaded.

"I have one plan to get their support," he informed.

"What is it? Please tell me," I eagerly asked.

"We will have a Reception after the Court marriage on that day. What do you think?" he suggested.

"Good idea. How many people do you recommend to attend?" I asked.

"We will invite our close family and friends around 100 people. We should not get any complain for not inviting them," he said.

"Great," I said.

"Is there anything else?" he inquired.

"No. That is what I have got," I told.

"Hmmm! We better inform them now before they call us," he suggested.

"Okay," I replied.

We left the balcony together to the hall and sat down at our respective places. His family looked at him and mine at me. Madhavi said in a low voice to Samarth, "Is everything alright?" she doesn't know I could read her lips. He shook his head up and down continuously.

Mr. Ranjan asked Samarth, "Have you both cleared your doubts?"

"Yes," he replied.

"What is it, can you explain?" he pressed him to elaborate.

"We discussed about the Wedding plan and decided to marry in court," he said calmly to all of us.

All were stunned to hear it, this was unexpected. Some were disappointed, some were silent and some were frowning.

Mother asked me immediately, "Why are you fussing about it? Don't you want it according to customs and traditions?"

"We thought about those things but it is an economically simple process and considered legal in every Country," I explained to all.

"If you thinking about huge expenses please leave it to us," father commented in a low tone.

"It is not about costs. I wanted it to be simple and elegant. Doesn't a bride have their marriage arrangement to consider?" I complained.

"Yes, you can. It is your right, though we have to give reason to our relatives and friends for not inviting. What do you say?" Madhavi questioned me.

Before I could say a word, Samarth interrupted, "We discussed that we will invite them to our Reception fixed on the same day the Marriage will occur. In the Afternoon, Court marriage will be conducted and on the night, the Reception will be implemented," he elucidated with a fine smile. I appreciate him for standing by my side; still, we have not concluded yet.

Everybody is quiet, I think Samarth's idea is working. I have to be patient till the end.

Mr. Ranjan opened his mouth, "It is a good idea. What do you say, dear?" he turned to his wife and signaled her through his eyes for strange approval. He made a weird face and I sort of felt some secret is going on between them.

"Yes. I have no problem. We must listen to others' decisions," Madhavi hesitated.

My family members were lost in their thought, and at last, Mother said, "Okay. The marriage will take place in Court. We will visit you in Ooty soon. And there, we will discuss the Engagement as well."

Uncle Rakesh said, "Even I will come along with them to Ooty. I am excited about Leena's Wedding wherever it takes place."

"So, we will leave you now," Mr. Ranjan happily replied. He rose from his seat to leave and others followed him.

We raised ourselves from the couch for mutual respect and I could see that Uncle Rakesh and Samarth have the exact height. Rashmika reaches her Mother's height; she might be around 5.6 feet. All were longer than me, I feel like a dwarf in front of them except young boys.

Mother and Madhavi hugged each other and Mr. Ranjan with Uncle Rakesh and Father as well. Their children shook hands congratulating me as I will be their future Aunt. Mother insisted they stay for lunch; though they declined. They left the hall one by one before Samarth took my hand to shake by saying bye.

Chapter 7

The Engagement and Court Marriage

Mother planned for this coming weekend to see the house where I will be living in the future. She packed all her and Father's clothes and sweaters. Uncle Rakesh will be accompanying them for 2 days in Ooty. The train leaves at 8.45 pm on Friday and they will return here on Monday morning.

There they will discuss the Engagement finalizing. I suggested they conduct it at our house rather than in Ooty or the ceremony hall in Chennai. I hope they all shift to the idea I applied.

Mother insisted on staying with Aunt Tejaswini but I informed her I would be staying home alone. Aunt Tejaswini will not welcome me even if I agree to stay with her. She intends to avoid our family at all costs. I would not blame her; it was my Father who showed her his bad behavior that leads her to believe Mother and I have same manners like him. I know she is judgmental.

As I recall when Father lost his job in the mill, Uncle Rakesh was the one who gave him the job of Supervisor in his hard-earned own Clothing Showroom. He neither worked nor thought about Uncle's dignity. He took his job for granted by creating chaos with staff and insulting his brother for unnecessary points, even in front of his wife, Aunt Tejaswini. She suggested her husband to fire his brother and Uncle Rakesh has no choice. His and his company's reputation was getting low month by month due to Father's continuous harassment.

Father lost his cool and had a huge fight with Uncle Rakesh and Aunt Tejaswini. He even complained to Uncle by saying wife's slave. This made Aunt Tejaswini decide to boycott and refuse to speak to Father. She sarcastically behaved with us too. Her son Aakash treated us exactly like her. Father's egoistic nature affected us all. It was Uncle Rakesh and his daughter, Abhi both forgave my Father despite what he has done and never changed their behavior towards us.

After all this drama, Father got disappointed with his brother for not supporting him. It was the father's fault; must apologize to Uncle Rakesh for his actions. He neither said sorry nor felt remorse; he started drinking alcohol from that moment. It is my Father's repeated drinking that made it worse for me and Mother. His verbal abuse and constant complaint started like torture to Mother. Her blood pressure got increased due to his actions. This matter happened after our last family Vacation to Ooty when I was 15 years old.

Things got better after he found a job but it lasted for a few years. He returned to his drinking habit forever. I despise the smell.

I commenced the job, started saving, and balanced the expenses. I hope he finds a job again after I leave this place. He should not be dependent upon rent support only.

They reached the spot safely; I called her in between work on Saturday to ensure their well-being. They took shelter in Mr. Ranjan's hotel and had breakfast and lunch. Mr. Ranjan and Madhavi specially supervised them. Both of them escorted my Parents to Samarth's house. He was not available in the house then and went to work in the factory. Mother informed me that the house of Samarth is three times bigger than ours. Furnished materials, items, and fittings are lavish and spacious to fill more things.

In the evening, they will be visiting the tea factory to meet Samarth. During our Vacation, we went to three tea factories. I asked her if we had visited his factory before, and she said no. Samarth was welcoming to them. He gave the history of the tea factory. His Paternal Grandfather is the founder and started the business when he was 26 years old in 1960. Father and Uncle Rakesh drank more than two cups of tea. It is like heaven to these brothers. After the visit, they went back to their hotel.

Mr. Ranjan and his wife requested to come to their house the next day for lunch and they have accepted. I reminded her to take an exotic gift basket while visiting and Mother thoughtfully bought it on the way to Ooty. She told me that the house space is a replica of the Samarth house but the built-up and interior design is different.

Samarth joined to have a family lunch with them and talked about Engagement. She has not given any further information by phone but will after she returns.

On Monday, I went to the Office and returned home early. Mother has ordered food online to spare time for me to discuss the Engagement. She was both excited and upset about it. It was decided to conduct the Ceremony in our city after 10 days on Friday by the first week of November or else they have to postpone till January third week due to Samarth's business. She said it will be hectic for two months causing due to the heavy demand for tea and coffee every year. She was upset because it will take place in our house with limited guests. She made a list to invite around ten people from our side excluding us and a few guest from Samarth's side.

I inquired about his Parents with my Mother and whether they have met during their visit. She said that they have not come and only seen their photographs; though they may appear during the Engagement ceremony. I hope his parents attend it as I am looking forward to meeting them.

We did shopping in a day for Groom's ring, dress and other things to gift them. She took the ring size of Samarth in Ooty and I have given ring which I never liked.

Today is the day of the Ring Ceremony. We fixed the timing around 2 pm and after that lunch will be served. It was the best timing for a simple function. If we keep it in the night; we have to summon every Relatives, friends, and Colleagues and our house isn't big enough for more than twenty Guest.

I have purchased a light cream beaded with stones Ghagra Choli to match a stone gold jewelry set and it suits me. I covered the head with a heavily stitched net dupatta. Parents were hurrying to complete the work before Samarth's family and Relatives arrive at our house. Uncle Rakesh, his wife, his son and Father's cousin brother, his wife and their two daughters who are around 19 and 16 years; another Father's cousin sister, her husband, and their only 21-year-old son have been invited. Abhi is happily married to Arush, a Mechanical Engineer, could not come due to her hectic work schedule in Singapore. I miss her.

They entered the house around 1.30 pm settled down to their seats. My cousin's sisters entered the room to pick me and I followed them to the hall. I walked slowly and sat next to Samarth on the couch. He was admiringly staring at me and I was doing the same. He was wearing a navy blue silk kurta suit. All their eyes were set on us when he appreciated me; I blushingly admired him as well. His sister's whole family and other relatives were present. As I scanned the hall, his Parents are missing.

Mr. Ranjan introduced his cousin sister, her husband, and their twin sons who are younger than Rashmika. They appreciated me for how pretty I looked. The tea table was set with juices, sweets, biscuits, chocolates, and snacks, and for the lunch, Roti, butter chicken, Pulao, Palak gravy, Desserts and starters like panner tikka, Dahi vada has been ordered. His relatives and mine brought us packaged gifts that were not necessary. They could have saved it and given it on the Wedding day.

The time was precisely 2 pm and Uncle Rakesh nagged us to start the Ceremony. We exchanged our rings slowly and were applauded by others with claps and whistles. I have chosen him a single-stone diamond ring and mine was a heart-shaped single diamond with a 15-20 minute diamond around it. It was sparkling on my left-hand finger. I came to know that Samarth has chosen it. He has good taste.

Our relatives begin giving us gifts and we accepted them shyly. Everybody was busy talking to each other. I excused myself from sister gossip and asked Samarth whisperingly, "Where are your parents?"

His cheery face turned to sorrow as though I have said something awful. He went into deep thought for a second and said, "They are busy in London and won't make it this month due to their business."

I thought what kind of parents are they that their business is too important than their Son's Engagement?

"Will they come to our Wedding?" I inquired.

"Yes. Probably," he replied.

"Probably? Why?" I questioned.

"It depends according to their work schedule, if they are busy; they won't make it," he explained.

"Don't you complain about it to your Parents about their way of thinking," I angrily said in a low tone.

"I did many times. But we are used to it," he calmly said.

I want to ask him more; Father distracted me by announcing lunchtime. We left the couch and went to the dining table, his family, relatives and I sat together. Father, mother, and Uncle Rakesh served the food to our guests, the rest will eat after them.

I understand now why his face is in remorse when I asked about his parents; I would like to talk to them and protest if they didn't attend our Wedding.

After lunch, Our Elders rounded up to plan the wedding date. Uncle Rakesh informed us that getting a date in Court marriage is not easy. Samarth confirmed that he will be free after the second week of January. He said that the date must be from or after 16 January. I hope my Parents manage to fix the date on his birthday, there will be a double celebration.

In the meantime, I showed the room to Samarth leaving us alone with others to give us space. He looked at the room admiringly and was amazed that I have not kept any favorite actors and celebrity posters as his sister and niece kept in their rooms. I admire and watch movies of my favorite actors; never go to the extent of keeping posters. I told him the intention to get married on his birthday. He said he is hoping the same. He wanted to marry at the end of this month because these two months his dealers demand bulk orders which gives more profit to his business than the rest of the months.

I said even if he is ready this month, I won't accept it. He asked the reason for the denial. I told him I had to shop for the Wedding, reception dress and other clothes, invitations, and arrangements will be tough for us.

We exchanged our phone numbers, he reminded me not to call him as he will be busy the whole day and night even on Sunday. He will call me when he is free, he only gets time to sleep; sometimes he slept in the factory office a few times. He consoled me that he will not sleep in the factory after marriage, and will return to the house as soon as possible. I asked him the motive for such huge demand; he explained that due to the winter season, festival gifting, and Corporate Gifting like Diwali, Christmas, New Year's Eve, and others which give this business is a high priority. I can't believe my ears that tea and Coffee can be used for gifting. I have received diaries, Mugs, and calendars only in the working station.

I understand him as he is the sole owner to take care of his Grandfather's business. His Father was not interested and does not want to follow in his Father's footsteps. He started his own RO plant Company and his wife supported him which excelled after Samarth's birth. Samarth had one younger brother Abhinav who died at the age of 7 due to pneumonia. If he was alive, he would have taken care of it or joined his Father's RO plant in London.

Mr. Ranjan came to my room informing Samarth that they are leaving now. I want to know more about his brother but had to part ways. He took my hands with both his hands making me shiver with his touch; he said farewell.

It was 5.30 pm when the entire Guest left us; I changed my dress to formal. Mother called me to unwrap the presents. She handed me the first gift that looked like a chest box. When I opened it, it was filled with eight assorted different flavors of tea.

"Who gave this?" I asked Mother.

"Samarth," she said.

"When?" I asked her.

"While you were in the room after they entered the house," she replied.

"Why didn't you tell me?" I inquired.

"Sorry. I was busy taking care of the Guest. It is not the only present he brought," she informed me.

"What else are there?" I was curious.

"I am opening it; it is a red Kanchipuram silk sari. It is beautiful," she said flatteringly. I went near her to glare at it. It has an excellent design with a Zari maroon border. I inquired her to show me the other presents from Samarth. They were a few wrapped gifts; I removed them one by one. It is a Perfume, Leather Jewelry box, Scented oil, and candles. I was ashamed of not buying any presents for him. Mother showed me the other people's package.

Mr. Ranjan and his wife gifted us a basket filled with exotic homemade chocolates, fruit Champagne, different flavors of jams, dry fruits, and cookies. The Guest gifts were a set of pans, an Aromatic spice gift box, and other ceramic showpieces.

I thought to call him to express gratitude. His phone was ringing continuously. I tried again after a minute, "Hello," he said.

"Huh! It is me, Leena. Are you busy?" I asked him.

"No. I was in the bathroom; I reached here at the hotel ten minutes before," he replied.

"Oh! I called you to say thank you for the gifts especially the sari is gorgeous," My voice was flattered.

"You don't have to say thank you. It is a custom to bring the present to the Bride," he informed. That is true, how could I forget as I have already seen it many times.

"Still I want to thank you and sorry for not buying you anything," I apologized.

"Don't say sorry. Besides, I don't want anything," he cleared it.

"Do you like the ring?" I said to lighten the conversation.

“Yes, I heard you have selected it. Do you like my ring?” he questioned me back.

“Yes, the Sari too,” I replied.

“I want you to do me a favor if you like the Sari,” he asked.

“What is it?” I inquired.

“Can you wear it on our Wedding day in Court? If you are comfortable with it; you can wear anything during the Reception,” he answered.

I thought for a moment, “Okay,” I told.

“Great. I will be looking forward to seeing you,” he said. I could hear the happiness in his voice.

“Me too. Bye,” I said hanging up. I don’t fancy wearing the sari though I want to gift him by wearing it, by making him happy.

I went to Mother as she was sitting on the couch. I said, “Did you inquire about Samarth’s Parents today from Madhavi?”

“Yes. I did,” she told me.

“What did she say?” I asked oddly.

“They could not come due to their busy schedule in business in London that is getting hard to complete,” she replied.

“That’s it. Have you asked further?” I said.

“No. What is it, dear?” she asked seeing the stress on my face.

“Don’t you find it odd that the Parents miss out on their Children's Engagement? The day every Parent enjoy or takes advantage of something they eagerly waited for,” I doubted.

“I understand what you are saying. I feel the same as you. I am concentrating about you and the Groom's matchmaking only. I do not consider the Parents right now,” she said calmly.

"You should take into account about his Parents to Madhavi. Samarth said that they may or may not be attending the Wedding. Who does that? Which Parents do that? What do people say when you and Father are not attending their daughter's marriage?" I said.

"Okay, I will ask her. What to do if she says they are not coming?" she questioned.

"Tell her that you would like to talk to their Parents. Compel her to give the number no matter what. We will interrogate them for such carelessness. What are they proving by not attending the Wedding? What is the motive?" I said hastily.

"You are right. It is weird to think Parents do such a thing. I will meet them and ask about it if they are coming," she replied.

"Good," I said.

Father and Uncle Rakesh went to Court the other day with the necessary documents to secure the date of the marriage. After discussing with Groom's family, they concluded on 21st January 2019 on Monday. The Reception will be organized by the Groom's Family in the evening. They planned to conduct it in the Hotel for the Reception; they will be staying for the night or two before the Wedding. I find it expensive.

Samarth called me after 10 days and wanted to know my well-being as I got a fever the day before. Of course, Mother said this while contacting Madhavi and she said to him.

He said, "How are you feeling now?"

"Better," I lied. My head was aching a little.

"Have you consulted the Doctor?" he inquired.

"Yes," I said.

"Did you drink the organic tea I gave you?" he asked.

"No," I told the truth.

"Why not?" he demanded.

"You know, I don't drink tea. I thought you had given it to my Parents," I said.

"It is for both you and your family. Please drink and tell me which you like the most?" he requested.

"Okay," I said.

"Believe me you will surely not resist this one. You will feel good in your condition, try the tulsi tea," he said confidently. I feel like he is playing the tea game.

"Sure," I said approvingly.

The Wedding date is coming near; I still feel unprepared for it. We have printed more than twenty less than thirty reception cards. Mr. Ranjan said that they needed only nine cards. Uncle Rakesh and Father took the workload to distribute it, giving me a few cards for my friends and Colleagues. I have planned to invite a few close friends from my College and School-Saranya, Udaya, Priyanka, and Mayank who are settled in Chennai, the rest I could not ask as they are settled out of the station and Country. The office staff will be Mrs. Raheela, Mr. Vivek and others, especially my boss.

I have given my job resignation to the office and card at once. I am going to work till Pongal Holidays on January 16 and I have to train my new replacement. I have bought the Reception dress, heels, and other necessary dresses and items to live in Ooty. This time I bought a present for Samarth and his whole family. Mother called Madhavi to inquire about their parents; she said they are coming. I am relieved to hear it.

On January 16th, I called him to say happy birthday as he is turning 33 years old. He responded with warm words but told me that he find it very uncomfortable to celebrate it. Men leave behind their birthday celebrations when they become mature. Though I bought him his birthday gift and will give him on our wedding day.

On January 17th, office staff organized the farewell party for me as they do for every retired staff. I am truly delighted about such a party as I am not retiring but starting a new path. I am gonna miss my work, office, and staff, especially Mrs. Raheela for being there and guiding me.

On January 19th, Samarth checked in to the hotel near the airport with his sister's family. There is no news about his parents; may attend on Reception. I have packed every necessary item amounting to up to two big suitcases as I will be traveling by Airplane to Coimbatore on 22nd January morning. I prefer by traveling train; Samarth insisted and planned according to save time. He has called me three times from Engagement till today. He is a man of few words. Mother advised me to adjust whenever, wherever necessary particularly for two months as he will be busy in the future.

The Designer applied henna on my hand the day before the Wedding. This is my last day as Leena Kumar; tomorrow I will be Leena Kumar Karthik. I am nervous, sad, and excited and sometimes my feet get cold. I have not known him very well in this limited time. I have no other choice than to leap to marry this guy.

I found Mother hiding her tears whenever she looked at me. Sisters and Brothers surround me except for Abhi, who got her tickets delayed by her husband, who may meet at the Wedding. I miss her as I am close to her apart from others. I want to talk to her in person as I could not complete the conversation through a phone or video call. I started missing this house and will be difficult to leave every corner, every wall, and every stair.

On January 21st, we were getting ready, and I find it hard to wear a sari. Mother wore cement color silk sari and helped me wear it. She was angry and insisted I go to a beauty parlor before and I refused it as I can do my makeup professionally. Father has groomed himself by now with a kurta set, continuously reminding us that the time of signing is 2 pm. We have to reach before or at exactly 1 pm for our presence. I kept the packed birthday gift inside the handbag. We left the house at 11.30 am along with Uncle Rakesh and his family. Other relatives will join the Reception as Uncle Rakesh gave an opinion not to overcrowd the Court. He wore a light purple shirt and black pants, his wife Tejaswini wore a purple Benaras sari, and his son grey shirt and black pants. We rented a car for us while Uncle Rakesh brought his own.

We arrived at the Court at 12.50 pm and I could not find Samarth. Today was a sunny day; I could feel the sweat running down my forehead spoiling my makeup. Maybe I am nervous until I find Samarth. Father saw the spot for us to sit and wait as they will do the rest of the procedure. This wait is making me agitated; every second is beating my heart like a clap of thunder. The corridor of the premises was filled with many couples along with their Families.

Uncle Rakesh could feel my tension and took out his phone to dial Mr. Ranjan. I see closely toward the back of him, Samarth arriving. He was wearing cream color silk Sherwani set; his sister's family followed him. I got up from my seat praising his face, features, and dress. He smilingly greeted my family and he looked over me exhaling said "Wow." He stared at me intensely making me shy. He took out his white handkerchief handing me to wipe the sweat. I forgot that I have it distracted myself by his physique I was admiring.

I addressed Madhavi, her husband, and their children; Rashmika and Siddharth came forward to tell me that I am looking gorgeous. Madhavi wore heavy work green sari, her daughter was wearing a golden stone studded gown-type churidar dress. Mr. Ranjan and his sons wearing light blue, yellow, and aquamarine kurta sets.

Father notified us that it will take more than half an hour for our turn. I sat again at my previous place; Samarth sat beside me. His family and mine gave us space standing a few steps distance away.

He begins, “Are you okay?”

“Yes,” I said awkwardly.

“And you?” I asked.

“I am fine. You look.... beautiful,” he said slowly staring directly toward my eyes.

“Thank you. You look beautiful too,” I said stupidly.

“Beautiful?” he questioned me raising his eyebrow.

“I am sorry, handsome. It's just that I am a little nervous,” I replied.

“I can see that,” he said hinting at my forehead.

There is still some sweat appearing on my forehead; wiped it again and I see the foundation cream on the white handkerchief. I took out the gift box from my bag meant for his birthday and handed it to him.

“What is this?” He asked.

“Belated Happy birthday to you,” I gave wishing him.

“You shouldn’t have bought it,” he took it disapprovingly.

“Open it,” I commanded. He unwrapped the gift box slowly, his face lit up when he saw the Gold watch.

“I loved it. Thank you,” he said appreciating my choice.

“You deserve it,” I said

As he was admiring the present, I could see his face seem different; like he has done something to glow.

“Have you done something for your face? I could see it is dissimilar like you have done facial,” I asked.

"Um! What? No," he guarded himself.

"Your face is deeply cleansed," I interrogated.

"How...How do you know that?" he hesitated.

"I can smell it," I replied.

"You can smell it?" he questioned surprisingly.

"Yes. My Mother is a beautician; her hand was always covered with the scent of beauty creams," I explained.

"Your mother is not working for the past ten years, then how did you recognize it is facial; it could be After shave or other things?" he asked.

"Mother has done to me facial hundred times; I know how I look like after it is completed and the smell is easier to catch what kind of cream it is," I elaborated.

"Well, what do you smell on my face? Which flavor can you tell?" he challenged me. I came close to him to sniff which made him uncomfortable.

"It is a fruit facial," I answered after a few seconds.

"Amazing," he was astonished.

"Thank you," I said.

"I never wanted to do it but sister insisted," he informed me.

"Do you always listen to her?" I had to know how close he is to his sister.

"No, not always. She guides me when it is necessary and never compel about it. This time she threatened me that she won't allow my wedding without facial," he chuckled.

"I am glad she had done that," I approved of her suggestion. What is a man who does not clean himself perfectly on his wedding day?

Uncle Rakesh came near us informing to get prepared as our turn is near. We steadied ourselves. A man approached him with two garlands in his hands. Samarth introduced to us, Mr. Raghav. He is the manager and friend of Samarth working in the tea factory, both are school buddies. He is around 5.8 or 5.10 feet, has red skin, looked a little older and leaner than Samarth, though good-looking. I am pleased to meet his friend accompanying us.

We went inside the Court Room led us by Uncle Rakesh in front of the Marriage Registrar; we were standing side by side. We were handed the garlands to exchange, Samarth leaped to put it and then I did. The Registrar showed us the spot to sign in the Registration book. Father, Uncle Rakesh, and Madhavi became our witnesses. Everybody applauded.

The Ceremony itself was over in minutes. One by one hugged and congratulated us, Mother was crying happy tears so does Madhavi.

This man Samarth has become my husband and I am his wife. My life as Leena Kumar is over. I can't believe this moment will ever occur in my life especially with one who is handsome, rich, running a fine Business, and with a sense of humor and morality. I don't understand the combination of the Man who has Ten Crores Tea Company with a 90 lakhs annual turnover deducting expenditure along with 4.5 crore house pairing the Woman who has 15 lakhs earned bank balance, 21 lakhs jewelry and a 2.5 crore house which gives us 60k rent per month that belongs to my father's name and will be mine after his death. He is ten times wealthier than me. Probably I am lucky.

Chapter 8

THE RECEPTION

Finally, the Marriage Ceremony is over. We all left the premises of the court to reach the Hotel to begin our reception. We went near the parking lot, and they prepared two rented cars, one was a large Maroon Innova and the other was a white Prime model decorated with jasmine and rose flowers. They thought it will be a burden to bring their vehicle as we will travel by plane tomorrow. As I went near my rented car with Mother, Samarth requested to accompany him. I did not refuse, though I hinted him that I'll travel with Mother for now. Mother was furious; she and father lead me to the garlanded car. She reminded me that I must follow him as he is now my husband. I was a bit annoyed by it as we will have more time together once we will leave this city tomorrow.

Samarth sat next to me in the car and whispered, "I am sorry for not letting you go with your family."

"It is alright. It is not your fault, it is mine. I am just so used to riding with them, I almost forgot about the tradition to ride with a Groom after a Wedding," I said.

Our driver started the engine of the car and I was perplexed as others are not coming with us. I asked him, "Is one of your family not coming with us? There is a lot of space here."

"No. That car is big enough to carry seven people and my sister's family total is five," he explained.

"I know that car is huge. Isn't it obvious that one of your families should travel with the Bride and Groom?" I told him.

"It should doesn't mean it must," he said sternly. I recognize that he wants to ride with me alone except for the driver. It will take time around thirty to forty minutes to reach there.

Ten minutes have gone, and we spend the moment staring at the passing view. I thought he will ask me something as he wanted me alone, though he looked at my side several times. He cleared his throat to start the conversation with all his strength. I never intended to meet and marry such a shy guy.

At last, he got his guts, "Are you okay?"

"What? Yeah! I am fine," I said calmly.

"Are you happy?" he asked staring directly. I thought like happy about what?

"I am happy. Why are you asking?" I questioned.

"It seems you are not behaving like every Bride should, Energetic, full of joy, fear in their eyes. You are calm like it is not even your Wedding," he described.

"I could ask you the same. You are behaving like you are going to attend the business meeting, very silent, composed," I targeted him.

"I am usually always like this shy, calm like to spend time by myself," he chuckled.

"I think I am just like you, introvert. When it is coming to Weddings, I am persistent to go properly without any dispute. It is like a task for me to complete it without hurdles," I cleared all my theory.

"I want you to enjoy it rather than taking it as an assignment," he advised me.

"You have not seen me enjoy other events, it is our Wedding that I am quiet," I said teasingly.

"What did you do in Social Activity?" he asked me curiously.

"Haven't Mr. Ranjan told you anything about what I did at my cousin sister's Wedding? What did he say about me then?" I asked him.

"He said that you are beautiful, naturally energetic, clever, and honest," he said.

"That's it?" I was curious.

"Yes. Is there anything else he forgot to tell me?" he hastily asked me.

"He never said that I am impulsive and straightforward; I will dance like a maniac if it is my favorite junk music," I said with a smile.

"Oh," he went to his thinking.

"Do you think you can handle that kind of wife?" I teased him.

For a moment he was silent and said, "Yes, I can," smiling at me.

"Do you feel betrayed for not expanding details about me by your brother-in-law," I asked him cautiously. I had to know his meaning.

"No. I am glad he met you," happiness appeared in his tone.

We sat silently after our brief moment, reaching our destination. The Hotel seemed Grand when we stepped into it. We all went inside the restaurant of the hotel to have lunch. I ate lightly as I don't want to throw up due to stomach ache. Samarth separated from me after lunch to get ready in his room. His sister and niece took me and my Family gang to the Reception Venue. Inside the venue, there is a bridal room. Mother gave me the bag of Lehenga Choli dress; I bought the pink stone studded design with silver lace.

Madhavi has arranged a make-up and hairstylist, but I declined it. Madhavi insisted as she has paid the amount in advance. I had no choice but to follow.

I got ready around 6 pm. The Hairstylist did a braided-up bun hairstyle on my hair. Abhi arrived and came to the room to congratulate me. She reached here around 5.30 pm. I showed disappointed for not attending the Engagement and Marriage. She apologized to me many times. I forgave her.

Abhi told me that she and Arush met Samarth and he is more fine-looking than her husband. I interrogated about her husband's whereabouts; she said he is having a conversation with Samarth and will meet us on the stage. She has booked a room in this Hotel and will be accompanying me till the Airport.

Madhavi, Mother, and Abhi took me to the Venue, on the stage. When I entered the place, Samarth was in a black Tuxedo suit with a bow tie. He looks like a Christian Groom. I don't know how to react except smile. He has a high-quality taste in dressing. My Lehenga weighed a lot to lift while stepping on the stair of the stage, and Rashmika helped me to go. Samarth was smiling continuously at me while I smiled for a few seconds. I was nervous so was Samarth.

Our Reception occurred after the welcome drinks had been served by the waiter to us. I feel relaxed now. All I need was a refreshing Smoothie.

Mr. Raghav, his wife, and children who are 8 years old boy and 4 years old girl came to us to wish. His wife has darker skin than Mr. Raghav, his children looked similar to him. Madhavi, her husband gifted me the long diamond earrings to me and the Gold bracelet to Samarth.

The whole hall started filling up with people; his relatives and mine were intermingling. His family and mine were taking care of the Guest, and only Rashmika was by my side helping me by handling the presents. She was making me relax in between the arrival of the visitor who was wishing us.

A middle-aged couple has come from Samarth's side. He introduced them as his Grandmother's friend Mrs. Lincy's son Mr. Scott, Daughter-in-law Mrs. Scott, and Grandson Samuel Scott. The son said that his Mother could not make it due to a cold fever. I heard they live in Ooty.

Many close and far away relatives attended, one handed us a big wrapped package, while the other a small wrapped box. A few people gave us cover filled with cash while the latter flower bouquet. The Photographer and Video person took our stills. Samarth's few friends, factory staff, and my Colleagues came in a group; only my friends have not come yet.

Samarth excused himself to take a bathroom break and the Guest was not visiting us for the past 10 minutes.

It was 8 pm and I am hungry. I should have eaten something in between when I was getting dressed as we will be the last to have dinner after all our Guests have gone. Rashmika could see the tiredness on the face.

“Are you okay?” She asked me.

“I am fine,” I said. I don’t want to burden this little girl as she has done a lot for me today.

"No, you are not fine. You look pale. Do you want to go to the bathroom?" she worriedly asked.

"No. I am hungry," I explained.

"Oh, I see," she said. She immediately took her bag, and begin searching inside; there she was holding a chocolate bar. She gave me the bar to eat. I am so thankful to her, she is a lifesaver.

"Thank you. How long have you keeping this chocolate?" I asked her in the middle of taking bites.

"I just bought it yesterday for you," she said.

"Why?" I was stunned.

"I knew you feel hungry as my mother fainted at her Wedding as a result of starvation," She elaborated. I am amazed by her thoughtfulness.

"You are so sweet, Rashmika. You are a good bridesmaid. Do you want some chocolate?" I offered her.

"Thank you. I am not hungry. I have two more chocolate slabs with me just in case you need them," she told me.

As I was eating the piece of it, a sound that I could recognize said, "Eating alone. Do you mind sharing the chocolate?" It was Mayank, my best friend.

He shook my hand and hugged me. He exactly appeared the same when I met him 3 years before for his Wedding.

"Of course," I gave him a few pieces of it.

"Thank you," he said. He ate it in one full mouth.

"This is my husband's niece, Rashmika. This is my friend, Mayank," I introduced them to each other.

"How do you do, Rashmika?" he asked.

"I am good. Please you two carry on," she said and left us to arrange the gifts accordingly.

"I am so happy you came," I was excited.

"It is my pleasure. You look lovely," he praised me holding my both hands with his.

"Thank you. Where is your wife?" I asked him.

"She is talking to Priyanka," he said.

"Priyanka, when did she come?" I asked him immediately.

"We both arrived at this place at the same time. They got carried away talking from the parking spot to the hall. I left them to their chat to meet you," he described.

"I believe that your wife is still talkative," I teased him.

"Yeah, I know. She increased her banter after Marriage which is torturing my ear," he said. I could not help but laugh with him.

I was so involved with the giggles that could not notice Samarth was watching us. He came near slowly with a displeasure look. I introduced Mayank to my husband. They shook hands firmly.

Mayank teased Samarth, "All the best man for marrying an irritating woman." I punched Mayank on his shoulder. He was smiling continuously.

"Don't you worry, I can handle her," Samarth said calmly.

"I will assure you one thing she is less talkative compared to my wife. You are safer than me," he said with a humorous tone.

"You are married?" he asked him in a serious tone.

"Yes, I am. Look, there she is," he gestured toward his wife coming near us. Mayank introduced his wife to my husband. She wished us long life together. She commenced her talkativeness by praising me to Samarth about how I helped her on her wedding day. She went on and on, her husband thought that it was enough of a chat and Priyanka was waiting her turn to converse; Mayank came to our rescue. He excused himself and his wife.

Priyanka's conversation was a few words. I asked about her husband, she said he could not come as he went to Dubai for the project. She left us following Mayank and his wife to the food stall.

Samarth and I were alone on the stage, "Where have you met Mayank?" he asked curiously.

"We met in school. He and Priyanka are my childhood buddies," I explained.

"It seems you are very close to him," he said.

"Yes. He is not a usual person. Many boys in my class were having male gangs but he was blending with everybody," I said.

"I can see that when he was holding your hands," his tone showed the sign of jealousy which is a new thing I found in him. I must convince him that we are just friends before he makes up his mind about our relationship in a bad sense; though I have to wait to see the limit of it. How does this behavior end?

"Yes. He holds the hand of those who he is near," I said to boost his spite.

"Ok," he said coldly. His face becomes dark and severe as he is imagining. I don't want to create doubts on our first day.

"If you two become friends, he will hold your hands too," I said the truth about Mayank's friendship, his broadminded, his way of having fun.

"Really?" he was unconvinced.

"Yes, I am not lying," I said. Samarth laughed for a minute; I knew this will make him giggle.

"He is exceptional," he admired him.

Udaya and Saranya came late with their husbands and children. I introduced them as college friends to Samarth. They made their discussion lightly with us.

A few close Guests hung around at 9.30 pm. Mr. Ranjan took us to the buffet. Uncle Rakesh, his family, my parents, and Samarth's family accompanied us to eat. I kept a keen eye on Mother as she may consume oily food a lot, though she didn't. Well, I am relieved.

After dinner, all Guests left us; only my parents and Uncle Rakesh's family were present. Abhi and Arush didn't stay long and went to their room. Mother hugged and caressed us with a blessing and will meet us at the Airport tomorrow.

Madhavi gave all the presents to Mom and Dad and will keep them as we are unable to carry them by Airplane due to luggage limits. Samarth told my Parents to use up the gifts as it is not necessary. I agreed with him as I recall that his house is much occupied with everything. Mother insisted that she will send it through courier or bring it by herself. We said okay. They parted with a smile.

It was 10.30 pm, it is our Wedding night, and I have to share the bed with Samarth from now onwards. I was tired and nervous. We all left the hall together. Mr. Ranjan has booked three rooms in this hotel- one for them, one for their children, and the third for Samarth.

Samarth saw the uneasiness in me and advised Madhavi to let me sleep separately tonight. Madhavi unhappily agreed. She counseled Rashmika to sleep with me and Samarth decided to share the room with his nephews.

Is he always a gentleman? Isn't it every man's desire to sleep with his wife on the wedding night? Is it for his bashfulness? Or doesn't want to rush for it?

I could not sleep the whole night. It is not because of a new place, though it is about Samarth's nature. It was 4 am, and Rashmika slept soundly next to me. I should shut my eyes for a bit.

Chapter 9

A New Journey to Begin

I opened my eyes suddenly due to repeated knocks on the door. It was 7.30 am. Rashmika did not wake up for the hard work she did yesterday. I could hear it was Madhavi. I unlock the door immediately. Madhavi made us aware we get ready and meet them at the lobby at 9.30 am. The flight time is 12.40 pm; we have to reach the Airport before 2 hours departure.

I woke Rashmika and went to the restroom to bathe. When I returned, she has packed all her belongings. My two big suitcases are readily packed. I told her to shower slowly as we have more time. I charged the mobile and checked the whole room if we have left anything. She is a fast person to take a bath unlike me. We both got ready at 9.15 am. We left the room to check on others. Madhavi was combing her hair, Mr. Ranjan was packing the bag, and Siddharth and Vinay were idly playing as they are all set.

After a few minutes, Samarth came to Madhavi's room along with his bag. He wished us Good Morning. Mr. Ranjan advised Samarth to take me and Rashmika to the entrance hall and complete the checking out from the hotel and wait in the restaurant.

We all three left the room, Samarth called an attendant to bring the baggage cart for our bags. He helped us to the Reception area and tipped him a good amount. We waited on the lobby sofa while he did the procedure, it took only 15 minutes. We planned to wait for others in the Restaurant. Samarth called his Sister to inform our place and ordered breakfast for us. I declined him to order breakfast for me as I would not digest it by lack of sleep. He recommended drinking juice at least which I drank.

As we are eating up the food, Madhavi and others joined us. They ordered their breakfast. I waited to meet my Parents for the last time before departing. I called Abhi about her whereabouts. I want to meet her before we leave the hotel. She said she will meet me at the Airport as she got up now. She is a lazy bone during her leave.

We left the Restaurant and reached at 10.30 am. It took 15 minutes to add traffic and signals as we are nearby the Airport. I was searching every corner at the Airport front for a minute.

My Parents and Uncle Rakesh waved at us. My happiness knew no bounds by staring at them. They came closer to us, Mother's eyes were dripping with tears. I instructed her to stay strong. They arrived here before 10 am. Abhi and Arush arrived just in time. She promised me that she will visit us after a few months.

Mr. Ranjan informed us that it is time to leave. We embraced each other; Mother kissed me a lot on the cheeks. Samarth was watching us; his expression was deeply sad. I feel he is missing his Parents through our love.

The plane took off after we boarded it. Vinay sat next to me, I was in the middle, and Samarth was on the aisle side. I gave Vinay the window seat to view the scenery, and I informed him that I will take the nap. Madhavi, Rashmika, and Siddharth were seated in front of us while Mr. Ranjan was seated on the aisle side next to Madhavi's aisle seat.

Before boarding the plane, Samarth checked on me after parting with my family whether I am crying. Probably he thought I might drench the dupatta with tears. I was not weeping but I was sad. Usually, women cry after a Wedding and I don't know why I am this detached. I used to cry a lot when I was a teenager, but now all the sentiment is blank. There is something wrong with me or else I became so strong that there is no room for sensitivity.

Samarth woke me up as we are close to landing. I still feel sleepy. We went to the parking lot of Coimbatore Airport. Two persons came near us who looks like the staff or driver of Mr. Ranjan or Samarth. They handed the Car keys to us and left. So, they are the staff. One car belongs to Samarth and the latter belongs to Mr. Ranjan. I traveled with Samarth in SUV Car alone while Mr. Ranjan, and his family in an Innova Crysta car followed us. I could see the mountains and it is the point to ascend. I usually get scared whenever the vehicle driving on the peak road.

"So tell me. How was your work? Did you love your job?" he questioned me distracting the fear in me.

I sighed "Satisfying," I replied to him.

"That's all. I was expecting a few sentences or paragraphs from you," He was expecting more than I revealed it.

"It is not that much interesting. It is just a job," I compromised him to leave the subject but he was determined by looking at my face to expose more.

"You know you should not talk while driving and keep your eyes on the front," I reminded him.

“Don’t worry about that, I am a good driver,” He replied enthusiastically.

“Do you always chat with others while driving or is it me who you want to have a conversation with?” I was curious to know now as he was still driving.

“Both,” he told me. It is obvious that it is his habit to speak while driving.

“You should concentrate on driving now, we can talk later. It is said that ‘even the best driver can make accidents',” I could feel he is disappointed due to my sarcastic quote. There was silence for a few minutes and he deliberately glanced in between at me. I had to ask him for his continuous glare.

“What is it?” I asked him.

“Why are you so scared of my driving?” he asked.

“I am not afraid of your driving,” I told him.

“Yes, you are. I can see on your face,” He pressured me to reveal the lean road he is driving on which scares me a lot.

“Do you feel safe driving on this narrow road while discussing with people?” I said in a tense tone.

“Yes, always,” his eyes were on the front.

“But I don’t feel secure mounting on the road through the mountains, viewing the scene from the top of the car which makes me dizzy,” I explained to him and he gave away nothing when he recognized my fear.

“You don’t have to worry about it. I have been driving this hill for my whole life,” he ensured me with his smile.

“So, are you driving this hill for 33 years?” I asked him hiding my smile to know his reaction to the humor.

"What?" his reaction was questionable at first and we chuckled together. I am glad he figured out my jokes about 'whole life'; only a few can understand the humor.

"Sorry, I mean I have been driving this hill for 12 years or more I think," he shyly smiled and apologized at the same time. He pause his talk for minutes and I was enjoying the view through the car. He was right about his driving, about the road, about the speed, etc. and I wouldn't judge him now; I need more time to know him.

"Leena," He distracted me.

"Yes," I replied.

"You have not replied to my question yet," he said.

"About what?" I had forgotten what he asked before the driving part.

"About your job," he asked again.

"Why are you not letting it go about the job?" I sounded irritated this time.

"It's just that I am curious about it," He replied with a smile.

"Okay. My work was good and nearly satisfying, but it is always repetitive which is boring for me. There is nothing new but the pay was good. I was expecting a little change in work that will be exciting," I explained the boring speech to him.

"So, you want some challenge in your job," He repeated in a short form.

"Yes! A small change couldn't hurt. Too much of challenges can make me annoyed and not have enough patience to handle them," he was listening to every word I uttered.

Samarth stayed quiet the whole trip after our brief talk, I feel the cold shiver in my hands. He hinted that we are almost there. It took more than 2 hours to reach his house. The road was getting lonelier and bushier trees on the side as I could not see one person walking. He turned right to the small lane which will be enough for the big truck to move and one blue house situated on the corner of the starting lane. We moved further inside the street, I saw a big bright yellow single-story mansion type with one balcony located at the end. He got out of the car to open the gate. He parked next to his old red car. I got out of the car to have a better sight of the house. I turned to see another big house cottage type which is in white situated on the left side of our house separated by a plant fence. The white house was thirty yards far away from us.

I inquired about the white one; he said it belongs to Mr. Aasif Khan, our neighbor. He has one car and one scooter bike parked outside the house. Only three houses situated in this 500 meters long street, it will probably take approximately 6 minutes to walk, to get out of this lane.

I was willing to ask more about our neighbor, Mr. Ranjan's car arrived. He and his family got out of the car.

"Do you like the house, Leena?" Mr. Ranjan smiled at me.

"Yes. It is beautiful," I admired it.

"Well, you have not seen inside, the interior is magnificently designed by Madhavi. First, we have to unload yours and Samarth's suitcases," he explained.

Samarth and Mr. Ranjan started removing baggage from the car. Madhavi instructed Rashmika to stay with me and went to unlock the house with her children. Rashmika said that her mother went to arrange the Graha Pravesh items. Samarth and I waited outside for the traditional ritual. It was 4.15 pm, and the climate here made me feel chilly as if the temperature has dropped 1 or 2 degrees minute by minute. I hope it gets over soon, as I can't stand here.

Once we were inside, I see it is not a house but a genuine mansion constructed with wood flooring. The hall was big and furnished with two sets of sofas with a tea table, a vast three-chest drawer, and a 40-inch flat screen on it, a dining table near the kitchen room on the right side, near the fire chimney on the left side two large single sofa chairs. The back of the sofa chairs have wooden stairs attached to the left wall. If I move further inside the right side of the hall, there is one locked room next to the kitchen. The whole wall is covered with scenery painting, a cordless landline phone, and a lamp on the mahogany table next to the stairs, attached two or more candle stands with two candles on every corner; I think the current light goes out here sometimes. A mini crystal kind chandelier hung on the ceiling. There is one window next to the entrance covered with drapes. The children sat down on the sofa. As Mr. Ranjan said, it is magnificent.

"You are right, Mr. Ranjan. This interior is beautifully designed by Madhavi," I said in an amazed tone. She has studied Bachelor of Science in interior design and I must say she has a talent.

Madhavi smiled, "Thank you. I have done only a few changes, the rest was done by our Grandmother long ago. If you want to change anything, go ahead," she said.

"No, no. It is perfect," I assured her. Samarth smiled at me broadly.

"Do you want to see the back of the house?" Mr. Ranjan asked me.

"Sure," I said.

There is a back door covered with long curtains next to the locked room, Mr. Ranjan leads us the way. He widely opened it to show the garden view. It was big enough to play badminton or Kabaddi. A gentle wind was touching my face.

Before they move forward, I said, "Please wait, I will wear the sweater."

I removed the sweater from one of the suitcases I packed. All children went out without wearing warm clothes, it seems they are accustomed to this weather.

I went outside with Madhavi and Mr. Ranjan, Samarth following us. There are two trees and lots of plants growing in pots and in the Garden. There is a garden table chair set with a huge umbrella attached to the Ground near them. The area of the Garden must be two-thirds of the house and a long fence on the border. The white cottage house looks near from here. I recognized a few plants that are jasmine, hibiscus, rose, and aloe vera on the pot; I cannot guess the others and the trees.

"What are those trees' names?" I asked.

"The one on the left is an Orange tree and on the right is a pomegranate," Mr. Ranjan said.

"Do these trees give fruits?" I was curious.

"Yes. The fruition timing is from March. It gives you bulk," he said.

"Who plucks the fruits?" I asked.

"Nobody," Samarth said.

"Why is that?" I questioned.

"We rarely come here to stay and Samarth is busy enough to take care of the house and work," Mr. Ranjan said.

"Why not we consume it if the tree is giving us fruits?" I asked.

"Well, I pluck one or two oranges to eat," Madhavi said. Her children are running and playing.

"What about the children?" I asked.

"They will pluck it only if the chocolates and desserts are growing on this tree," Mr. Ranjan scoffed at his children. I laughed slightly.

"I think we should order lunch. Leena must be hungry and the children ate all the snacks on the way," Madhavi suggested to Mr. Ranjan. She is right, I am famished. You feel like vomiting if you eat on the way to the mountains.

"I already did," Samarth said.

We went inside the house; Madhavi informed us that they will leave after lunch. I insisted they stay with us tonight, but they declined it. Mr. Ranjan took our luggage upstairs after I gave all the presents to them. I bought a tea set made in silver for Mr. Ranjan and his wife, a gown with matching artificial jewelry for Rashmika, a Volcano science kit for Siddharth, and a racer car for Vinay.

Samarth was picking up the food in the doorway from the delivery guy. The food was hot and tasty; I feel like I could eat more but I didn't. After lunch, they prepared to depart from us.

The sun is about to set, they left us at 5.45 pm. Samarth went inside to start the fire chimney while I stood there watching the barren road. I am afraid to get inside but I could not stand there as the wind blew heavily. I am nervous, alone with Samarth in this Enormous house.

He lit the fire and I was standing there watching the hall. I searched for the remote of the television screen inside the drawer to pass time. As I was looking for it, Samarth came near me.

"Do you want to see the rest of the house?" he asked.

"Umm, okay," I said. He was about to take me upstairs though I stopped him that I want to see the locked room next to the kitchen.

"Oh! That one. It belongs to Grandparents," he said it taking out his house key from his jeans pocket. He lead the way, and I followed.

When he opened the door, the room was furnished with a mahogany queen size Bed with two small drawers on each side with lamps on it; there is a window exactly the shape of the entrance hall window covered with long curtains. There are three wooden cupboards built on the wall across the bed and a long five-rack of cupboards stacked with books. There is slight dust when I touched the drawer.

I stayed with him appreciating the room, "Shall we go upstairs?" he asked suddenly.

"Okay," I have no choice but to obey. I cannot stay here. He locked the room and hurried to go upstairs. I climbed slowly on the stairs watching a few framed photos of the family on the wall; I paused to see one of the childhood photos of Samarth, Madhavi, and his late brother Abhinav and they all were laughing. Samarth on the above two steps followed my eyes.

"We took that photo when Madhavi completed her 10th standard; I completed 3rd grade and my brother 1st grade," he said. I see the happiness and pain both on his face.

"What was the occasion on that day?" I asked him.

"We got the result of Madhavi's 10th exams; she became the topper of the school. Grandfather and Grandmother took us to Kanyakumari to celebrate it. We took it here after we returned from the vacation," his eyes glowed when he talked about the moment.

"Where are your Parents then?" I asked.

His face tensed whenever I asked about them, they never attended our Wedding, and their photos are not there on the wall. I have to know what the issue between him and his parents is.

"They were busy then," he said carelessly.

"Why? I don't understand this. They have not attended the Wedding as Madhavi informed us that they surely will," I interrogated.

"I don't know," he said.

"You don't know? Samarth, they are your parents. You ought to know their whereabouts," I advised him.

"I have never talked to them for a while," he told me.

"If you have a dispute with them, please clear it as soon as possible. Have you informed them at least about our Wedding?" I questioned.

"I did not inform them, Madhavi did. Leena, please leave that subject now as I am tired," he said leaving me behind on the stairs.

I would not argue, so I started climbing. There are three rooms upstairs. He opened the first room on the long corridor that belongs to Madhavi and was precisely like the Grandmother's room, the second room was slightly small like the kitchen that is filled with two children's beds and toys, and the wall was decorated with cartoons. He said that it belongs to him and his brother when they were young. Now, Siddharth and Vinay live here whenever they stay which rarely happens.

The third one is a Master Bedroom belonging to Samarth and me to stay. As I entered the room, our suitcases were next to our doorway. As I scanned the room, it has a king-size bed, two table chests on either side of it with a big lamp on it, and four attached cupboards on the wall for clothes. There are two cushion chairs with a small table in the corner of the room, next to it there is a balcony door closed with curtains. This is more spacious than others.

The night surrounded the house, and the room was getting warmer owing to a chimney fire. I feel awkward alone with him in this room, seeing the bed makes me sleepy. He looked at me in between. I have to clear him about my intention on the first night as I don't want to disappoint him.

"Do you want to sleep?" he asked distracting me.

"No," I said. He looked intensely into my eyes. I took out the suitcase to unload all the clothes before he could move closer to me.

I kept busy with the work as he watched me patiently. He showed me the two empty cupboards reserved for me.

It was 7.30 pm when I unpacked all of the clothes and things from the Suitcases and so did Samarth with his. I went to the bathroom to clean myself; there are four bathrooms in this house. One in Samarth, one in Madhavi's room, one in Grandfather, and the last is the Common Bathroom situated on the back side of the stairs in the hall. This bathroom was half the size of our bedroom.

After I came outside the bathroom, he asked, "Are you hungry?"

"Yes," I said. I am still starving. I don't know what he will think about me as I just ate a few hours before. Maybe, he is starving too.

We went downstairs to the kitchen, there is leftover food. Samarth helped me find the utensils to warm the food. I ate slowly as I could not leave the dining table. He was ravenous in his every bite which got over so soon.

"Do you want to eat ice cream?" he asked.

"Do you have it now?" I asked.

"Yes, Madhavi bought a week before for us," he said.

"Yes, I would love to eat," I said. He brought the family pack of blueberry flavor from the fridge.

"Why you have not offered Madhavi's children?" I questioned.

"She bought it for her family too which is stored in her house. They will eat there," he explained.

I went inside the kitchen to wash the utensils; he stopped and reminded me that the maid will come tomorrow to clean it. I cannot make excuses now to go to his bedroom with him though I can sit here near the fire chimney to get warmer. I told him that I want to stay here for a while, and he accompanied me. I sat on the left sofa chair. He paused there standing near the first step of the stairs looking at me astonished as if I have done something terrible.

"What is it?" I asked.

"It is nothing," he sat across me.

"Did I do something wrong?" I was curious.

"No. Why did you choose this sofa chair to sit in?" he asked.

I chuckled and said, "Why? Is there something special on this seat?"

"Most of them I met sat on the couch or sofa chair where I am sitting. They find it comfortable. You are the first person to sit here since.... So I am asking why you choose this?" he asked.

"Well, I could see the stairs, the whole hall from here. From your seat, I can see the closed entrance door and a window that might be boring," I said.

"Great. You talk like her," he said.

"Whom do I talk like?" I asked him.

"My Grandmother, she said exactly the thing you said now which is incredible," he said.

"So you are saying nobody sat here after your Grandmother, right?" I inquired.

"Yes," he said.

"Wow," I said and paused for a moment.

I begin, "You don't have to stay with me," I said tucking my hands in a sweater pocket as it started freezing, the weather.

"I would like to stay here," he said.

Every second was ticking like a minute or hours; I am thinking about how to make him understand my uneasiness about mating as I am not ready yet. I was looking at the fire, how it is getting on my skin making me soothe. Strangely, I stayed away from the heat in my city; here I am wanting to touch every hot object like this burning firewood. I don't want him to wait for me, make him astray. It took strength to tell him.

"I want to tell you something," I said.

"What is it?" he asked staring at me.

"It might bother you," I told him.

"Just say it," he said with an eager tone.

"I want you to give me a few moments until I settle here; I might be bold in behavior though I am shy in this first-night thing, about mating," I said quietly. He looked at me for a few seconds.

"I told you before you can ask me anything, as I said I will do according to my wife's comfort and you are my wife now. I will give you how many moments or days you want," he assured me.

I was astonished to hear that, "Are you ready to do that, to wait?"

"Yes," he smiled. It depends upon how much longer will he remain patient.

I rose from my seat to go to the room as I am feeling sleepy. He didn't hover this time when I left him there. Maybe he is thinking about the decision he gave me tonight whether he hustled it too soon. No, he was not. He is dropping more wood into the fire when I reached upstairs. I went to the bedroom and applied balm on my head.

After a few minutes, Samarth entered the room and went straight to the bathroom. As I was preparing the bed for me, he changed into a grey T-shirt and Track pants. There are four pillows on the bed in which I gave him two pillows and a blanket to sleep on. He stared at me with doubt.

"Why are you giving me this?" he asked.

"It is for you to sleep with it," I said.

"Okay. You can keep it where it was before," he told me. Now, I am confused. He told me he will give me space till I settle; now he wants to stay.

"I thought you will sleep in another room," I said hesitantly.

"This is our room. We should share it to understand each other. We won't if we sleep separately," he said.

"You said that you will give me space," I inquired.

"Yes, I did. I said that I will give you time but I didn't say about leaving the room. This is a big bed where three people can sleep comfortably. We are just two people," he explained.

He was right; I have to follow him without involving further. I slept on the edge of the bed; I can see he has slept soundly. I put one pillow in between us as I spread my hands and legs a lot.

Chapter 10

Life in a Week

The next day he woke up before me. It was 8.30 am when I went downstairs. He was preparing breakfast. The man who lived here alone by himself for several years might know some cooking as he informed me during our first meeting. Probably his sister taught him. There was egg and toast, fruits like apples, grapes, strawberries, and orange juice on the dining table. He has not prepared for himself but for me too and I was 'Wow' in my mind. I could see he is a morning person.

"Good Morning. How are you?" he asked.

"Good Morning. I am fine. I should have gotten up with you," I said.

"It is no need. You got to rest," he smilingly placed the plate on the table. I got distracted by the sounds of utensils and plates clanging together in the kitchen. It was the maid who washed the dishes. Her name is Madhu. He called out her name Madhu to introduce me. She was wearing a synthetic sari and a brown sweater above it. She must be around 35 to 45 years old. He said my name to her; she welcomed me by folding her hands. I did the same. He said that I will be managing the house from now onwards and she had to follow the order of whatever work I give according to her convenience. I confirmed that I will not bother her by giving extra to the regular work. She uttered a few words and I could see she is shy to talk in front of Samarth. She might open herself later. She smiled and went to continue her work.

He reminded me to have breakfast before it got cold. We sat down to complete it. After we have done it, Madhu took the plates to wash them before she leave. She minded her work which was beneficial for us, unlike Mother's talkative maid. She informed us about leaving. She left the house alone for us.

I interrogated him about her day-to-day work in this household. He said that she dusted, broomed, and mop the house, wash the utensils, and put the clothes to dry from the washing machine. He also informed me that she cleans the rooms of Madhavi and her children a day before if they are staying with us for a while and Grandparent's room once a month on Sunday when he is at home as it gets filled with the web. He further informed me about the salary he gives and her 12 years of work experience here. She works two more houses after us. She reaches here before 8 am every day as he has to be at the factory before 9.30 am.

He planned to visit the factory for a few hours today to check on staff work. He left me around 10 am. I called my Mother to inform her that I reached here safely. She gave me a few missed calls yesterday but I was tired to call her back. She understood the circumstances. Father came on line to talk casually for a few minutes with me and gave back the phone to Mother. She asked about the first night and I explained the whole thing. She was shocked and awed by saying he is a gentleman. She advised me not to make him wait any longer as men become crude and angry later.

I hung up the phone and went to take a bath. I bought only three sweaters, I must shop for a few more as I am gonna need them here.

I came outside the house looking for sunshine and heat; found the exact spot to sit near the front porch steps. I closed my eyes enjoying the sun ray heat giving relief from the cold lingering here which is difficult to obtain it. After a few minutes, I can feel slight sweat coming from my head. I hate to sweat, I really do, but here I was craving for it. The release of sweat from my body makes me active enough to enjoy the sun.

Two quarters have passed here, and I think now it is enough for me to stay here. I get back inside the house to the kitchen to prepare lunch. I searched inside the fridge; it has leftover ice cream, a few vegetables, fruits, jams, butter, eggs, chicken, and varieties of sauces.

I intended to prepare chicken gravy with boiled rice and a salad; I hope he likes the recipe. I have done the cooking. I went to the back of the Garden to pass time when Samarth come. I took pleasure in viewing this scenario.

Suddenly, I got curious to know about our neighbors, to know them. I might go there and introduce myself to whoever living there. Maybe later, but first I have to ask Samarth or Madhu about them.

Just before noon, I could hear the car approach the front yard. I got inside the house to open the front door. He pressed the bell button and called out my name. I immediately unlocked it. He smiled handing me the packet of black currant berries as it is one of my favorites.

"Is everything fine?" he asked.

"Yes. Thank you for bringing me this fruit," I said.

"No need to thank me," he said.

I wasn't sure whether he is hungry or not, "Will you eat lunch now?"

"Did you make it so soon?" he questioned.

"Yes," I replied.

"I don't eat early afternoon. Besides, you don't have to cook for a week and Madhavi instructed me to make you settle down in the beginning," he went to the kitchen and brought the water bottle to pour it into a glass.

"I have nothing to do here except cooking. So, please let me do the work from today," I said.

"Okay, it is up to your wish. If you are comfortable, go ahead," he sat down on the sofa to drink it.

"If you are not busy, would you show me around the shopping place after lunch?" I asked.

"Do you mean the food market?" he inquired.

"Yes. I guess," I shrugged.

"Okay," he said.

I sat next to him one step apart to ask about our neighbor, "Shall we go to meet our neighbor?"

"Who?" he asked shrinking his eyebrow.

"The person who lives in the white Cottage, you said his name is Mr. Aasif Khan?" I replied curiously.

"Why?" he asked.

"Don't you want to introduce me to him?" I asked him.

He indifferently said, "It is not necessary."

"Why not?" I questioned him.

"I don't talk to him. I always keep to myself," he said.

"Well, I am not like that. I always want to know my neighbors. Will you come with me?" I enlighten him.

"No," he replied.

"Why?" I asked.

"He and his family are not in the house. They went to Hyderabad," he said while sipping more water.

"Oh," İ said disappointedly.

"No need to worry, he will be back after one week," He said.

"How do you know?" I asked.

"He informed me all before leaving," He kept the empty glass on the table.

"So, you do talk to him?" I inquired.

"Yes, rarely," he cleared.

"Ok," I said.

I have often wondered what this man has been doing if he doesn't mingle with his parents, and his neighbor, I hope he is having contact with his friends at least or is estranged from them too.

After Lunch, Samarth drove the car down a narrow lane to the main road; he explained the history of the location wherever he drives through. It seems he knows this place, this area his entire life.

He glanced my way in between for the approval to continue his chat. I replied to him with acceptance. He doesn't want to annoy me by talking as I am scared of this sloppy hill road. I kept count of time; it took almost twenty minutes to reach the market. He accompanied me inside the supermarket. I watched him shop with me as he is fluent in everything he buys. He knows what is necessary. We shopped for food items for a week, sweaters, and other necessary products.

Over the next few days, I saw Samarth leaving for the factory and returning early in the evening, at the house sweaty and hungry. When

I inquired about the lunch, he informed me that he usually eats from the Restaurant. I must make him lunch as I don't want him to eat outside which will make him sick. We ate dinner together at the table. After eating, He always took an hour to work on his business. After he finished, he watched the news for a few minutes on TV before he goes to sleep.

During the day, Madhu comes and does her work diligently. I tried my best to make her talk with me, but she only replied with 'Yes' or 'No'. She kept to herself just like Samarth. It will be no use to asking about neighbors from her.

On Saturday, I prepared lunch for him and put it in the steel container to stay warm. As I handed him the container informing him about the lunch, I could see he is happy like never before. He didn't expect this from me. I know, I know, sometimes I do surprise people.

On that day, I was getting bored of browsing the internet on my laptop which is a gift from Samarth as I am keen on browsing. Samarth has given me a bunch of extra keys to this house and I thought of checking other rooms apart from the kitchen, the hall, and the backyard which I am very well aware of it. First, I went to Madhavi's room but I could not find anything except the bed, empty drawers, and cupboards. Maybe, She has vacant the whole room before her marriage or after. Next, I went inside the children's room, which is empty except for the beds, drawers, a few toys, and a wall painted with cartoons. I went downstairs to check on his Grandparent's room.

As I was going through the five rack books cupboard, it was filled with biological research and findings, some fiction, some non-fiction, etc which might interest me to read. I opened the drawer next to the bed, I found old times antique gold chain clock that might belong to his Grandfather. Another drawer was empty. I wandered toward the wooden wall cupboard. I tried to open but it was locked. I wonder if Samarth has given me the key to this. I checked through the keys and found a little one. I hope it is the cupboard one. And it is indeed the cupboard key.

I opened it wide; it was dusty and filled with webs. I coughed and coughed till I was back to normal. I could see it was occupied with Photo Albums of his Grandparents, his parents, his and his sibling's childhood, school, and college. His parents looked younger in this and I expect to see them in person. In one of the family photos, his mother is holding his baby brother. Samarth looked handsome from the rest of the family. Some documents belong to this house, factories, some drawing notebooks, etc.

I found two Jewelry boxes, one containing a Gold Necklace with Earrings. Another box was bigger than the other, it contain long gold jewelry designed with enamel and a set of bangles. I think it is owned by his Grandmother or Mother or Madhavi. If it is Madhavi's, then why she has not taken it with her? I kept the jewelry back inside the box. I don't want any fuss about it from Samarth and it doesn't belong to me.

I locked the cupboard and the doors of the room the way it was. I went to the kitchen to prepare dinner.

Samarth came early that evening. I was about to tell him about his Grandparents' room, but he distracted me by saying, "What do you say we go and visit my sister's house tomorrow?" he waited for me to reply. This is a good idea to go out of this house. Perhaps I have not seen his sister's house yet.

"Yes. Sure," I replied. He smiled and headed for the bathroom.

He thought I needed a change or that visiting his sister's house will make me distracted from the soundless neighborhood.

When he returned from the bathroom; I asked him, "Are we going for dinner?"

"No. We are going for lunch," he said.

"Did you inform them about us visiting their place?" I inquired.

"No. They invited us yesterday. Sorry, I forgot to tell you," he said.

"Okay," I said. Tomorrow is Sunday; everybody will be free from work and school. He wanted me to blend with his family which is a good idea. So, I can ask Madhavi about their parents.

During dinner, I enlightened him about the Grandparent's room and that I have gone through their belongings without his permission. I felt guilty when I said it.

"I am sorry. I don't know what to do. I was getting bored, so I was roaming around the house going through things to pass time," I said

"Are you kidding me? This house belongs to you now. You can roam wherever you want. That is why I have given you the extra key," he calmly said.

"Thank you. Do you know your Grandfather has a unique collection of books in his room?" I said enthusiastically.

"Yes. I agree with you," he said.

"I have gone through the wall cupboard as well. It has a photo album of your Parents when you were young," I said curiously for his reaction. He is blandly eating his dinner.

I feel, he doesn't care about his parents anymore. So, I changed the subject and informed him about the jewelry of Madhavi I found to be the most high-quality design I have ever seen.

"What? Madhavi Jewelry," he asked again.

"Yes. I saw a necklace set in one box and a long necklace with a set of bangles in another box," I said. He chuckled for a second.

"Madhavi will never leave her jewelry here. She might leave her husband but not the jewelry," he explained.

"Is it belonging to your Mother?" I asked doubtfully.

"No. It belongs to my Grandmother," he said.

"I knew it. She has good taste," I said smilingly.

"Thank you," he replied. I went back to finishing my dinner. Samarth was keenly looking at me between every piece of food he is taking. After dinner, I went to the kitchen to put the plates on the sink. Samarth was next to me standing.

"Please come with me. I have to tell you something," he requested, leaving me to think about what his intention is. I have no idea but to follow him.

He went straight to the Grandparent's room door and took a key from his pant pocket to open it. I went near him before he entered the room. As I went inside, he was unlocking the wall cupboard. His look was stern while searching it inside the cupboard.

"Huh, I found it," he said excitedly. "Come here, Leena," He asked.

I stood near him viewing the things I found this afternoon. He opened both the jewelry box and said, "My Grandmother's father was a goldsmith in Coimbatore and my Grandmother has a talent for designing jewelry. These pieces of jewelry are made with her designs through her father. It was made for her marriage. Isn't it beautiful?" He said sensitively.

"Yes, it is quite unique," I said admiringly.

"It is not the only jewelry she brought from her father. It is the half of it lies inside this cupboard," he said.

"Half of it! where is the remaining?" I inquired.

"Madhavi has it," he grinned at me.

"Oh," I said.

"My Grandmother had given us instructions before dying about her jewelry that half of it belong to Madhavi and the other half given to me," he said giving me a shock.

"So, you are saying she left it for you to use," I asked in amazement.

"It is not for me, she meant it for Granddaughter-in-law; that is you. It is yours now. She clearly ordered to share her jewelry equally," he gave me the jewelry. That is true, How come he is gonna wear it? I am so stupid. I think he will not use it for a loan or sell it for his business either as he is sentimentally attached to his Grandparent's item. Everything in this room is old-style. I probably think he has not changed anything even after their death. As I watched him, there is always a spark on his face when he talked about them.

"Wow. Are you sure?" I asked with doubt.

"Yes. I want you to wear it tomorrow," he said.

"It is incredible," I said while touching every corner of the necklace.

"I am sorry," he said eventually.

"For what?" I inquired.

"I should have given you a few days before. Madhavi advised me to give you after marriage. I am so preoccupied with my work, I could not remember it," he said caringly.

"It is alright. Thank you," I said with a big grin on my face.

"Please wear it tomorrow. It will make her happy," he requested.

"Sure," I said.

"This is what is left of my Grandparents in this room," he continued.

"I presume you are attached to them closely," I asked.

"Yes, very much," his face became glad to harsh. He is missing them.

"Tell me more about them," I insisted.

"What can I say? There is so much to tell," he added.

"Tell me how your Grandparents married," I asked. I love people's history, especially about the strong couple. How they met, how they fall in love, how they continued their lineage when they barely know each other before getting hitched.

"Grandmother was living in Coimbatore with her father helping in his Gold smith business through design. Have you seen her notebook which is full of Jewelry designs?" he asked me.

"Yes, I have seen it. It is remarkable," I appreciated.

"Grandmother was rich while my Grandfather was totally the opposite. He was born and lived poorly in Ooty but he has a keen interest in biology which got him a scholarship to study in College. He was 17 years old when he met her during one of his friend's marriage. She was attending her relative's marriage. They liked each other. Her father came to know about this and did some research. He was not glad about his background except brilliant student tag on his head in class, and college. His Professor's appreciation made my Great-Grandfather think, to give his daughter to my Grandfather," he said.

"How old she was back then when they met?" I was curious.

"I don't remember well. She was 14 or 15 years old and studying in the Ninth or Tenth class. She got married in between her twelfth standard in school. Grandfather insisted she completes her school after marriage but never stepped inside the College which she never regretted," he added.

"Why is it so?" I interrupted.

"They were like two peas, they loved and cared for each other. College was not prioritized before for women, technique or skill made their name. She continued her drawing work even after marriage and she earned it from her father. He, on the other hand, worked as a Botanist Researcher after College for a few years. He bought the land little by little through their savings to commence the Tea work.

At first, it was a loss for one or two years. You know business drawbacks like Impatient Employees, poor Growth, poor marketing, etc. One day, Grandmother helped him by giving free samples to her relatives and friends in and around Ooty and Coimbatore; that is a common strategy to lure people to buy. Through that, they got a dealer who ordered bulk due to the best quality they produced. We are continuing the exact quality till now.

After that Profit was taking its peak one by one, bought this land, and built it as their home. Grandmother's father died when my father was 7 years old. As she was his only child of him, the house, Gold, and money came to her as an inheritance. Through that, she helped her husband expand the tea business by buying machines. The profits of his business never made him greedy. He balanced his family and work perfectly, they both did equally," He stopped.

"I feel that you are proud of them," I said.

"Yes. We are what we are because of them. What we have, is because of their hard work and dedication. I have not earned it, but they have. I am just continuing what they have started," he became serious.

I know now that his parents never took care of them but their Grandparents did. I guess they lived here most of the years. He suddenly changed the subject.

"I think we should take a rest now as we are leaving tomorrow early after breakfast," he said.

"Okay," I said before I could further ask him.

We left the room and he locked it. I was carrying his ancestor's jewelry to my room to wear tomorrow. I kept it inside the cupboard box that was made to keep jewels. I don't understand, so much happened in a week. My life would take a turn as I have never imagined it. I still feel lonely here as I have nowhere to go. Samarth does his best to comfort me. I hope I would probably do the same.

Chapter 11

THE WHOLE SUNDAY

Samarth got up early as usual. While he showered, I chose to wear a green color Knee length chiffon dress with black jeans and a grey overcoat that I bought while shopping before marriage. This is the first time I ever wore a coat. Thus I never needed it in Chennai. I combed out my hair into a ponytail and applied slight makeup. I wore the necklace as he suggested.

As I got ready, he came out dressed in his full-sleeve Turquoise blue slim-fit T-shirt and khaki color trousers. He combed it while it was still wet.

I had to go downstairs to cook a simple breakfast as advised by him. I made toast, an omelet, and orange juice.

Finally ready, He and I slid into the car. I reminded him to stop by the sweet shop to buy dessert. I don't want to enter their house barehanded. I was enjoying the view as he drove silently. All the long trees were covering the sun. I saw nothing except the road in between the forest trees, a few cars passed by. We were heading west as I browsed the map online. Pine forest has left us.

The trip took us nearly fifteen minutes of travel down the road of segregated Villas. I kept the windows down for a better view of the Luxury houses.

At last, we came to a halt near a green-colored Mansion type house; you cannot recognize it as it is surrounded by green trees. Madhavi and her husband greeted us with smiles and handshakes; I presented her with blueberry cheesecake. Their house looked similar to ours. Mother was right except the house is bigger than us. It had two story added which reminded me of separate rooms for their children. Their children sat on the sofa watching TV in the hall. When they saw us, they greeted us one by one. Samarth and Mr. Ranjan left me to join the boys to watch TV. I guess I should leave him with them. Rashmika looked over me for a long time with bright enthusiastic eyes.

"Where did you buy the dress?" She asked.

"In a store," I replied.

"Is this readymade," she asked again.

"Yes," I said.

"I like your dress. Mother doesn't want me to buy readymade as she thinks it might get ruined easily due to bad stitching and never fits perfectly," she said.

"Huh, tailored dress always is the best. The cloth might get ragged but the stitch stays intact," Madhavi interrupted.

"That is true, I buy readymade only if it is western," I agreed with Madhavi.

"See. She is with me on this topic," Madhavi replied.

"But I want one like this. It is pretty," She said.

"Thank you. I will bring it for you when I find anything over here or back in Chennai," I promised her.

"Oh thank you," She said leaving us behind.

I removed my coat as I felt warm inside the house. Madhavi's sudden stare went toward my collar, she was looking over the necklace I was wearing. Her eyes lit like a glowing moon.

"Samarth has remembered what I said about the Jewelry. Do you like it?" she asked.

"Of course. It is really pretty," I said.

"I thought he might forget to give you as it has been there in the Grandparents' room for a long time. After seeing you wear it, it reminded me of my Grandmother. It is her favorite necklace," she enlightened me with the history.

"Do you miss them?" I asked her.

"Yes, always," she said. I could see a few tears oozing out, but she stopped them from coming out. I smiled and changed the topic to make her comfortable with the sentiment.

"I heard you have taken half of her jewels," I asked.

"Yes. I bet Samarth told you all. Do you want to see it?" she asked.

"Yes, please," I followed her to the stairs which are on the first floor of the house. She showed the whole cupboard filled with Sarees, Coats, and dresses. She opened the huge box attached to the cupboard where she kept the ornaments. She withdrew the long narrow velvet box and opened it wide.

My eyes glittered at the sight of the beautiful thing. This is quite bigger than the jewel I have, but the design was not more striking as mine.

"Why you have not taken her favorite necklace?" I was curious. Rashmika entered the room joyously with a tea and a biscuits tray in her hand.

"I loved her jewel all of it. I could not decide what to take along with me during my marriage. So, I took these instead of yours," she explained.

"Oh, I see. Was she alive then?" I said.

"Yes, she was alive. She died after a year," she said in a sad tone.

"I am sorry," I said.

"It is alright, dear. You know she got annoyed when I took a long time to select her jewels; Grandfather advised me to take them all. Though I resisted," she said.

"Why didn't you take it?"I advised her as I can see she is very fond of it.

"Well, I wanted to be fair with my brother and his wife," she said with a smile. Yes, she is fair-minded from the start when I met her.

We three of them enjoyed the tea gossiping about the shopping place, sightseeing, you know women talk. She took out the Photo Albums of her marriage, old faded of their Parents and Grandparents. The photo of their parents reminded me to ask what is keeping them apart to meet me. What is it Samarth doesn't want me to meet them? I enquired Madhavi with a stern look in my eyes. Rashmika has not left our side when I questioned her mother. She became silent at that moment. I could see there is a deep problem rooted in their heart, especially Samarth or is Samarth the cause for not inviting their parents? One question increases more suspense here.

Finally, she advised me to be patient and calm when Samarth is ready to blend with them, he will let me meet. She said he will explain to me once he is prepared. So, Samarth is the main reason they are not invited. I was right. How long should I be patient? A month, A year, or whole life. It is aggravating in my head, making me dizzy.

Madhavi shook me off from my thought asking if I was alright. I assured her that I am okay.

Madhavi reminded me that we are going boating after lunch. I was blinking, and Samarth has not told me about the plan.

Lunch was served early. Rashmika and I helped her in the kitchen. The table was full of starters, food, dessert, and fruits; except for little space left for plates, glasses, and spoons. I overheard Samarth and Mr. Ranjan discussing business endlessly. Samarth talked about the tea and Mr. Ranjan about hotel management. Two boys were watching cartoons.

Madhavi called out to everybody when the table was set. All came to the dining table in a jiffy, especially those boys.

I asked Mr. Ranjan about life before marriage, relatives, and their whereabouts while eating. I don't want to spend this visit talking about food and business.

He was energetic when he recalled it. He said it was his most memorable life when he was young. He also said that having a family is the most important part of his life and we should cherish it always. I don't understand, is he hinting at me or Samarth; probably both of us? We two creatures were doubtful about the marriage and still are. We have not settled down yet.

Mr. Ranjan made humorous remarks about his children, which make them shy or embarrassed. His boys never back by embarrassing their dad too. It was like a debate between young and old. Samarth, Madhavi, and I were enjoying this scenario, laughing. I have never seen Samarth this much happier. He always smiled or stayed silent.

The food was warm and tasty. I could not believe I have eaten a lot. I relaxed by helping Madhavi in the kitchen after lunch; it is the best way to digest food in this cold weather.

After a few minutes, the whole family was preparing themselves to go to the lake. Samarth and I were left hanging in the hall watching TV to pass time. In the meantime, I interrogated Samarth about the boating plan. He apologized and said it was a last-minute plan.

We all drove to the lake. We went to the opposite side of the tourist boat. I was keen why we have stopped here when the boats are on the other side of the lake. When I got out of the car to check it, Madhavi's children were running down the slope losing their sight. Samarth told me to follow him accompanied by Madhavi. When I reached the spot, I could see the narrow deck with two boat ropes tied to the large wooden stand. One boat can fill eight people and the other boat can have five people in it.

Madhavi's family got on the big boat except for Vinay. He wanted to sit with me while Samarth was busy removing the rope off the wooden stand attached to the deck. I assured them that I will take care of him but Mr. Ranjan compelled him to get in the boat with them. Vinay has no chance but to follow him. Certainly, they rowed away from us. It seems they want to give us privacy. Samarth and I got on the other boat. He handed me a life support Jacket to wear. He tightened his jacket efficiently.

Truthfully, I never liked boating especially on the water which is cold like freezing ice that gives you shiver with one finger touch. Samarth dipped the oar gently on one side and then on the other. He had much practice before without disturbing the boat's movement.

"Is this your boat?" I asked him.

"Yes," he said.

"What about the other boat?" I asked.

"It is not mine. It belongs to Ranjan," he said while rowing the boat.

"Is it safe to keep the boats here? What if they got stolen?" I inquired.

"It is a private deck, especially for a few people. You could see a chained door before getting down to the slope," he said.

"Yes, I have seen it," I confirmed to him.

"It is done by a security person who by my instruction has opened it today," he said.

"So, you two own this side of the deck?" I asked.

"No, it is private for those who have bought the boat for personal, not for business. For business, you can see the other side. You have to pay them yearly fees for security to keep our boats safe from thieves or any damage," he explained.

"How much do you pay?" I questioned.

"Rs.5000 per year including discount," he said.

"Oh, Okay. How much does the boat cost?" I asked more.

"I think it is around 2 lakhs," he said carelessly.

"Wow. You should have bought the motorboat," I suggested.

"Motorboat is for sea. I bought this for the lake. Besides, I love rowing; it makes my muscle stretch and mind serene," he said.

"Do you come here often?" I asked.

"Yes," he said. I scanned the lake but there is no one around there. Others boats are far away look like a minute toy on the lake.

"Alone?" I asked.

"Yes. Is there a problem?" he asked.

"Are you not scared of water?" I asked him with doubt.

"No. I am wearing a life support jacket if I drown and I know swimming," he said.

"Still, the water is icy cold. How do you survive that even if you float?" I asked him.

"Well, I don't have any drowning experience," he teased. I flinched at the word.

"Please don't say that word. I request you to not come here alone," I insisted.

"Please don't worry. I know how to take care of myself," he said.

"I insist," I pressed him.

He reluctantly said, "Okay. As you wish," He bowed down.

The lake is surrounded by pine and eucalyptus trees. The sceneries are perfect. I kicked the shoes to the bottom of the boat and stretched my legs. I leaned back sniffing the fresh water smell. I closed my eyes enjoying the cold breeze and the sun rays together pouring on my face.

After a few moments, I could feel the movement of the boat had stopped. I opened my eyes to an unexpected change. He has ended rowing, halting in the middle of the lake, and his eyes are on me.

This sudden glare made me shiver. He smiled admiringly at me. But I had to look away. I have no idea what to say.

"Are we staying here longer?" I asked.

"Yes," he said without looking away.

"Where are others?" I questioned.

"They went north side and will return after an hour," he said.

"Are we not going there?" I asked him.

"Do you want to go there or stay here?" he asked me. I thought we will be following Mr. Ranjan's lead. He brought me here alone, to understand what I like, to make me comfortable. I am grateful for this ride.

"I think I am fine here," I said shyly looking into his eyes. He saw uneasiness in me turning into discomfort.

"You can relax," he said, after that, he shifted his body to the right side giving me privacy. He was viewing the sun which is about to set in a few hours.

I got back to closing my eyes, "Thank you for bringing me here." The surface of the lake has become still which is easy for me to stretch more. To my surprise, I enjoyed this day.

"You are welcome," he said without turning. I don't know what he will assume about me as I am not ready for his stare too. As a husband, he is entitled to look at me. But I have not allowed him yet and he understands too. It is a constant problem for me as I am not willing or eager to be his wife.

I closed my eyes, I don't know for how long. A gentle wind was touching the skin before but now it has become strong poking like a knife which reminded me that the climatic degree was dropping. My hands started shaking. I wrapped my hands around body. Samarth too was enjoying this day, even the tough breeze he handled like a bear.

I could not bear the wind anymore, so I called out his name and informed him that we should leave. He obeyed instantly without arguing. Maybe my posture revealed everything.

He started rowing rigorously. After fifteen minutes, we arrived at the deck. First, he got out of the boat to tie the knot on the wooden stand. Then he gave his hand to me to help me climb the deck. I could not balance my leg because of the water wave though he pulled me swiftly to his body. He was concerned and asked if I am okay. I said

I am fine. He let go of my hand and body. It is my first clumsy moment with him. He shyly looked at me and then at the lake.

We waited for his sister's family. Samarth called Mr. Ranjan regarding their whereabouts. He said it will take more than half an hour for them to reach this spot. Till then we went to the roadside where our cars are kept. He hinted to me the tea shop was situated nearby. We both went to drink the tea as the evening is getting colder. And we returned to the deck. The wind was blowing heavily on the face; the sun is about to set within a few minutes still no sight of them. I asked Samarth to call them again as my mobile has no service; he said they will be fine. I prayed for them to return safely.

At last, I saw their boat coming closer and closer. There is no sign of tension on their faces, and here Samarth and I were getting anxious for their return. Out of concern, I asked why it is taken so long. They explained that they stopped another side because of the strong wind blowing. The boat became shaky. Now, I understand the arrival delay. Samarth pulled everybody one by one out of the boat. I hugged Rashmika, the two boys, and Madhavi for arriving safely.

We all went to the car after tying the knot of the big boat. I locked the window of the car immediately to get myself warm. After a few minutes, Samarth started the engine to go to the restaurant to eat dinner. Mr. Ranjan's Car was behind us.

We parked our cars on the Ooty-Mysore road. There were many fine restaurants situated everywhere. The boys were asking for the pizza. Mr. Ranjan did not respond to their demand. We all went inside one of the barbeque restaurants. When we entered, it was not crowded.

We sat down in the family lounge. Vinay and Siddharth were not pleased to come here.

I asked them, "Why both of you are sad?"

"We want pizza. Father has not taken us there," Siddharth said cheerlessly.

"You two had pizza two days before. I don't want to ruin your tummies by having pizza always. It is time to get some proteins," Mr. Ranjan said immediately.

"We want pizza now," Vinay insisted.

"I said no pizza today," Mr. Ranjan commanded. The boys became silent after the argument.

"Don't worry. We can have it some other day. After dinner, we can eat ice cream. What do you say?" I said.

"Oh, yes," both of them were happy now.

We chatted, laughed, and ate dinner. At half past eight, we got out of the restaurant and said goodbye. Samarth and I thanked them for the beautiful day; I invited them to come to the house. They all agreed happily. We all went to our respective cars to reach the house.

Inside the car, I could see Samarth was in good spirits all the way while driving. I am pleased that he had fun today as he smiled rarely. I stayed silent for the whole ride watching endlessly the trees passing by which has become dark.

We arrived at the house. I took out the keys and got out of the car immediately after parking; heading towards the door as quickly as I can to avoid the cold air. It was freezing and my coat was not enough to make me warm.

I got inside it while Samarth was locking the gate gradually as if this cold wind could not affect him at all. I got rid of my shoes as it is making me itchy. Samarth was two steps behind me when I was about to place the shoe on the rack. I smiled nervously and he smiled back while locking the door.

"Did you like it today?" he asked coming near to me.

"Yes. The whole day was excellent. Thank you," I said happily.

"You are welcome," he said. I was about to climb the stairs, and Samarth touched my right hand suddenly which was on the handrail. His immediate touch made me turn to look at his face. He was coming near slowly toward my face to kiss me. I took my hand from him immediately; distancing myself. At first, he looked intense and cheery. Now, there is disappointment in his eyes. He braced himself after the rejection.

"I am sorry," He said silently.

I looked at him once and left him there without saying anything. I climbed the stairs as fast as I can. I went inside the bathroom of the room heavily breathing thinking the whole moment just happened now. His happiness showed that he was ready to mate tonight. He came near to leap into the marriage; though I am not ready. My body and mind reacted soon enough to take a gap from him.

I felt guilty when he said sorry. I know I was supposed to respond to him back, but I didn't. I became shaky after his surprise. I didn't know what to do, so I left.

I am attracted to him, not in a way that I am willing to share my body. I have to feel deep intensity toward him and it has not begun yet. I have to tell him to clear his mind.

I got out of the bathroom to confront him. Well, he was not there. I stood there still waiting for him to come, but he didn't come. I changed my dress to a night suit and went to bed keeping the door open for him. I slept early but I heard the sound of Samarth entering the room, then he went inside the bathroom. I opened my eyes to see. I feel that the rejection made him vulnerable or angry to see me. Maybe, he gave me space to think or himself think. I never meant to hurt his feelings. I will say sorry to him tomorrow and explain the problem. I shut my eyes quickly after I heard the unlocking of the door of the bathroom.

Chapter 12

The Neighbor

The cold is always around here even the bed sheet felt like it is soaked in ice water. There is no warmth in here as I feel I am paralyzed and I could not move an inch. My body was aching like never before in my entire life. I lived in cold weather back then in my city, it was soothingly good. This is like living under the cave of a snowy mountain. I hope the summer comes soon as possible; though I cannot tolerate this winter anymore.

Even my eyes are aching, so I slowly opened them. I scanned the room, but Samarth was not there. I got up from the bed rubbing my painful head. I heard a weird noise outside. I went towards the balcony to see it; it was Samarth washing his car and the tires were drenched with mud from yesterday. I went to the bathroom to get ready before he occupies it.

I went downstairs to make breakfast. Now, I feel like a stupid girl after looking at the fire chimney. The black flakes of the wood were more outside the chimney. As I remember, the floor was clean yesterday morning with little flakes before we left the house and Madhu vacuum the spot effectively. Samarth was not staying here because he was angry with me. He was lighting the wood fire to make the whole house warm. Thank goodness, he did that thing, or else I would be completely paralyzed today. How can I be so foolish? Still, I can feel he is hurt from yesterday.

I heard him climbing the stairs while I was making breakfast. I started serving the food on the table; he was getting down the stairs completely dressed to go to the factory. I looked at him saying that the breakfast is ready.

He smiled at me for a second and sat down on the chair without speaking. We ate silently. He kept glancing up at me in between his few bites as if he wants to say something. It is bizarre for me to stay silent for a long.

I asked him, "Do you like breakfast?"

"Yes," he replied.

I was looking for some words to say, "Will you come early today?"

"Why?" He asked.

"I have to buy groceries as it is getting over," I asked.

He hesitated to say something, but I declined, "No need. I will manage myself."

"It is not that I don't want to come. I do have work to complete. Maybe we can go after I come here at 6.30 pm," he said.

"It is not necessary. I will buy myself," I replied hastily

"How will you go?" he questioned.

"I will go by auto," I said. He chuckled instantly scratching his ear. Did I say something funny?

"You cannot get auto here. You have to walk a kilometer to find it," he explained.

"Oh. Is there ride app service here?" I questioned.

"No. It is restricted over here as 70% of people earn through tourism," He enlightened me.

"Oh, I see," I took a long sigh.

"You can take the red car," he said.

"I cannot," I replied.

"Why? Is there any problem?" he inquired sternly.

"I don't know how to drive," I answered.

"I heard you can drive," he asked.

"Only scooters and Bicycles, Not cars," I enlightened him.

"Oh. I misinterpreted it then. Why didn't you learn from your Uncle Rakesh? He has cars and you are close to him," he questioned. Uncle Rakesh has already done so much for us. How can I tell him asking Uncle to teach me will surely annoy his wife and will make matters worse for all of us.

"I never thought that time it will require now. I never imagined myself married to a person who wants me to drive his car," The words coming out of my mouth made him think about how many men are patriarchal. Only a few men want women to be independent.

"I can teach you," he said.

"Where? Here? No way," I said disapprovingly.

"Why not?" he asked.

"It is very risky to learn to drive on this sloppy road. I am scared of it," I said.

"The road over here is not bad. It will be easy for you once you learn," he encouraged.

"Oh no, please. I am sure I will create an accident," I replied.

He stopped eating and thinking about the topic. I glanced at him hinting towards the plate to finish his breakfast. He has no choice but to complete it. After we finished eating, I cleaned the table immediately. He rose to leave the house by saying bye.

I stopped him to hand over the lunch box, "Samarth, Thank you for considering me driving. I appreciate it," I said.

"Thank you. I am sure I will find a way to teach you to drive fearlessly," he said with utter confidence. I smiled.

"And I am sorry for yesterday. I hope not I have hurt you. It's just that I am not ready for consummation, I need more time," I said swiftly.

"I understand. Please be ready when I come at 6.30 for shopping," he said coolly.

"Okay," I said. He left the house instantly.

Madhu came late that day; she explained that her second son was the reason as he was not getting ready for school. I asked her before about her family. Her husband's job is driving the truck in a transport company. She has two sons, one is in college and the second one is in school. She said her first son is responsible while the other is naughty and immature, and is not interested in studies. Indeed, you always have even and odd people born in the family which creates balance or damage.

The day went as usual by browsing the internet or watching TV. I called my mother to check on her. I elaborated the yesterday's event. She was happy that I enjoyed it. Father was not in the house at that moment when I asked her. We laughed and teased each other. In the end, she inquired about the mating to which I lied that he did not initiate it.

“I am worried now. It is been more than a week,” she said.

“Ma, it is not a big deal,” I replied.

“You don’t know anything. Does he have any problem with mating?” she inquired further.

“Please stop it. I am the one who requested him to give me time, not him,” I shouted at her.

“I am just saying out of concern,” she said calmly.

“Please don’t investigate this topic again with me. I will tell you once I consummated,” I outraged at her.

“Okay, I am sorry. Please don’t be angry,” she changed the topic after the argument.

After I hung up the phone, I thought about the lie I said to her. He did try to kiss me, tried to come closer to me. If I say the truth, she will be more annoyed with me than him. I can keep her silent. What about others? What Madhavi will think of me if she knows the truth? Will Samarth tell her about us as he is close to her sister? Even if he keeps the secret, what if Madhavi forces him, to tell the truth? Or blurt out everything to others from constant pressure?

I trust Samarth that he will not disclose our secret; though I have known him for only a week. I should tell him about not sharing our private matters. Today, I’ll talk to him.

Samarth came exactly in and around 6.35 pm when I heard the car engine parked outside the gate. I was readily waiting as he informed me early. He called me by phone immediately once he stopped the engine. I picked up the call to ensure that I am set to go. I took the purse and keys to lock the main door. I sat next to him inside the car.

"How was your day?" he asked.

"Good," I replied.

"Have you prepared the list of groceries?" he questioned.

"Yes. I did," I said.

"Then, let's go shopping," he said like a child.

He drove the car, and brought me to the same supermarket we went last week. While shopping, I was getting itchy to talk about the secret we have. I want to wait till we reach our house, but my impulsive nature was resisting it.

I took the courage to talk to him. When I went near him, he was examining the vegetables holding in his hand.

"I need to talk to you," I said in a hushed tone. They were only a few people in the supermarket, but I was being cautious. He jumped when I came close to him.

"Yes, tell me," he asked.

"Have you told anybody about it? About?" I was finding words.

"What is it?" he asked again. I cleared my throat to say.

"Have you told anybody about my request in delaying consummation?" I asked quickly.

"I have not told anything to anybody," he said deeply looking into my eyes.

"What if your sister asks you about us? Will you tell her?" I inquired.

"No," he was stunned by my question turning his eyebrow V shape.

"Are you sure?" I asked again to confirm.

"Yes. You don't have to worry about my sister; she doesn't get involved in any of the private matters of others. I usually don't share everything with my close ones. As I said before, I always keep myself busy," he explained.

"So, you have not slipped any secrets of your loved ones to others?" I was curious.

"I never gossip," he said calmly.

"Hmmm! Do you have any secrets?" I was questioning him like a teacher.

"No. Why do you ask?" he inquired.

"I just want to know you more. So, tell me do you have any; I can keep it in my stomach," I teased him.

"No, I don't have it," his answer was direct. He walked away from me a few steps. This chat was getting interesting for me.

"I bet you do have secrets," I pressured him.

"Why do you think that I have? Give me one example," he stopped walking and turned to see me.

I came nearer to him and whispered, "The secret about your parents."

His face became from casual to deeply engage in his mind. I think I have hit the trigger point. I touched his hand to calm his nerves.

"Samarth, you can trust me. Please say it," I asked in a caring tone.

"Please drop the topic," he pleaded.

"Okay, as you wish," I stepped back from him letting go of his hand. It is not that he doesn't put his faith in me; he is not ready yet. I went back to complete the shopping.

We were silent the whole ride when we returned to our house. I watched the dark trees passing by at night and the moon was full white, flawless in glowing.

Inside the kitchen, he was busy helping me to stock the fridge and cupboard with groceries without saying a word. He went to the chimney fire by lighting it quickly. He was watching the fire and I was behind him watching.

"Samarth, I am sorry," I said.

"For what?" he said still watching the fire.

"About the argument we had. I don't know what is going on between you and your parents. It is none of my business as you know me for only a few months and I understand," I said carefully.

"Thank you," he never turned his face from the fire.

"Will you watch the news till I warm the food?" I said.

"You eat it, please. I am not hungry," he said and went upstairs leaving me perplexed. What just happened? I said sorry to him for not revealing his parents to me. He should be sorry, not me. He lied to me and my parents about his parents and that they will be meeting us at the engagement, at the wedding, at the reception, etc. These men know how to trick us into believing that we did something wrong to them. My head was spinning around when I was thinking. Probably, I am feeling hungry. I went to the kitchen to warm the food and I was so famished; I ate it fast. Why should I be abstaining from eating dinner when he is not hungry? It is his stomach, not mine. I am really angry with him now.

I went to the room to sleep, Samarth was sleeping quietly. When I saw his face, I forgot all the rage. I change the dress and climbed the bed without making any noise.

The next day I was experiencing the same cold weather as yesterday. Samarth was early as usual. I was rubbing my eyes continuously till it was opened. I went downstairs to check on him. He was in the kitchen preparing breakfast; I bet he is still angry to make his food. Men have an odd way to show anger, either they leave the house by not eating or preparing themselves food. Father used to do such things when he fought with my Mother. But we never fought, it was an argument we had last night. I went towards him to talk. He glanced at me.

"Good Morning, I made you breakfast today. I hope you don't mind using your kitchen," he slightly smiled. I am confused now by this sudden change.

"You mean to say 'our' kitchen," I corrected him.

"Yeah! Right," he said. I started setting the table. I could smell he has cooked the Omelet and bread perfectly.

We sat down on the chair together consuming the food slowly. He kept glancing up at me as if waiting to say something; I should ask him.

"What is it, Samarth?" I could not hide my frustration.

"What? I didn't say anything," he replied.

"You were glancing up at me continuously. You do that when you have something to tell," I said in a serious tone.

"I am sorry for the behavior at the supermarket and back home. I know I have lied to you regarding my parent. Yet you showed patience. I will tell you about them once you are open-minded," he requested.

"I am open-minded," I replied quickly.

"Yes, you may be but I haven't felt that way. Listen, I am not being judgmental. It's just that," He took a few seconds to say, "When we have not opened our hearts to each other? How come we can share everything in a week? I need time just like you requested me to give yours. Will you give that?" he explained.

He has a point and I should be fair to him. I know our situations and perspective are different from each other. I had no option; so, I said yes with disagree.

"Do you like it?" he changed the subject.

"Yes, it is tasty," I politely said.

"Thank you. I have found a way to teach you driving," he said.

Will he not leave this topic? He is desperate to teach me. "How?" I asked.

"This Sunday, we will leave the peak and reach the spot to drive easily for you," he explained.

"Are we going to Coimbatore?" I asked him in disbelief.

"No, we will not go that far. We will find the vacant place in Mettupalayam after leaving behind the mountains," he said enthusiastically. I think it is not a bad idea.

"You are ready to do that thing," I asked still doubtful.

"Yes," he replied.

"Don't you think it will take the whole Sunday by driving forth and back? Don't you wanna rest that day?" I inquired by taking bites in between.

"No. I will take a rest when you start driving here," he is very much anxious now.

"I hope I don't disappoint you," I said.

"No, you won't. I have confidence in you," he smiled.

He finished eating and went to the kitchen to put the plate on the sink. He took his wallet and keys to leave. I stopped him as it is early now and I have not prepared the lunch. He explained to me that he has pending work to complete; he will order the lunch from the Restaurant as one of his clients will come to meet him. He said bye and I reciprocated.

In the Afternoon, I prepared tea to drink. I opened the backyard door to enjoy the sun. The hot tea and sun could not hurt me my tongue and body as before did in the city. Instead, I was taking pleasure in the bitter less warmth in here. I walked on a grassy field to absorb the heat on my foot. In the distance behind the bush of the house, I heard noises of snickering. As I went near the bush, two girls were looking at something near the plants of the garden of the White cottage side. One of them was taking pictures of the plant on mobile which I can't see what it is. The other started drawing in her notebook.

I took another step closer to them and said, "Excuse me." They both jumped together at my voice.

"I am sorry. I didn't mean to scare you girls," I said calming them.

"It is ok. We never expected a person here," One of the girls who are taller than the other said.

"What do you mean?" I asked her.

"Ah, we never find anybody near the house. It is always silent," She explained. I remark that Samarth never talks to them, as he said he is a lone person; keeping busy at the factory and at home.

"Oh. What were you looking at on the plant?" I asked curiously.

"An insect, a blue bee which is rare to find," the small girl said.

I saw that they are nearly identical to each other with the same shade of fair color, exactly long black hair. I think they are sisters. They wore plain churidars with jacket-type sweaters, the older one wore black, and the other was bluish-grey. The older of the two has a round face with a few freckles on her cheeks. The younger one had a clear perfect oval face that looks more beautiful than the older one.

"Have you caught the bee?" I asked innocently. They both smiled broadly looking at each other.

"No, we don't collect. It is for the design," the older one said.

"Oh, Wow. My name is Leena," I said introducing myself and stretching my right hand toward them.

"It is nice to meet you. My name is Roohee Khan and this is my younger sister, Fahima," they both returned the handshake.

"Did I disturb you to miss the bee?" I asked her.

"Oh, no. I already took the photo of him," Fahima said showing the photo.

"The bee looks beautiful. What do you design?" I asked her.

"I design clothes. I am learning a fashion design degree in college," Roohee said.

"It is wonderful," I said appreciating her.

"Do you live there?" Fahima asked pointing toward my house.

"Yes," I said. They both looked at each other in surprise.

"When did you buy the house from Mr. Karthik?" Roohee asked.

I laughed for a second, "I don't have too much money to buy the house. I married Samarth Karthik; he is my husband."

"Oh, When?" Roohee asked in astonishment.

"I married him on 21st January," I replied.

"It happened last week," Fahima said raising her eyebrows. I assume they were not invited by Samarth.

"Yes," I replied.

"Congratulation," Roohee said smilingly.

"Thank you. Did my husband tell you anything about Marriage to your father?" I asked.

"I heard he got engaged. He never said he is getting married so soon," Fahima asked Roohee.

“Maybe, our Father has forgotten to tell the date,” she replied to Fahima. I could see in their behavior that Roohee is more polite and mature than Fahima.

“What is your father's name?” I asked to confirm.

“Our father's name is Aasif Khan,” Fahima smilingly said.

“Do you both want to come inside the house?” I invited them.

“No, Maybe later,” Roohee replied.

“Who else is there with you?” Fahima asked me

“It is just me and my husband,” I replied.

“Lovely. Have you started planning for your honeymoon or already been there?” she asked curiously. The word ‘Honeymoon’ made me uncomfortable. Roohee pressed her sister’s hand to stop asking me any further questions.

“Sorry. She didn’t mean to interfere, she is curious,” Roohee said politely.

“It is ok. We didn’t plan the honeymoon yet. He is busy at work,” I replied.

“It is true. It is been a month since we saw him,” Fahima said caringly. Roohee folded her notebook and glanced at her watch.

“I think we should leave now,” Roohee said.

“Please wait. Who else is there with you?” I asked.

“We two and father,” Fahima replied.

“Please do come to my house if you two are free,” I said when they are about to leave.

“Sure,” Roohee said.

They smiled and turned back to their house. I watched them as they walked away. I felt relief to have found the people near the house. I headed back to my kitchen to prepare lunch for myself. She was right it is silent here; I could hear the insects sound more loudly than others.

Chapter 13

Two Sisters

That evening, Samarth came late exhausted. I prepared dinner early. He washed his hand and sat on the chair of the dining table. I poured the food accordingly. He ate quickly as if he is hungry for a whole day. He devoured half of his food in six bites. I had nothing to say but to watch. I suppose he worked hard today.

"Are you okay?" I asked concerned over him.

"Yes, it was a critical day for me," he said.

"Why? What happened?" I asked.

"One of our workers got an accident in the factory. Two workers were having a dispute with each other. It got beyond when one person pushed the other to the wall next to the window. The Window glass broke into pieces and got stuck on his hand bleeding heavily. We immediately took him to the hospital," he said without a break.

"Oh, that is awful. How is he now?" I asked.

"He is fine," he said in between bites.

"Thank God. When did it happen?" I asked.

"In and around 5.00 pm," he said.

"Why didn't you tell me when I called you?" I asked.

"I don't want to bother you," he replied.

"What is the name of the injured person?" I asked.

"His name is Prasanth," he said

"Is everything got cleared between the workers?" I asked curiously.

"No. The problem is that Prasanth's wife wanted to complain about the worker," he sadly told me.

"Then," I asked waiting for the answer.

"I and Raghav suggested to Prasanth and his wife to drop it. It was an accident and he has to face him as they are in the same colony; and every day at the factory," he said.

"Did the worker say sorry to Prasanth?" I asked.

"Yes. When we were about to leave the ward of the hospital, the person came and begged Prasanth to forgive as it was not intentional," he explained.

"Did he forgive?" I asked anxiously.

"Yes," he replied coolly.

"I am glad he did that. I hope this never happens again," I said taking my plate to sink.

"I hope too," he replied.

After that he strolled towards the garden thinking, I cleared the table and went to the room. At half past 9, he came to the room and to the bathroom to change. Before I could say, he went straight to bed to sleep. I wanted to tell him about what happened this afternoon. He slept soundly and I didn't want to bother his sleep. Probably, tomorrow I will tell him.

Every winter morning was the same as usual; the same goes for my body, the aching. I looked from the balcony, I saw that the neighbor was about to leave in their car. I got down immediately to arrange breakfast. I saw Samarth drinking tea with the newspaper in the other hand. He was still in his T-shirt and pajama. I wished him Good morning and he replied the same. I asked him whether he is sleepy and drained from the last night. He said that he was alright.

I made him a huge breakfast that gives him strength. We sat down and ate slowly, "Yesterday, I met our neighbors, Roohee and Fahima,"

Samarth stopped eating, "Mr. Aasif's daughters?" he asked.

"Yes, I want you to introduce me to their father this evening," I asked.

"I will be coming late today. I have a meeting to attend," he said. Now, I stopped eating.

"I don't understand. I wanted a quick introduction; it is not that I will be chatting with them for a whole hour," I told him.

"Is it necessary?" he raised his head to see me.

"Yes. When I talked with those girls, they were oblivious that you got married. I am asking why didn't you invite them to our Reception?" I questioned him.

"I would have invited them but I didn't," he said warily.

"Why?" I asked.

"Cause you wanted a simple Wedding with a few guests," he said reminding me of my request.

"Yes, you are right. But three more guests would have not harmed me. There were only a few people from your side than ours," I said.

"Listen, I have a factory to run. If you want to meet them, so be it. Please make sure that you don't get involved often," he insisted.

"Okay, never mind. I will do it myself," I said.

"Are you angry?" he asked.

"No," I said without looking at him. He went upstairs to get ready and I to the kitchen to make lunch.

That same day, in the late afternoon, I went to the garden to see them. I found nobody except the white house and their garden filled with birds and insects. After a few minutes, I saw that they were walking toward me.

"Shall we come to your house, if you are free?" Roohee asked me politely.

"Of course. You can come," I said. As I can see, they cannot cross over the heavy border bush. It is not pleasant to greet people from here.

"We will come toward the front door," Roohee said.

"Okay," I said and went straight to the door to open it. They showed up smiling and looking beautiful as if they have come to a party. I welcomed them inside directing them toward the sofa to sit. I went to the kitchen to bring a Soft drink for everyone.

"When I was nine, I came to this house last time. Ever since I have wanted to see this place again," Roohee said finishing her drink and setting the glass down on the sofa table.

"I don't remember this house as I was only seven. This is the first time I am seeing this interior of the house," Fahima said.

“How long have you been staying in your house?” I asked.

“Since I was five and Fahima was three,” Roohee said.

“We came here when our maternal Grandfather died. He has nobody to look after his house as our Uncle; our mother’s brother went and got settled in the USA. Our Uncle never came here to claim the house as he became quite rich there. So, our Grandfather handed over the house to our mother before dying,” Fahima explained.

“How old are you two?” I asked.

“I am 21 years old and she is 19,” Roohee said.

“So, you are living here your entire life. Why didn’t you come after when you were nine?” I asked her more.

They looked at each other, “We don’t know. After Madhavi’s Grandfather Mr. Vijay Karthik died, we have not been invited since then,” Roohee said.

“Do you know Samarth's Grandfather?” I questioned.

“Yes. Our Grandfather and his are friends. We use to come here when we were little. Grandfather Vijay and his wife were good and caring toward us. Ms. Madhavi is lovely, allowed us to play with her daughter,” Roohee said enthusiastically

“Are you in touch with Madhavi?” I asked curiously.

“Yes, but rarely we meet. Through her, we came to know that your husband got engaged,” Roohee replied.

“When did she tell you?” I asked.

“Actually I didn’t meet her, our Father did. She and her husband came to our Father’s showroom to place an order for a suit,” she said.

“Does your Father work there?” I inquired.

"No. He owns the showroom of Suit for Men; we have a wide range of specialty materials. We don't deal only in Suits; we have Shirts, T-Shirts, Jeans, pants, etc. If you want to buy anything for men, please visit there," She said it like a TV host promoting the brand without taking a breath.

"I will come if Samarth wants to shop. When is the last time you met Madhavi?" I am sticking to the interrogation now.

She was thinking, "When she stayed here for a week last summer holiday. We met her in the garden plucking oranges from the tree and she offered us a dozen. We accepted it and their children played Volleyball with us except Vinay as he wants to become a referee."

Both Chuckled together as they are reminded of some sort of funny event. Finally, Fahima said, "Vinay is a bit naughty. He whistled around, play, and became a boss for all of us. He said to us secretly that he will make us win if we give him chocolate as a bribe."

"Really, he did that. What both of you do then?" I asked her in astonishment.

"We agreed but Rashmika and Siddharth felt fishy when he gave points to us even when we are not playing properly," Fahima said. We all laughed at his mischief.

Fahima continued, "We got caught and Siddharth was running after Vinay for his naughtiness. We had fun with them."

"Did she invite you both inside after the game?" I asked them.

"Yes. She requested us to visit her husband's house but not here," Roohee said.

"She never invites us here. I don't know why?" Fahima added. Roohee glanced at her sister irritably to keep quiet.

Her sentence made me realize something suspicious. Madhavi is always good to people, even when she is tense. She can manage anybody anywhere. Why she has bid them to come to her husband's house when she can summon them here which is near their house? Is it due to Samarth that Madhavi doesn't grant entry to neighbors? Why is he so aloof?

"Do you know Samarth's parents? Do they come here?" I asked.

"Very slight I know them. They rarely come here. Last time, I met them at Madhavi's Grandfather's funeral. After that, I have no clue," Roohee said in a low voice. It is been like 12 years since she met them. I am obvious that Fahima doesn't know who they are as she doesn't remember this house as well.

"When are you completing your College Graduation?" I asked Roohee changing the subject.

"This is my last semester; after that, I will do a Practical Diploma Course in Designing," she said.

"It is a good choice. What about you Fahima, are you in college?" I asked her.

"We are in the same college. I am studying Bachelor in Computer Application second semester," she said proudly.

"Well, she studies boys in College than books," Roohee laughed.

"Shut up. You are ruining my image," Fahima said in an annoyed tone.

"It is ok. You both can tell me anything, I am a secret keeper," I confirmed to her.

"I only hit at handsome boys," Fahima became comfortable. We all giggled.

It was a relief for me after I met them. They stayed here till early evening. They both asked me about my background, my journey of marriage, etc. I asked them the College life and their friends. Finally, we became friends. They invited me to visit their house to which I gladly agreed.

A few days were usual with Samarth. I got to see Roohee and Fahima at half past one every day after college. No College on weekends which is beneficial for me. I watched them and their Father leave the house at 9.

I barely see their Father from the window at 8 pm. Roohee said that she wanted to introduce me to him and he will be available every Friday afternoon at her house. She invited me and Samarth for a lunch this coming Friday.

I asked Samarth about it, though he refused to come. I excused Roohee that Samarth will not be available at that time. She didn't mind at all. She might know it was expected. But she and Fahima are glad to have me.

At last, Today is Friday. I dressed in a formal Anarkali dress after the morning chores. She invited me at 1.30 pm and I did go there on time. I locked every door of the house before leaving. It is five minutes walk on the lane to the cottage. The nearer I went; I could see the cottage's white color getting faded and old. I rang the bell at the door, and Fahima opened it after a few seconds. She welcomed me with a broad smile. I saw her father coming out of the room. He warmly invited me to come inside. The cottage doesn't look the same as the outside, the interior design is modernly built, a sophisticated one. It reminded me of the phrase, "Never judge a book by its cover."

Roohee heard the bell arrive quickly from the kitchen to see me. She showed me the L-shaped Sofa to sit on it. They all sat together after me. Their father congratulated me for getting married to Samarth. He praised Samarth that I am clever to have found such a good person.

After our few talks, I can see Mr. Aasif khan is a humble person. Roohee brought me a welcome juice in her tray and said that Lunch will be ready in a few minutes.

I didn't mind about the lunch, I want to see their house and meet their father. He may know about Samarth's parents' history.

After that, Roohee called out to the dining table. Fahima and her father rose from their seat to the table and I followed them. As I went near, I could smell the aroma of Biriyani. The table was filled with the finest dishes. We sat together except for Roohee as she is pouring the food to all. She sat down next to me and Fahima across me, and their father in his host chair. I admired Roohee for cooking the food deliciously. We were discussing the variety of food we ate in our life.

Mr. Aasif Khan asked me suddenly, “Do you find any problem settling here?”

“No, Uncle,” I lied.

“I am asking you that many people find it difficult to stay here, especially those who have come from the hot city,” he explained.

“I found it trouble at first. But now I am fine,” I lied again.

“Please don't be a stranger. If you need anything, ask us,” He said in a polite tone.

“Sure, Uncle. I am sorry that Samarth didn't invite you to the Wedding Reception,” I apologized.

“Please don't regret dear. I understand he is a busy man,” he replied.

“Actually, it is my fault that you were not invited,” I said slowly. All looked at me surprised.

“We don't understand,” Roohee said.

“Well, it was my idea to have a simple marriage which occurred in Court. I requested him as my mother is getting sick in between,” I said in a low tone.

“What happened?” Roohee looked concerned.

"She has a heart attack twice a year. I don't want it to happen again. So, we arranged it with a few close families," I explained.

"Oh, Leena. You did the right thing," Roohee supported me.

"Many youngsters don't think that way as you care about your family. Your parent is lucky to have you," Mr. Khan said.

"Thank you," I replied.

"You are strong to let go of the dream wedding," Fahima said.

"I am sure that Fahima will not sacrifice her dream wedding even when I become sick," Mr. Aasif teased her.

"Father, I am strong enough to sacrifice," Fahima said with confidence.

"I trust Roohee will give up but not you," he teased again annoying her. Roohee giggled and I smiled.

That afternoon was quite delightful; Mr. Khan accompanied us till 3 pm as he must go back to his Showroom. He talked about his young days and his neighbor's friendship with Samarth's Grandfather. Through him, I come to know that his father-in-law was not only friends of Mr. Vijay but also him. After he left, Roohee and Fahima showed me around their house. This cottage was filled with a vast hall along with four bedrooms and a kitchen. They took me to the backyard which I could not see before. There was a small cabin situated five yards away from the cottage. Fahima said that their father build it for them to play. Their garden was surrounded by roses, orchids, Jasmine, petunia, and many more near Pine trees. They said every flower's name. The name of flowers coming from their tongue rolled off like they are experts in it. I placed my wish to them to go beyond the pine trees though they declined as it is the end of the mountain which is sloppy and it is fenced with wood and wires. Roohee explained it is built for wild animals from entering the place. I asked have they come across any wild animals entering around here. I feel safe when she said no. I don't want to see that might cost me trouble.

We came back inside their house; Roohee brought a set of photo albums of them, their ancestors, friends, etc. I turned every page analyzing the photos while Roohee and Fahima gave details of the time and place they took it. I could see a teenage boy standing next to them in a family photo. I asked them who he is. Both faces turned from excitement to despair. I waited for a reply.

At last, Roohee said, "He was our brother."

"What do you mean by 'was'?" I asked.

"He is dead," she said with a heavy sigh.

"I am sorry. When did he die?" I showed condolences.

"It was three Years before," she said sadly.

"What is his name?" I asked.

"His name is Mohsin," She replied.

"What happened to him?" I asked her in a soothing tone.

Roohee didn't reply, there were a few minutes of silence appeared and I think they were mourning.

"What happened?" I asked again.

"He was murdered," Fahima said aloud.

"Fahima, stop it. He was not murdered, it was an accident," she said annoyingly.

"Why are you lying to her? He was murdered," Fahima argued.

"You need to stop right now. We should not fight in front of our guests," Roohee reminded.

Tension was growing on me; I had never seen them angry before. There is some serious issue between them regarding their brother's death. Fahima says he was murdered while Roohee says it was an accident, which one is correct? If Fahima is right, who killed his brother and why? If Roohee is right, Why is Fahima saying that he was murdered? Perhaps I should ask this later.

"I am sorry. She thinks he was murdered, it was really an accident," Roohee explained. Fahima was still frustrated and could not quarrel despite her wanting to.

Many people never fight when the Guest is near. It was a sort of respect shown towards the visitors. I guess Roohee never want to disclose their family matters to me and I understand that as I am a new person to them. She should feel a strong trust to open stuff like that to me. Probably they tell me later when they are ready and I should not bother them.

"Okay, how old was he?" I said.

"He was 17 years old," she continued.

"It must be heartbreaking to see your loved ones die this young," I asked.

"Yes, it is," Roohee agreed. Both of them stayed quiet, thinking.

I asked her changing the topic, "You said you are learning fashion design in college. Have you sketched any clothes?"

"Yes, let me show you," She took me to her room while Fahima followed us. She took out her sketch pad handing over it to me to see. As I turned every page, it is remarkable to see how talented she is in her work. The drawings were filled with insect patterns in dresses, Gowns, etc. People say that Insects tend to be evolving rapidly due to the environment. She has chosen a good path for boosting her career in the future. As I can see this world is a place for passion in fashion.

"It is extraordinary work you have done," I said appreciating her.

"Thank you," she replied gladly.

She showed me a few dresses which were meant for the College project. The clothes were designed with yellow and black butterflies pattern, red ladybirds, etc. I found Lady Bird is the best dress from others.

After the discussion, I thought I was getting late; though I have nothing to do besides cooking dinner. After a quarter minute, I informed them that I should leave. They insisted I stay longer, but I declined. They understood and gave me packed food for Samarth when I was about to leave their house.

They dropped me at their threshold and said goodbye to each other.

Chapter 14

The Birthday Party

After I reached my place, I went to the bedroom to lie down rewinding the situation that happened in their house. Some sort of tragedy occurred in their lives which shattered them to discuss with others. Probably I should ask Samarth, he might tell me.

Samarth arrived at the usual time. I warmed the packed food Roohee gave me and I have not prepared anything for myself except a large coffee. Samarth ate the food vigorously. He inquired about the empty plate I have. I informed him that my stomach was full as I ate plenty which is difficult for me to digest in this cold environment. I informed him that I had a good time with them and missed his company. He apologized and will be there for me when they invite us again.

I asked Samarth about Mr. Khan's Son when he got to take a nap in our bedroom. I told him the whole topic happened in their house.

He listened and didn't reply. I pestered him for the answer. Finally, he said that I should not ask him about their issue especially when it is critical. He also added that it is the right of our neighbors to disclose their matter directly to me than asking others. It means he knows; he doesn't want to gossip about it. I have no choice but to stay silent.

The next day I did my part of the work. After Samarth left, Madhu entered the house. I inquired her about Mr. Khan's Son after she completed her chores.

At first, she hesitated and then she told me that Roohee's brother did a terrible crime and suggested I stay away from the family. I got displeased at her suggestion and ordered her to come to the point. She said that he killed two Police officers. I asked her why and she replied that he was dealing drugs and selling them at the school campus to students. When the police officer found out about it and came to the house to arrest him. He ran away from the jeep in the middle of the road taking the police pistol with him. They exchanged firing bullets. Then, he killed two officers and ran away from that place.

I was shocked to hear this news and asked her more about how he died. She continued that he stayed hidden for a few days and the Police tried to search him but could not find him. After a week, they found him in his backyard house. His family was helping him to hide. The police arrested him, again and he tried to run away. The police have no option but to shoot bullets at him. That's how he died.

I suggested to Madhu that the family must be unaware of his hidden place. The Police might have followed him every place. He had thought to stay out of sight; he found his cabin is the best to conceal him. At last, the Police searched the house which leads them to catch him easily.

She disagreed with me and ensures that the Police told the Media news that they found the food plates in the backyard house. So, the family was helping him.

"You should not blame the entire family, he lives in that house. He must know when to get inside the house when his family is not around. He might have stolen the food, and taken it to the cabin. Think about it," I enlightened her.

"Maybe or Maybe not. I am sure that the family was helping him, they never left the house," she said.

"You should not be judgmental if you don't know the truth. The Police might have thought that the family was helping the boy," I advised her.

"You may be right. I don't want to interfere in their personal life. I feel that they should have locked him up instead of hiding him if they found him in the backyard. I know a family will do anything to help their blood. What about others' blood being spilled like it was nothing? Just think about the two police families he made orphans," she explained.

I didn't argue further as she got the point. What if Madhu is right about the whole thing; about Roohee and her family hiding her brother after he killed? He was not only carrying the drug problem but also killed two officers which is devastating. He was not a fugitive to them though a son and a brother.

Right now I am dealing with a heavy scandalous story. Samarth would have stopped me from meeting them, but he didn't. He knows his neighbor for many years more than others. He neither mingled nor judged them; though he talked to them rarely. He believed that they are innocent. My husband is right; Roohee or Fahima will tell me their truth than ask others about it. I should wait for it. Till then I should not be negative toward them.

I met my neighbors that day in the garden when we first met; we talked about our likes and dislikes. I never tried to ask about her brother. I inquired about other neighbors where the house is situated on the corner of the starting lane, the blue house. Roohee informed me that the old couple Mr. & Mrs. Kaushik lives there. They have one daughter and one son who live in Bangalore. The daughter married the Bangalore guy and settled whereas the son followed the sister to Bangalore for a job and he too settled there. Their son and daughter visit them during holidays.

"Do you visit Mr. Kaushik's house often?" I asked Roohee.

"No. I meet them rarely," she said.

"Are they good?" I asked.

"Yes. Do you want to meet them?" she asked me.

"Yes. Shall we go there today?" I asked her.

"Sure. They always stay in the house as they have no one here to visit," Roohee said.

"Fahima, are you coming with us?" I asked her. She is busy chatting on her mobile.

"No," she said disapprovingly.

"Why not?" I questioned her.

"She is scared of their cats. They attacked her when she went there to give their misplaced postcard," Roohee explained.

"Mr. Kaushik has cats in his house," I asked her.

"Yes," Roohee said.

"The cats will not attack you this time, Fahima as we all are going together," I teased her.

"I will not come. You two carry on," Fahima replied without glancing at us.

We left her in the Garden and proceeded to go to the blue house. I thanked Roohee for her company; asked her if I should bring anything as I am visiting them for the first time. She said that it is not necessary as they are welcoming to others; though they will be glad if I gift them any kind of Cookies or a small amount of gratuitous food. I thought it is a good idea.

Before leaving, I went to the kitchen and opened the packed cookies filling in the bowl. We walked slowly, the blue house looked lovely as we got closer. I always come across their house before leaving the street to the main road. I have not got the chance to look closer except today. Roohee pressed the doorbell button two times. After a while, an old lady around her fifties opened the door. She must be Mrs. Kaushik, she looked weaker and wrinkles surrounded a lot on her face.

Roohee greeted her and introduced me to her. She knew Roohee and allowed us both inside her house. We followed her to the living room where an old man sat on the single sofa. He wore an old type of glasses watching his mobile sincerely. He must be Mr. Kaushik. He stared at us for a fraction of a second. He recognized Roohee and greeted her to sit on the sofa. I followed Roohee and sat next to her.

"It is been so long since I saw you Roohee. Where is Fahima?" He asked Roohee ignoring me.

"She could not come as she is busy with her studies," Roohee replied lying about her sister.

"Who is this lady with you?" he inquired about me.

"She is Samarth's wife," She replied.

"Who is Samarth?" he asked.

"Samarth Karthik, Our neighbor," She reminded him.

"Oh, The silent boy. How are you Mrs. Karthik?" he asked me directly. I think he has given a nickname to my husband as a silent boy.

“I am good, Uncle. Please call me Leena,” I replied.

“Please don’t mind my husband, he could not recognize people with names nowadays,” Mrs. Kaushik apologized to me.

“It is ok. I don’t mind,” I said. I gave Mrs. Kaushik a bowl of cookies; she appreciated and accepted the bowl.

Mrs. Kaushik brought us tea and a pound cake to eat. We all talked about our past, especially Mr. Kaushik. He even remarked about Samarth that he will never get married as he was too shy. Their hospitality was good and comfortable. Hours have gone swiftly and we took a leave from them. Mrs. Kaushik happily hugged me and reminded us both to come whenever we are free.

As we are returning to our house, Roohee said that she feels miserable to see old couples living alone by themselves without their children to take care of them. Her words rang like a blow in my ears, which made me recall Samarth’s parents who are living alone like Mr. and Mrs. Kaushik. It was not only about Samarth’s parents but also mine. I miss them. I called them immediately on my mobile after I reached the house.

Today was Sunday, Samarth informed me yesterday about the driving lesson. I agreed without a choice. We got up, dressed quickly, and ate our breakfast. Samarth seem pleased though I was not. We left the house at 10.30 am.

The hills have left us and we have reached the Starting edge of the highway. I could feel that the speed has been increased which makes me bumpy. I looked at my husband; he was staring back at me for a second and back toward the road. I looked at the speedometer of the car shows pointing above 90. He said nothing but I have to ask him why is he driving so fast.

"Are you in a hurry?" I asked him.

"No! Why?" He looks confused.

"You are driving so fast which makes me wonder that you are in a hurry," I asked him.

"I always drive like this," he replied me with a smooth grip on the wheel. I am confused now with the reply.

"But you never drove fast before, not even on the first day after marriage," I recalled him. He smiled at me for a second making me a little bouncy through his maniac driving.

"I don't know whether you enjoy speed driving; we barely knew each other at that time and I don't want to scare the new bride on the first day after marriage. You almost got scared to have a conversation with me while driving on the first day mounting the hills. If I drive like this that day, you would have surely run away from me," I felt embarrassed when he reminded me of that event, and how nervous I was. His statement made me more worried does he drive like this on the mountain; I have to ask him.

"Do you drive like this when we return to our house? I mean driving in the mountains," I was serious about it now.

"No, I don't drive fast on mountains which are exceptions. It will create accidents,"

"I want you to slow down the car now," I commanded him loudly.

"What?" he questioned me.

"Please slow down," I requested him.

The speedometer shows pointing 70 now. I am glad that he did as I requested him to do. He drove slowly and reached the bland spot. He got out of the car, requesting me to do the same. I sat in the driving seat and he sat next to me.

He commanded me to put on the seatbelt. He told me step by step about the car driving part names and instruments. Theoretically, he said how to switch on the engine, how to press the clutch pedal with my left foot, how to change the gears, etc. I am relieved that he brought me to the empty spot so that I can drive easily. Before commencing to drive, he told me to relax.

After an hour, I drove smoothly without his instructions. I was feeling hungry as the time struck at 2 pm. I appeal to him to put a stop and continue it after lunch. He agreed with me and will continue next week.

He surprised me after lunch that we are going to the theatre to watch a movie. I thought it was a wonderful idea since we have not spent time together outside alone. He bought snacks along with cold drinks. I enjoyed the movie besides the intimate scenes which made me embarrassed as Samarth sat next to me. I thought he will put his arm around me as most of the theatre seats were empty and men take it as an opportunity to get close; though he didn't do it. We reached the house around 8.30 and I had a good day.

On Monday, he took me to his factory, showed his cabin, introduced me to his staff, etc. He was full of pride for what he did in his business. I appreciated him for his hard work. I changed my mind about working together and pleaded with him to allow me to work in the factory as I have got nothing to do in the house. Oppositely, he turns down the offer as I have to take care of the house which is more important.

Every Sunday he carried me to the same place to teach me to drive; I was getting better at it. On 5th Sunday, he informed me to drive on the mountain road which I refused as I am not ready yet.

I have spent two months here with Samarth; it passed like 2 years for me. It is like I am used to this place for a while and I started liking it. Samarth has always been patient with me during this time. In between these days, he tried to touch my hands one or two times. I didn't respond and got rid of his grip. He didn't complain about it.

We spent our days visiting Madhavi's house which is rare, shopping grocery, learning to drive, etc. Besides that, I have Roohee and Fahima for companionship. We have grown close to each other like true friends, especially Roohee. We both have the same behavior, taste, and character; understand each other well.

At the end week of March, I drove the car on the mountain road confidently. We celebrated it by eating ice cream. On the way back to our house, Samarth asked me for a fee for teaching which I promised without any idea.

That night, he asked me for a kiss as a toll. The promise I made to him was hitting like a hammer on my head. I should have asked him before giving the word. I thought he might ask me to cook his favorite dish or some sort of gift. Then my brain reminded me that the man who has everything will not ask for any materials or goods. I would have kissed him though I don't want to do it as it is not correct. A kiss is a token of Love.

I have to feel something about him; I want my first kiss to be special and not to be treated as a fee. So, I excused him that I could not give him what he wants. He understood and slept on the bed. I feel miserable and angry with myself. He is doing his best while I am acting like a stubborn chauvinistic woman.

His goodness makes me want to hug him, and be near him but I have not accepted him which is a bad impression for me. I slept silently next to him.

The next evening, Samarth returned home late. He took out the card from his coat and placed it on my hand. It was a birthday invitation card. He informed me that Mr. Raghav is conducting a birthday party for his daughter who is turning 5 years old on the 1st of April evening and we are invited. Only five days left to buy a present, Samarth told me that we are gifting cash. I advised him to gift both cash and a toy which he approved.

On the 1st of April, the climate around here was getting warm and I could feel the summer month has started. The trees started growing

Orange and pomegranate fruits in the garden; within a week they will ripe.

Samarth came early at 5 pm to pick me up to go to the birthday party. On the phone, he suggested I should be ready before he reaches home. I had done what he instructed.

Mr. Raghav's house was not far away from our place, it took only ten minutes to reach there. When I entered, the whole living room was crowded and DJ music was playing aloud. Mr. Raghav saw us and escorted us to his Garden which was least empty than the living room. The garden was decorated with lights, Pink and blue tents. Under those tents, Buffet tables and chairs were laid. He invited the whole staff and their family which I am slightly familiar with. I could see Madhavi and her husband Mr. Ranjan with his family entering the garden. Samarth and I joined them.

At 7.15 pm, we all gathered in the living room to celebrate as Mr. Raghav's daughter proceeded to cut the cake. One by one gave their gifts, took photos, and waited for dinner. Everybody was having a piece of cake and beverages before dinner.

Mr. Raghav's house is enormous and the living room is big enough to hold fifty people. Madhavi and her family left us to have dinner. Samarth and I stood on the corner of the hall far away from the main door entrance finishing our cake slice.

Suddenly, I saw a woman standing on the porch looking elegant in her dress and ornaments. She smiled and went to Mr. Raghav to congratulate him, handing a wrapped gift to his daughter. They were talking close to each other. I assume she is his best friend or sister. They don't look similar as she has fair skin than all of us.

Mr. Raghav said something in her ear, to which she turned her face to our side, scanning the room. She glanced directly toward us beaming. I have the feeling she knows us or knew Samarth. I saw Samarth's face which gave a stern look as if he saw a ghost.

Slowly, she walked toward us passing the jam of people. She greeted Samarth with a 'Hi' and he did the same to her.

"How are you?" She asked him. Her voice sounded like a chime.

"I am good. How are you?" he asked her calmly.

"I am better than fine. I heard you got married?" She inquired.

"Yes. Meet my wife, Leena," he introduced me. She glanced at me and smiled. Her face is smooth like a porcelain doll and her eyes can strike any man to love her. I feel envious of her beauty.

"Hi, Leena. I am looking forward to meeting you," She gave her hand to shake and I returned it.

"Thank you. Your good name," I asked her.

"My name is Ragini Desai. Samarth, Raghav, and I studied in the same school and college," she explained.

"Oh. I am glad to meet you," I replied.

"Ragini is a classmate and a friend of Raghav and me," Samarth said in a relaxed tone.

"Best friends. I have known your husband and Raghav since 5th grade and we three have been close friends since then," she said confidently.

"Oh, I see. Have you come alone?" I asked her.

"No, my husband is with me. He is somewhere....," she turned and scanned the hall and said, "Here he is. Suresh, Please come over here," She called him aloud.

She waved at her husband to see and he walked past the crowd. He looked handsome though not more than Samarth. He wore a branded collared sweatshirt with a long sleeve and blue jeans.

She introduced him to us as Suresh Desai. By way Samarth and Suresh talked, I believe they are meeting for the first time. He then turned to me to speak after Samarth introduced me to him. Mr. Desai complained to my husband for neither attending their marriage nor inviting him to our wedding. Samarth explained in a formal tone. Ragini tried to stop her husband to drop the matter as it is nothing important. I support Suresh in mind that he is right about best friends inviting each other to their weddings. I suspect there is some dispute between Ragini and Samarth.

After a brief discussion, they both left us to meet others. I found Samarth relieved once Ragini left us on the spot. I ignited the topic that Suresh protested before.

"Is she your best friend?" I asked Samarth.

"Yes. She was.. back in college," he said cautiously.

"Why didn't you invite her as you have summoned Mr. Raghav to our wedding?" I questioned him.

"I would have but she is settled in Bangalore and I was busy," he said.

"You could have called her through the phone. Many people get invitations through one call," I told him.

"Actually, we are not in contact since college," he informed.

"Why?" I asked.

"Because we fought then we never talk to each other. Is it enough?" he got annoyed. From that moment, I closed the subject and concentrated on the party. I have friends; I do fight with them and get along later once both of us calm down. This is totally strange to see Samarth not console the matter after a fight or Ragini never tried to finish the conflict. Maybe, one of them is immature, I guess not who might be.

Half of the guests in the living room are gone to either have dinner or home. The children had enough space to dance to the music played by DJ. Samarth and I watched them enjoy it; even elders joined.

He saw my leg that was tapping the ground at the beat of the music.

“Do you want to dance?” Samarth asked me.

“No,” I replied.

“You said you like dancing. Join them,” he said.

I can’t bear his thoughtfulness. His caring for me let me lose my grip on things. Are there any men like him who care about their wife’s interests?

“I will dance only if you join me,” I asked him.

“I don’t know how to dance,” he stared at me this time.

“I know you do,” I stared back at him.

“I don’t think it is a good idea. I might embarrass you,” his voice is serious now.

“I don’t mind. Please dance with me,” I insisted.

“Alright,” he said. He shakes his hand and moved his leg slightly along the thump. Through this, I came to know he is not a bad dancer.

We both danced until we are exhausted to breathe. We sat down on a sofa for a while and he took leave from me for a restroom break. Before he was gone, I informed him that I will be available in the Garden as I am famished.

Chapter 15

The Secrets I Must Know

In the Garden, I took the plate filled with necessary food and desserts; planning to join Madhavi and her husband. Before I move further to them, I saw Ragini eating alone at one of the vacant tables and her husband was nowhere to find. So, I decided to join her and extend our presence as we have not recognized each other properly.

I went near her, "Do you mind if I join you?"

"Oh, no. Please have a seat," she pulled the empty chair next to her for me to sit.

"Thank you," I said.

"You are welcome. Where is Samarth?" She asked me.

"He is on a bathroom break. Where is your husband?" I asked her.

"He is socializing with others, talking about his business as usual. It is boring to me to stand there and talk about work. So, I moved from him to have dinner," she explained.

"How long have you two been married?" I inquired her.

"It is been four years," She replied with a sigh.

"Do you know your husband before marriage?" I inquired.

"No. It was an arranged marriage for me and him," she replied in between bites.

"Don't get me wrong, are you happy with him?" I asked her caringly.

"Why do you ask?" She questioned me.

"I mean to understand what it is like marrying a stranger as you did," I hit the straight point.

"At first, it was difficult for him and me. Then, after a year we became close and understand each other. You know, marriage needs compromise, without compromise it is tricky to adjust," she said.

"Yes, you are right. I have to cooperate with Samarth as he is still a stranger to me after ten weeks," I said recalling his behavior regarding the parents.

"I would not worry about that as I know Samarth and he is best in everything he does. He is better than I am in friendship. So, I approve he will be a good husband to you," she confirmed.

"You show faith and confidence in him whereas he is the opposite about you," I replied.

"Like what?" she asked me raising eyebrows.

"That you and he fought during college days and stopped being friends. Why is that?" I gave her a brief explanation.

She sighed as if there is a burden in her heart, “It is a long story.”

“Please tell me. I have time,” I insisted.

“It is better you ask him,” she said.

“It is a problem with Samarth, he never explains. Do you know he neither talk to his Parents nor invited them to our Wedding? I don’t even know what they look like in person,” I said in an annoyed tone.

“I am sorry, I cannot help you,” She apologized to me.

“So, you do know about his Parent's stuff. How long is he a stranger to them?” I asked her more. She didn’t respond. I stared at her, waiting.

“Since he was nine years old,” she said at last. Nine years old, is she kidding me? It is more than 23 years. Are they dead? No, they can’t be or else Madhavi or Samarth would have told me during our first meeting.

“What happened?” I questioned.

“I cannot say. Do you know why he is estranged from me?” She questions me back.

“I don’t know,” I told her shaking my head.

“I broke the promise by disclosing all his secrets to my brother. He got shattered when he found out and never spoke to me again. It was a sensitive subject and he trusted me by saying all his problems and made me swear. I thought my brother will help me by handling the matter; so I told him. Then my stupid brother confronted him,” She said.

“What is it?” I enquired her.

“Please don’t ask me more. I don’t want to break the promise again by telling it to you. He is angry with me for cracking it once and I deserve it. Friends always keep secrets from others; I guess I was not up to his friend. One day, I am sure he will forgive me,” she said calmly.

"You can't keep me hanging. Please explain," I pleaded with her.

"Please take my advice don't upset him by enquiring about his Parents. Samarth is a sensitive person and he has trust issues. Once he begins faith in you, I am sure he will tell you all. Till then you must have patience," she suggested.

Patience! Why do people keep telling me to tolerate it? First, my mother, my sister-in-law and now Ragini is guiding me. Is the problem with Samarth big enough to ruin our relationship? What is he hiding from me?

"Are you ok? You have not eaten anything," She asked me.

"Well, I am not hungry anymore," I drop the fork on my plate.

"You better start eating as Samarth saw us. Please don't discuss what I have told you now," She pleaded. As she said, Samarth walked toward us sternly.

"Don't worry, I will not tell him anything. You can count on me," I said relaxing her.

"Thank you," she said.

"Are you finished?" Samarth asked me standing across our table.

"I have not started yet. I was waiting for you," I told him.

"Well, I am finished and I will leave you two alone," Ragini left the table and went to her husband to accompany him. He sat on the chair next to me and started eating from my plate.

"Are you not bringing your plate?" I asked him.

"No. I am not hungry, I will have a few bites from yours, then I am done," he told me calmly.

"Okay, you can finish it as I am not hungry," I told him.

"You were hungry before. What did she say that ruined your appetite?" he caught me.

"Who? Ragini. She didn't say anything," I lied.

"I bet she said something," he insisted.

"Nothing, she was appreciating you that I got the best husband," I told him other true things.

"She did?" he said astonished.

"Yes," I change the subject.

"And?" he questioned me seriously this time looking at my eyes.

"That you are a vulnerable guy I will ever meet," I told him.

"That's all," he asked curiously.

"Yes," I said without blinking.

He dropped an intense glare at me and continued eating. I took a silent sigh as I was about to get caught by him. Before he can say it, I asked him about inviting her to dinner at our house. He declined and I insisted again to terminate their fight; it was no use to console him to alter his mind.

After dinner, we all left the party. That night, I was curious to ask him about Ragini. She seems like a good person by withholding the promise she made to Samarth. Once she had broken it and never wants to repeat it. I asked my instinct, What Samarth is hiding? What secret is that he only told her, not others? I feel he is close to her than other friends or did he love her? Yes, He would have loved her, look at her; she is beautiful in every way. She is like 8 out of 10, and I may be like 5 or 6 out of 10. If I score Samarth's physique and look, he is 7 or 8 out of 10. They would have become a perfect couple as their features were precise. They both had beautiful Children.

What am I thinking? He is your husband, silly. You are considering match-making with your husband and his best friend, Ragini. I don't know why but it is just that jealousy has not aroused in my heart.

I am imagining the past which is impossible in the present time. Now, I am his wife and he is my husband, that's it.

Before I think further about Ragini, Samarth came out of the bathroom. He was preparing to go to sleep.

"Did you love her?" I hit the main point.

"What?" he looked at me to proceed.

"Did you love Ragini?" I asked again.

"I don't understand why are you asking. She is just a friend," He hesitated.

"I know, I know. It's just that she has everything that all men want," I said cautiously.

"Like what?" he said uncaringly.

"Look at her, she is a beautiful, smart, educated, Independent girl which is a benefit for marriage," I said quickly. He sat close to me touching my hand.

"Leena. She was my friend. We have not seen each other like lovers. So, you don't have to worry about her," he said firmly.

"Was? What happened between you two that has become a barrier which is difficult to destroy?" I asked him angrily.

"It is nothing to fret about. We had a fight, which was tough, and went our separate ways after college," he explained.

"Can you tell me the reasons of the fight?" I pressed him again.

"I think you should drop this topic as it is none of your concern," he told me deeply.

"None of my concern? I am your wife. I have the right to know everything about you," I sort of yelled at him. He stood up from the bed.

"Leena. Have I forced you into anything? I did what you asked me. You wanted a simple marriage, I did. You said you wanted space, I gave it. You said you need time to mate with me, and I obeyed. Is it not enough for you?" he reminded me.

"Oh, Please. Don't mix it with what I ask. This is different, that is different when it is compared. I opened all my secrets, everything. I communicated with you about my likes, dislikes, friends, and even my parents," I said loudly.

"What do you mean?" he asked furiously.

"You know what I mean. I am asking about your parents. Where are they? What is it eating you to tell me?" my rage was showing in my eyes as I stood up to him.

"I can't tell you," he looked away from my stare.

"Why not?" I asked him intensely.

"Please stop," he begged me.

"I won't stop today. You owe me an explanation," I said with gritted teeth.

"Explanation? Then listen, I hate my parents. I don't want them around me or anyone whom I love. They are the worst people you will ever meet. I am saving you from them," he released a sigh.

"Why do you hate them? What did they do? Please tell me as I can't ask you again and again," I begged him.

"For now, this much I can say," he replied.

"I know there is more. Please trust me," I said pleadingly.

"How can I trust you when you don't trust me?" He said calmly. I am confused by his words, but I do trust him.

"What are you saying? I trust you," I said.

"Really, Then why you have not allowed me to touch you? I gave you more than you asked for and yet you have not given me a kiss," he constantly stared at me for a reply.

"I....I....," I became dumb. He is right.

"No words. It is easy to ask others to open up about private things. To share those things, you have to become intimate. You have not shared your innermost possession with me," he said calmly. He picked a blanket and a pillow leaving me alone in the bedroom.

I stood there perplexed by his objection. He has a point I don't believe him. I do like him regardless. After a moment, I crawled into the bed to sleep. I have nothing to say, but to cry.

The next morning, Samarth didn't have breakfast. He left early after I woke up. He is angry with me which I usually understand. I don't understand the part about his parents. Maybe, I should discuss it with my mother. No, it is not right. She won't mind if he is not close to his parents.

Perhaps I should ask my cousin Abhi as she has studied the Psychology of Human behavior. I looked at the clock, it showed 10.15 am. Singapore is 2.30 hours ahead of India and she might have gone to the office. I dialed the number and she picked up the call immediately. I asked her if she is busy as I have a ton to say. She informed me that she will call me after 10 minutes during lunch hour.

I waited and I waited for a call, it passed only 7 minutes though I felt like 7 hours. At last, she called me. I said everything about our relationship from starting till now even about Ragini. She listened without interrupting. In the end, she advised me to compel Madhavi about it as she is sure that Samarth will take lots of time to discuss it. As she talked about men's Psychology, they don't hide anything from their partners except the Love affair. If they do, it must be susceptible. She even told me that men who hate their parents must something to do during the childhood days that affected them till now.

She is right; he has not talked to them since when he was 9 years old. After the call, I planned on visiting Madhavi before lunch. I took out the car keys and drove myself to her house. It is my last chance to know the secret from her. If she doesn't say, then I must drop it forever.

As I arrived, Madhavi stood at the threshold waiting for me. I called her before I left the house intimating very urgent. She welcomed me and made both of us tea. I asked her about the children, she said that they are busy studying in their rooms for the Annual exams which will start in 2 days. I am glad they have exams and won't disturb us. After one or two sips, she asked.

"What is it, dear? You said it is urgent," she asked me casually. I kept the teacup and saucer on the table.

"Yes, it is important and it is about Samarth," I told her.

"What about Samarth? Is he okay?" she asked me in a concerned tone.

"He is fine though our relationship is not fine between us," I told her calmly.

"Why? Has Samarth done anything wrong with you?" She questioned.

"Yes. I feel like he is not happy getting married to me," I told her.

She desisted, "I don't agree, dear. Samarth is in cloud nine since he married you. I know he is not a jolly type of guy doesn't mean he is unhappy."

"Then why has he not touched me till now," I lied to her. I know it is deceitful though I had no choice but to bring the truth into her mouth. If I asked straight about the Parents; she obviously will refuse to tell me.

"What? Are you sure? You two have not mated?" She doubted. The word made me cringe, discussing intimacy with my sister-in-law is what I hate now.

"Yes, I am sure. It was me who asked Samarth about postponing the first night for a few days and he agreed. But now, it is been more than two months; and he has not approached me," I lied again.

"Oh, dear. Maybe I should talk to Samarth about it," she was upset.

"No, No. Please, don't tell him what I said. I am not concerned about it as he is keeping me comfortable. What I worry about is that he is not communicating with me. I feel like he loves someone or he doesn't trust me and that part is abstaining him from mating," I stopped her.

"What should I do then?" Madhavi asked me.

"It is not correct to ask you about his problems. You must tell me why is he like this introvert. I am living with a roommate, not with a husband. I know it has something to do with the past and you know about it. If I ask about his Parents and Ragini, he doesn't want to talk about it. So, please tell me what he is hiding from me," I insisted.

"Please be patient. You ask Samarth about it after a few months, and he will tell you," she advised me.

"No, I don't think he will say even after a year. He and I fought last night when I confronted him. Only you can explain his behavior," I pleaded.

She hesitated for a minute, "I am sorry, Leena. I can't tell you as it will complicate matters. If I say it, then he will cut ties with me. And I won't let it happen. Please understand," she pleaded more with me.

Now, I lost the last chance. I should pick up the handbag and leave this place as I am disappointed. No, I must not give up easily. So, I gathered my strength to manipulate her.

"Okay, I understand. I have no choice but to divorce him. I won't live with a man who is physically and mentally not available with me," I said calmly.

"Oh, no. Please don't take hasty decisions. You will find a way to tackle it or I will talk to him," she said.

"Please don't talk to him. If you want this marriage to work, tell me or notify the person who knows about it," I asked her once more.

There was a huge silence in the hall, and through her firmness, I can say she won't tell a thing. I will waste the time if I stay longer. I pick the bag and rose to leave the house.

Finally "Wait, Leena," Madhavi said.

"Yes," I looked back.

"I will tell you the person who can help you. First, you have to promise me that you won't tell Samarth about it ever," She opened her right hand to me and I put the right hand on it to prove.

"I promise you that I will not say anything to Samarth or anybody about what happened here and his secrets. So, tell me who is the person?" I inquired.

"Sundar and Bhavna Karthik, Samarth's and mine parents," she said it intensely as if she is guilty about it. His parents are the ones to cause him this estrangement and the question is will they tell me?

Chapter 16

I Am Shattered

Madhavi took out her mobile and dialed the number. First, she wants to introduce me to her Parents. She was four steps away from me while she talked to them, so I could not listen to it. Apparently, she is connected to them except for Samarth. Probably, there is a dispute between Samarth and his parents, not Madhavi.

After a while, she walked towards me and handed me her mobile. I took it, "Hello, I am Leena speaking," I hesitated.

"Hello, Leena. How are you, dear?" it was her mother, Bhavana Karthik.

"I am fine, Aunty. How are you and Uncle?" I asked her gently.

"We both are fine. We both are eager to meet you in person. We only saw your picture," she replied. I looked at Madhavi with a minor doubt; perhaps it was her who sent them my photo.

“Oh, that’s good. When shall I meet you, then?” I was curious.

“It will be difficult for you to meet us; as we are far away from you, dear,” Aunt Bhavana said.

“Which place are you residing now?” I asked her.

“We settled in Pondicherry for the past 8 years,” she replied.

“Pondicherry?” I said loudly. She is right, it is far for me.

“Yes, dear,” she confirmed.

“Will you tell me what is the problem with you and Samarth?” I inquired her.

“We will talk about that later. First, tell me Do you love my son?” She pondered a hard question which is tricky for me to answer.

“Let me be clear I like your son. I am not gonna lie about that,” I told her.

“Hmmm. I appreciate your honesty,” she praised me.

“Thanks. Are you gonna tell me now about him?” I asked her again.

“Will you not wait for Samarth to tell his problems? Is it necessary to know from us?” She replied.

“Yes. It is necessary for me or else I won’t be familiar with him at all,” I said the truth.

“Are you sure, dear? Samarth will be devastated if he becomes aware of the link between you and us,” she enlightened me.

“Don’t worry, Aunt. I am ready to take the risk. Please say it,” I strongly accepted to face the consequence.

“I can’t tell you over the phone, some things cannot be said over the phone. I have to meet you in person. Will you come to Pondicherry?”

Aunt Bhavana firmly asked me. I have no answer, how can I go to Pondicherry without informing Samarth?

"It will be tough for me to reach there. Will you come over here to meet me?" I genuinely asked her.

"I would love to come but my knees are aching and my husband walks rarely as we both have reached the age above 60 years. It is your decision now," She added. I almost forgot that they have become senior citizens. I froze for a minute to reply here.

"Okay. I'll let you know once I make the plan," I said.

"Please do the plan, dear. I am eager to meet you. Do you want to talk to Uncle Sundar?" She asked me.

"Of course, Aunty," I said. After a few seconds, I heard a crooked voice.

"How are you, Leena?" he asked me.

"I am fine, Uncle. How are you? I heard from Aunt that you barely walk," I inquired him.

"I am ok, dear. Aging is really a burden for a few people; Apart from that I am healthy," he said.

"I am glad you are healthy. One day, I will surely meet you both," I replied to him.

"Please visit us soon. Let me inform you that Samarth and you will always have our blessings," he said with passion.

"Thank you, Uncle. I will call you again," I said it.

"Bye, dear," he hang up the phone, and so did I.

It truly felt good to talk to them and to know that they sincerely care for their son. I find them frank and decent. Then, why does Samarth hate them? Only they can reveal the story.

But first I have to arrange the plan to meet them and it is a risky task for me. As I was thinking about it, Madhavi was looking at me uneasily. Is it because of her Parents mingling with me or Samarth Fury when he comes to know about it?

"What are you thinking?" I asked her calmly.

"Nothing," she replied sadly.

"You can tell me, Madhavi. Please," I asked her again.

"I am scared, Leena. What if Samarth identifies what I am doing? He will not talk to me. Gaining his trust back is hard," she looked into my eyes asking for the answer.

"Samarth would not know it only if we say it. As you made me promise, I will keep it till I die. So, it is your turn to promise me that this will be our secret. Do you agree?" I asked her.

"Yes, I swear," she reluctantly said it thinking about the consequence.

"Good, I will be leaving now. Take care of yourself," I said in a hurry.

"Leena, wait. Won't you stay for lunch?" she asked me out of courtesy.

"No. I am not hungry," I replied.

"Are you sure?" she asked again.

"Yes. See you soon," I said and left the house. Madhavi accompanied me to the entrance door waving me sadly.

After I reached the house, I was thinking of a way to go to Pondicherry. I should come up with a good plan so that Samarth won't doubt my intention. Afternoon arrived, I still could not prepare for the journey.

I heard a knock at the door. When I opened it, Roohee and Fahima were standing at the entrance smiling at me. I welcomed them as usual and prepared tea. My mind was aloof and both of them caught it. Roohee asked if they have disturbed me. I said nothing and lied about being tired.

Fahima asked suddenly if I miss my parents. I said I do miss them every day. Roohee suggested the idea of visiting them as they won't be meeting me the next week, as their exams have started. They will be busy for two weeks studying and completing the examination.

This clicked in my mind that it is a good thought. I thanked them both for the suggestion that this visit will help me meet Samarth's parents.

That night, Samarth arrived home late. I cooked his favorite meal and he agreed to eat it when I requested him. I sat near him on the dining table chair. While he ate, I informed him politely that I want to visit my Parents for a week. He stopped eating, gazed at me directly, and asked the reason. I said that it has been three months and mother is missing me and wanted me to visit her.

"Do you want to go?" he asked me while playing with the food through his spoon.

"Yes, I will be back after a week," I told him.

"When do you want to leave?" he said in a depressing tone.

"Perhaps next week," I replied to him.

"Ok, then. I will book you the tickets," he slightly smiled.

"Thank you. Do you like the food?" I asked him.

"It is delicious," he calmly said.

"Then why are you not eating it?" I asked curiously.

"I just lost my appetite," he said playing with his food.

"Is something wrong happened in Factory?" I asked him.

"No," he replied uncaringly.

"What is bothering you? Please tell me," I asked him again.

"Are you happy here living with me?" he asked me after a few seconds.

"Yes, I am pleased to stay with you," I approved.

"Why do I feel like you are not happy with me?" he inquired intensely.

"You believe me or not I am really happy," I firmly said.

"Then, why are you leaving me?" he asked disappointingly.

"I am just leaving you here for a week," I chuckled at him.

"I feel like you are saying goodbye forever," he touched my left hand and this time I didn't pull out it from his touch.

"Please trust me I will be back after a week," I said it placing my right hand on his hand confidently.

"Are you positive?" he stared into my eyes making me shiver.

"Yes. If you want to come with me, I'll be delighted," I lied to him. I hope he says no to it as I have to interrogate his parents alone.

"So, you won't mind me coming to your parent's house," he questioned me testing the behavior.

"I won't mind. Please come," I unintentionally said it.

"I can't come, I have work here. You go alone," Finally, he gave up.

"Thank you, Samarth. Everything will be alright once I visit them," I said with care.

The next day, our day was usual and Samarth brought me Airplane tickets, round trip. He has to be sure that I return to him and that the return ticket has been booked after the week. I kept my cheery face from revealing it to Samarth. This made me think that he is worried about the marriage, about me. I appreciate his authorization over me, but what if I want to stay a few days longer? Will he let me stay?

I started packing the bags and necessary items for a week. I informed my Parents about visiting them. I said farewell to Roohee and Fahima a day before the departure date as they will be busy the next day studying. I met Madhavi's family on the same day. Madhavi's children demanded clothes and gifts after I return. I assured them that I will buy it.

On the departure date, Samarth accompanied me to Coimbatore Airport. His behavior was not letting me leave him. He drove slowly so I can miss my flight. It is heartbreaking to see him like this weak, helpless person though he said nothing. I don't want to leave him, but I need answers only his parents can provide me.

At the Airport, he said a few words that still rang in my ears the entire trip. "Leena, I may not be a good husband, but I'll try my best. If you think I am good enough for you; please come back."

How could he say that he is not a good husband? In my opinion, he is the best man. Actually, on the vice versa I feel like I am not good enough for him. These feelings made me miss him already. I wanted to call him, though the Hostess abstain me from calling. I waited to call after the Flight landed.

On the way to the house, I called Samarth to have a casual talk. I detested my Mother picking me up from Airport, as I am Adult enough to reach home. After I arrived, Mother started crying seeing me after a long time. She informed me to take a rest. Actually, I was not tired at all. I messaged Samarth immediately that I have reached. He video-called me to check that I am fine and talked to my parents. I appreciate his protectiveness.

I told the mother that I'll be meeting my friends this whole week. She advised me to meet them later as our Relatives are inviting me for a few days. It is a ceremony that happens after marriage, a newly wedded bride or a couple will be invited for a feast. In my case, Samarth does not throw away time in these ceremonies. I am glad he didn't come or else he would get irritated by talkative Aunties and Uncles.

I planned the visit to Samarth's Parents on the fifth day after concluding the feast which means I have two days left. In between, Samarth and I called each other. I lied to my Parents that one of my friends has arrived here in Mahabalipuram to stay with her Parents from Dubai for a month. I visited other friends on the fourth day to make them believe me. I should have told my parents that I am traveling to Pondicherry than Mahabalipuram as the situation goes I don't trust my mother's tongue which might reveal everything. And I don't want to give any hint of suspicion to Samarth.

On the fifth day of the week, I booked a round-trip cab to go to Pondicherry. Mother was concerned about me traveling alone. I assured her I will be back before 8 pm. The distance between Chennai to Pondicherry is approximately 3-4 hours by car. I started my journey at 10 am. So, I'll be reaching there at 1.30 or 2 pm. Samarth's Mother gave me a complete address to reach there.

I had a light breakfast and bought a sweet box on the way. Finally, at 1.45 pm, I arrived at their house. The house was big, built with Pillars, colored light green with a small garden at the front gate. I knocked at the front door; a young lady wearing a Saree opened it. I gave her my identity; she smiled and said that Uncle and Aunt are waiting for me. When I entered inside, the structure and interior were the finest in design. I followed the young lady wherever she took me. The hall of the house was at the end. There, on the hall sofa, Uncle Sundar and Aunt Bhavana sat together.

They both rose together to welcome me. Aunt Bhavana was faster than Uncle Sundar approaching me. She held both my hands with her and hugged me tightly. I handed her the sweet box to her which she gladly accepted. Uncle Sundar showed me the way to sit on the Sofa.

I did what he asked. I could see he walked slowly back to his seat. I understand now that traveling is hazardous for them.

As I examined them, Uncle Sundar has more wrinkles than Aunt Bhavana. Uncle Sundar wore trousers and a shirt, Aunt Bhavana has grey hair cut into a bob style and she wore a plain printed white Saree. Samarth has his father's eyes and the face is the replica of his mother. She looks beautiful even in her sixties. I assume how Samarth got his handsome face; While Madhavi is the combination of both Father and Mother or their Grandparents I think.

"How was the journey, dear?" Uncle Sundar asked smiling at me.

"It was good," I replied to him.

"How are your parents? I heard your Mother has a heart problem," Aunt Bhavana asked concerning my mother's health.

"It happened before. Now, she is fine," I told her. I asked them about their health, to which they replied that they are not concerned about it at all. I appreciated their house and the interior. The young lady brought glasses of fresh juice. Aunt Bhavana hinted at me to take it. I hesitated at first and drank a few sips later. I told the cab driver that I will be back after 2 hours and the huge clock on the wall strike 2.10 pm. I should probably begin the conversation.

"Aunty, you know why I have come here to meet you," I asked her.

"We know dear. First, we will have lunch together. You must be hungry after a long ride," she asked me.

"I am not hungry," I lied to them. In fact, I am starving.

"You will get sick if you don't eat anything. Please join us," She advised me. I did it as she insisted and Uncle Sundar nodded with a smile. It is really awkward to meet in-laws without your spouse.

They both showed me the way to the dining hall. We all sat together and Uncle Sundar want me to sit near him. Two more servants entered the dining hall serving delicious food, dessert, etc. They have provided the whole buffet with more than eight food varieties. I am famished but my stomach is not big enough to eat all of it.

I guess they are showering love on me as their daughter-in-law who has met them for the first time. Their maid poured food one by one onto the plate. I stopped her once I thought I had a sufficient amount. I ate slowly tasting every flavor and I must say that is a more delicious food than the feast provided by my relatives.

After lunch, they took me back to the same hall. Aunt Bhavana ordered tea and cookies from her maid. I declined to drink after the heavy lunch as it still digesting in my tummy.

Now, I don't have the patience to wait as the time is ticking. I asked her the question that why Samarth is estranged from you both. What is the reason he does not want me to meet? Why does he see you both like an enemy?

Uncle Sundar counsel me to have the endurance to know it all. I explained to them that the cab driver is waiting for me and he might call any time after 3.30 pm. I promised mother that I will return before 8 pm and the worst thing is Samarth will call me any time as he does every day. Within a few minutes of the meeting, I could not ask them.

She understood what is bothering me the whole moment. Before she can commence; the maid brought with her a tea tray and cookies. Aunt Bhavana ordered her maid to close the door before leaving us. This showed me a sign that it is a vulnerable matter to expose.

"What Job did you do before getting married to Samarth?" Aunt Bhavana inquired me. What kind of question is this? I have not come this far to discuss the previous job I did.

"I worked as an Admin professional in a Multinational Company. Why do you ask?" I asked her.

“Do you love your job?” she inquired again ignoring the question I asked.

“Aunt Bhavana, I have not...,” She stopped me mid-sentence. I looked at Uncle Sundar for support though his face is composed.

“Just answer me did you love your job?” she repeated.

“Yes, I loved it,” I answered it.

“Please tell me will you be ready to sacrifice for your ambition by abandoning your family?” she asked me.

“No, I won’t abandon them for the sake of the goal,” I replied to her.

“Why not?” she questioned me gravely.

“Cause Family is more important than anything in the world. They may be an irritating, fussy, attention seeker, etc. When the bad time comes they act as the pillar to hold the roof to avoid the rain entering inside the house,” I told her without hesitating.

“You have said fair words. But there is one thing; Family will not support you when you have stopped earning money. What will you do then?” she inquired me like an interviewer.

“I am not saying I will stop earning. I always provide for them. I will withdraw the thing that does not make balance in life. Job is important but the difficulty arises in that which leads to dumping family is not worth it. I will find another job where it makes balance both your Personal and Professional life,” I answered like a pro.

“You know how to live life; though I was not. I mean, we both are not like you to think the same,” she replied.

“What do you mean?” I asked her.

“You know why Samarth hates us because we both avoided our children in their childhood for the sake of our Ambition,” she said with a glimpse of sadness.

"I don't understand. What happened?" I pressed her.

"If I tell you everything, you will start hating us too," she said in a depressing tone.

"I don't hate people easily, it takes time. Please try to tell me," I requested her. She looked at her husband to say further, and he nodded at her.

"When you are educated, you want to do something in your life. When we both got married, we came to know that we have the same determination. Sundar does not want to work in his Father's Tea factory as he studied Mechanical Engineering and I was good in Science and Management even when I passed 12th standard. Sundar and I wanted to start our own business together by organizing RO Plant Solutions. We got profit after Madhavi was born and it was good. When we saw the luxurious life of our friends and competitors, we craved more profit. We became greedy in our ambition after Samarth was born and we both avoided them little by little.

Our maids and my mother took care of them while we were managing the business. We send them away to Sundar's parents, and my in-laws during the holiday vacation. My mother died when Madhavi was 9 years and Samarth was 2 years old and I was pregnant with the third child, Abhinav. It was really difficult to take care of them as Sundar could not manage the business by himself as it started growing. Madhavi somehow managed to take care of Abhinav after he was born but her grades were getting low.

Sundar's parents visited our house suddenly and he saw that the children are left alone with housemaids. He got shocked when Samarth and Madhavi spoke bad language learned from the maids. Sundar's father insisted with us many times to take them to Ooty to nurture and we both declined the idea as we don't want to lose them by sending them far. We regret till now for refusing it," she stopped.

"Why? What happened?" I asked her. She didn't say for a minute. She pressed her hand with another as she is nervous.

"Tell her, dear. She has the right to know," Uncle Sundar encouraged her.

"Promise me, Leena. You won't say a word about it to anybody, not even with Samarth. If he knows that I told you his past, he won't forgive us forever," she stared intensely at me for the reply.

"I swear it, Aunt Bhavana. I won't say anybody," I assured her. She took a deep sigh.

"When Samarth was 7 years old, our business was reaching a high level and we got the offer in London through our neighbor Mr. Bejoy who is a businessman like us. He and his wife become so close to us like a family and he suggested that we apply the idea of opening a branch in London to provide RO service to the top business companies. Obviously, we became busy and the children were left alone with the maids. Madhavi, Samarth, and Abhinav used to visit our neighbor Mr. Bejoy and his wife. He provided our children with toys and Chocolates and his wife used to adore them as she does not have children of her own. One day, Samarth went alone to his house to play and Mrs. Bejoy was not available at her house at that hour. Mr. Bejoy allowed Samarth inside his house to play and then he touched my son inappropriately his main parts," she stopped again.

"What? You mean to say?" I could not speak.

"Yes. Mr. Bejoy raped our son that day. And we hate that person till now," she said. I could not say for a few minutes. Is she telling me the truth? No parents will bluff like that ever. It is better to think before I speak.

"Did he tell you about the incident?" I inquired.

"Yes," there is shame in her eyes when she told me.

"And?" I asked.

"I didn't believe him; we both didn't believe him," she felt humiliated.

"Why didn't you? He is your son. You must trust him for what he says," I sort of yelled at her.

"That is why we regret it every day. But Samarth was not honest with us either when he was young," she replied.

"What do you mean?" I asked her.

"Do you know 'the boy who cried wolf' story?" she asked me.

"Yes," I said. I don't understand why she switched to one of Aesop's Fables stories.

"Samarth used to make up stories to get our attention. He was mischievous back then; just like the boy who repeatedly fools villagers into thinking a wolf is attacking his herds. When he told the truth, nobody believed him. As we ignored it thinking Samarth is telling us a lie again but he was telling the truth," she explained.

"You cannot make excuses yourself for not believing your son. He came to you to tell his pain for what happened to him and you both waved him off," I asked them both looking into their eyes.

I continued, "Children don't deceive their parents like that especially when they are so young." Aunty took out her kerchief to wipe her tears. As angry as I am, I could not see her crying and Uncle is silent with sadness.

"You are right," Uncle Sundar replied.

"When you both got sure that he was telling the truth?" I asked both.

"After we didn't believe, Samarth took the support of Madhavi. He told her everything. Madhavi advised him to stop visiting the house and he obeyed. One day during the summer holidays, Bejoy came to our house when we were not there. Our maid went outside to buy groceries leaving Madhavi, Samarth, and Abhinav alone. Madhavi was a grown-up girl and she took care of his brothers easily. She helped Abhinav take nap during the afternoon. After entering the house, he asked Madhavi for tea so he can be alone with Samarth; though Madhavi was clever enough to never leave him alone with Bejoy. She called Samarth to accompany her into the kitchen. This made Bejoy suspicious that Samarth has told her.

Abhinav started crying after getting up from sleep. She went alone to the room leaving Samarth behind. Bejoy grabbed him and tried to rape but our maid saw from outside the window of this house what he was trying to do. She got inside and yelled at him. He left the house after confronting him. She locked the house and called us and my parents immediately," He explained.

"Where were you then?" I asked him.

"We both were in London. My parents reached the house after hearing from the maid and I am glad they called the police. We returned to India immediately. When the police inquired about him, he denied our Allegations by appointing the best lawyer. His wife was shocked when we accused him. We applied a secret trial to safeguard our children's modesty. However, his lawyer won the case by telling Samarth and the housemaid are lying to the Court by bribing him with money. That monster left Pondicherry and his wife divorced him. After a few years, his wife married another man. We never saw him after the last trial. I should have beaten him after getting away from punishment," he replied furiously.

"How Samarth was feeling?" I asked him.

"Odd. He became estranged from us slightly and my Parents insisted to take care of our children in Ooty while we were away, though we denied it to them again. They got disappointed and when the father and mother were about to leave the house on the last day, Samarth packed his luggage and requested that he will stay with his Grandparents. We reluctantly agreed to it. After a few weeks, Madhavi started missing Samarth and she and Abhinav too left us to stay with my parents for a while," he replied.

"And both of you let them stay there till now?" I inquired him.

"No, No. We went there after the summer holidays to bring them back to Pondicherry for School studies. Samarth became stubborn that he wanted to stay and learn in Ooty and Madhavi agreed with him. Abhinav insisted to us that we all should stay in Ooty," Aunt Bhavana said after recovering from crying. I listened to her while she continued.

"Well, we didn't listen to them and ordered them to stay with us. Abhinav and Madhavi agreed to come in the end but it was hard to convince Samarth. At last, he decided to return for the sake of his siblings. Things got better after a few months for everybody. Children got busy with their school work and we got back to our routine," she paused.

"What happened after that?" I curiously inquired her. She didn't respond to the question denying eye contact with me and Uncle was looking down heavily grieving. I asked her again after a few minutes, "Please tell me."

"Abhinav died due to Pneumonia when he was seven years old. It shattered us all. Samarth could not recover; it was shocking for him to see his younger brother die. He even blamed us for his death," She cried again.

"I am sorry for your loss. It is not logical to blame you; it was not your fault," I gave my condolences.

"It was our fault. We were not with him when he was sick," she replied.

"Where were you then?" I asked her immediately making me tense.

"We were in London. Madhavi called us right away after checking with Doctor. He informed me that Abhinav is in the first stage of Pneumonia. It was a monsoon month and we could not able to catch the flight to India caused of heavy rain at the end of November. Though she called her Grandparents right away and they reached the house and took care of him. Doctors tried their best to save him by giving him Antibiotics. However, it got worse after we reached here. His body was sweating a lot. We saw him alive only for a few hours. I got traumatized seeing my last child dead," she paused again.

I could not say anything. All I feel is sorrow and sympathy for them. It is the worst sadness for parents to see their kids die and I feel that it impacted Samarth more. If I recall the photo frame hung on the wall of the stairs, after the vacation of the Kanyakumari; their happy faces reminded me that their Grandparents took care of them more than their parents.

Chapter 17

The Guilty You Feel

I returned to my cab at 4 pm and he drove faster as he can. I didn't mind his driving, all I think about was the moment of spending seconds with Aunt Bhavana and Uncle Sundar. After spilling all the secrets of Samarth to me, I find it difficult to cope with it. I didn't answer them, as I needed time to believe. It was not the secret as well but the mistakes done by the parents. The mistake committed of being too ambitious lead them to live alone here away from children. Samarth desist his parents as they desisted their children when they were young.

Now, the question is what should I do? What should I tell them to lower their pain from losing their children? Madhavi is still in contact with her parents. What about Samarth? First, he got raped; never trusted by his parent which is heinous. Second, he lost his brother at a very small age. I believe he has not forgiven them after the second incident.

What they did is unforgivable. I thought my father is the worst parent. After hearing this, I concluded that he is better than them. He was with me when I got sick and took care of me. He irritated me but never abandoned me. I feel like I have been harsh with him the whole time, especially with my Mother and I am grateful to have such parents.

Uncle Sundar asked me about the verdict should I conclude. I have nothing to say. When I see them in their old age, I feel pity and when I think about Samarth, what he is doing is acceptable. I cannot conclude and never will. All I said was that time heals all wounds. One day, Samarth will forgive them and embrace both. I neither judge Samarth nor his parents for the decision they have taken. Both Aunt and Uncle are longing to meet Samarth; though he doesn't care about them anymore. What I want to know is how their dispute will end.

I took leave from them after the driver called me. Aunt Bhavana hugged me tightly and Uncle Sundar kept his hand on my head to give the blessing. Aunt Bhavana gave me her gold bangles as a tradition to gift to the daughter-in-law. I refused to accept it; though she insisted me to take it as a token of love. I reluctantly agreed. I assured them the next time, Samarth and I will come to meet them. They both smiled and accompanied me to the gate. I said goodbye.

I kept aside the thought of my in-laws and concentrated on my husband. I could not imagine people doing such horrendous crimes to a child, destroying their innocence, and childhood.

I thought women are not safe in this world, but neither men nor children can be protected from vile people. I understand now clearly why he hates his parents, Why he is never rude to me when it comes to sex, Why he kept his distance from his neighbors, etc. The trauma he has gone through cannot be mended by anyone.

I feel guilty for being unfair to him. Funny how I thought I will never love anyone. Perhaps, I have fallen in love with him when I married him. I miss him and I want to hug him.

Secrets make the relationship apart if the person knows about it or make it closer if it is a good one. I never kept any secrets from my beloved ones, I always disclosed them.

I dislike people who keep hiding it from me, doesn't mean I hate them. I will understand it if they are honest with me, even if the words are harsh to handle for me. At least I will know they are not forged in loving me or hating me, I will consider it as being realistic. I have always been frank with everybody even with someone who went against me.

But this time, I have to keep furtive to save my relationship with my husband. Secret that he had hidden from me, now I know about it. He would be devastated that I know his past even when he doesn't want me to. My head is aching to think about the event, his face filled with shock and pain; I don't know what he will think about me.

Keeping apart the event, I should never reveal anything about it to anybody. Now I know why people carry on secrets, it makes you keep other people safe, especially loved ones. If I was in his shoes, I would have taken time to bare it or not at all.

Evidently, I am not in his situation and never want to be; though I will take care of him whenever, and wherever he needs me.

As I watch the evening turning into night, I never stopped thinking about Samarth. His sense of humor, his view of people, his manners, etc is a sign of a perfect man.

Suddenly, my phone rang bringing me to this world from my imagination. It was mother who called me, I picked up the call. She gave me shock that Samarth has come to Chennai to my house to surprise me. She informed me that it has been only a few minutes since he arrived there and asked about me. She told him what I told her that I went to Mahabalipuram to visit my friend. I am relieved to hear it and she asked the whereabouts. I lied to her that I left my friend's house ten minutes before. The driver was watching me from the rear mirror for lying. However, I ignored him. I asked Mother to put Samarth on the line to which she declined saying that Samarth still wanted to surprise me even when I am not available. He doesn't know that she secretly called me to come home soon. As I checked the time, it shows 6.20 pm. I assured her that I will arrive before 8 pm; I hang up the phone.

I asked the driver when we will reach Chennai. He replied that before or after 8 pm including the signals and traffic. I got tensed as minutes passed waiting to reach home. I am surprised that he will visit me today. I was glad when he has not called me today. Now, I know he wants to surprise me. What I worry about is that I have not informed him yesterday that I am meeting my friend today that is far away. He must be disappointed for not updating him.

I reached the area around 8.12 pm and I requested the driver to drop me 100 meters away from the house. He did what I said. I deleted all the details from the mobile that leads to information about the Location on my way, though Samarth never touches my mobile.

I reached the house exhausted from the trip. Samarth was sitting on the sofa talking with my father. He broadly smiled after I entered and I acted stunned to see him.

I said, "Wow, I never thought you will come here. What is this sudden surprise from you? Do you have a business meeting here?"

"No. I came here to surprise you," he replied.

"Well, it is a good surprise," I told him.

After a few conversations with him, Mother informed us that dinner was ready. I was hungry as usual. Samarth sat across me on the dining table and Mother was next to me. He watched me in between I took bites. I reciprocated by smiling at him.

I went to my room after dinner to hide the bangles and it is not a splendid idea to hide here as Mother always checks the room before cleaning. She will surely inquire me about the gold bangles. I cannot take it with me to Samarth's house as he uses all the cupboards and drawers. One thing he never touches is my handbag; I better keep it there until he forgives his parents.

As I was thinking, Samarth entered the room frightening me. He said sorry for scaring me. I accepted his apology and opened the wardrobe to keep the handbag inside it. He was glancing at my every move and asked, "Are you okay?"

"Yes, I am fine. It is weird, I never expected you here," I told him the truth.

"Are you not happy to see me?" he asked me.

"I am pleased you have come," I smiled at him.

He smiled back and took out his track pant and top from his suitcase to change. I went to the bathroom after he came out. I brushed my teeth and changed into pajamas. When I got out of the bathroom, Samarth was locking the door. He looked at me intensely when I dropped the clothes inside the laundry basket. He came near me closely and I know what his intentions are.

I moved back from him to the bookshelf to support myself as I am trembling with fear and I asked him, "Aren't you tired?"

"No. Do you know why I have come here? cause I have missed you," he came closer again and touched my cheek with his right hand. He looked into my eyes stroking the face gently.

I didn't respond but I wished to push him away. I am not saying I am not ready, it is just that I never want to mate here when my parents are next to this room. What if they hear us moan? It is uncomfortable to think about it.

If I pushed him away, he will think that I still have not accepted him. I don't want to disappoint him again. I took courage and closed my eyes giving him a hint to kiss me. He pulled my chin up to kiss me and I responded. He hugged me softly while he kissed me. He took out his top and started undressing me slowly. I became stiff when he removed all his clothes and mine as well. He stepped back to watch me naked and I blushed to glance in his direction as he was naked too.

"You are beautiful," he appreciated me. I cannot say anything to him as he had seen me wrapped around clothes over the months since marriage. I gulped down the saliva forming in my mouth making me shiver from his deep stare. He came closer again to kiss me passionately. His arms around me were getting tighter, our skin touching each other. He took me to the bed to make me comfortable as my knees were shaking with his touch. I lay down myself and he was on top of me covering us both with the bed sheet. I felt his breath on my face and he was hard. He got inside me, fondling every part of my body and all I could do is moan. I don't understand this sweet pain causing me to forget everything around here.

He buried his face into my hair on the shoulder after loving me. All I could hear was his heavy breathing; I stroked his sweaty hair gently to make him relax. After a few seconds, we curled together and I began to feel sleepy. I closed my eyes and let myself enjoy the weight of him over me. Finally, he turned over, lifted himself, and stretched out on the bed behind me. I felt him against my butt and he is still hard. His hands are curved around me, kissing me on the neck lightly.

In the morning, Samarth was still sleeping next to me even though the clock struck at 8.10 am. This is the first time I got up before him. I lay still for a minute as I am naked in bed. I feel shy even to get out of the bed sheet. What if he opens his eyes suddenly to see me nude again?

I got up fast as I could from the bedroom, took my clothes, and went to the bathroom. I bathed quickly and wore churidar as I planned to meet my Uncle Rakesh's family this afternoon. And Samarth will gladly accompany me. I got out of the bathroom and saw Samarth was awake lying down under the bed sheet. He glanced in my direction smiling deeply.

"Good Morning," he wished me.

"Good morning to you too," I shied away. I was drying my hair with a towel to avoid eye contact with him. I don't know how to react after last night. I sat on the dressing table to wear jewelry. He was glancing at me through the mirror and I could not tolerate his continuous gaze.

"What?" I asked him.

"What?" he asked back.

"Why are you staring at me?" I questioned him.

"Why should I not stare at you when you are beautiful? Besides I am your husband, not a stranger," he replied with a mischievous smile on his face.

"If you are my husband doesn't mean you can watch me all the time. It is making me uncomfortable," I stood up to face him.

"Really. You know I can make you uneasy more as I am still without clothes," he tried to remove the sheet. I stopped him immediately, "Please stop," I pleaded with him.

"Why are you so shy, Leena?" He avoided my request and rose from the bed naked. I turned my face away from him as I could not recover from last night's pleasure. He came close to kiss me and I gave in. After a moment, I tried to push him as I am getting late to make breakfast. He held me tightly like never before.

I pushed his face away from my lips and pleaded, "Please let me go. We can do it later. I promise."

"I can't wait," he kissed me again. He started fondling my back, my breast, and my butt and I could not hold back either. I caressed the back of his hair with my fingers and rubbed his shoulder back and forth.

Suddenly, I heard a knock on the door; it was my mother shouting breakfast is ready. I made him stop mid-way through lovemaking. He reluctantly obeyed me and went to the bathroom to shower. I informed Mother that we will be there after ten minutes.

At half past 9, we gathered all together to have breakfast. We got ready to leave for a visit to Uncle Rakesh. After we have reached, Samarth was hanging out with Uncle Rakesh and it seems he is in a good mood making jokes with everyone. Aunt Tejaswini showed hospitality towards us, especially to Samarth.

We had a fabulous lunch made by Aunt Tejaswini, and it is been a long time since I ate her handmade food. We left early as we were supposed to leave, while Uncle Rakesh insisted on staying for dinner. Samarth declined as we have to catch a flight tomorrow afternoon and joked that he doesn't want to sleep the whole day tomorrow after a heavy dinner. We all laughed at his humor.

We all were so tired after the feast today afternoon and took a nap for an hour in the evening at our house. I ordered a lite dinner online and we spend our time together watching a movie. My parents left us alone to sleep in their bedroom. As I was changing channels through the remote, Samarth was gazing at me like he had done today morning. I know his intentions and it looks like he was waiting for the opportunity.

He got up from the sofa chair and sat beside me placing his right arm around the shoulder and his left on my lap. His touch on my lap felt like a cold shock increasing my blood flow. I didn't react to his action though he recognized my behavior as I am avoiding his advances. He reminded me that I had promised morning about sex.

I playfully ignored it and acted to forget about the promise. He swiftly started tickling my waist, making me laugh like a young girl. It has been years since I was tickled that way.

I gave up and said yes to him. He carried me in his arms. I think it is the first time the way he carried anyone as he is holding me tightly as I will slip away. He put me in bed like a fragile baby. I closed my eyes for a minute when he locked the door. When I opened it, he was stripping off his clothes letting me watch his body. He doesn't shy as I do. He got inside the bed sheet I was under it and helped me remove my clothes. He was eager to find my lips to kiss them. I can taste the strawberry juice essence he had during dinner which I enjoyed kissing him passionately.

After we have done mating, I could not sleep for a few hours. Probably I had a good day for the past 24 hours happened which is unexpected for me. I looked at Samarth sleeping beside me, counting his breathing. When I watched him, all I think about was his pain when he was a kid caused by that disgusting person.

I wished I have time travel equipment; so I can journey to his past, protect him from the vulgar man, and beat him black and blue. And I know it is impossible to think of it but now I will be around him caring and protecting. I never thought that I would ever fall in love with him. Despite this fact, I married him to do the wife's duties. Now I know what love is and I love that feeling.

We got up early as possible to catch the flight on time. We packed our luggage and had breakfast; I could see slight tears in Mother's eyes. We said our goodbyes and left the house at 10 am as our flight departure time is 12.30 pm.

Samarth have already booked tickets with the same flight as mine two days before when he planned to surprise me though our seats were separate. Perhaps it will not take more than ninety minutes to reach Coimbatore and we will be back together after we arrive.

I began to shiver as Samarth drove on the mountains reaching our destination. We took a rest after unpacking the luggage in the evening. He came into the kitchen while I cooked dinner, hugging and kissing me on my neck. I sense he is in the mood again. After dinner, we went to bed early to make love again.

The next day, he went to the factory to work and I planned on meeting Roohee and Fahima. As the reminder came over me that they will be still studying for exams. Maybe, I should wait for them to call me. I called Samarth that I will be meeting Madhavi alone to give gifts to her children, but he didn't mind at all. Actually, he encouraged me to do the job.

I must go and ask Madhavi a few answers to clear which is annoying all along and her children will be busy with examinations. I thought it is a good opportunity to meet her. I called her before I could meet her. She said she will be alone to meet me from around 11.30 am to 1 pm. I drove my car immediately to the house.

She prepared tea for both of us and I asked the whereabouts of her children. She told me that the school has fixed an afternoon examination for a few class students and they went to write question papers. I handed her the gifts that I bought for them. She looked pleased as well as concerned.

I know what it is, my visit to her parents and hiding about it from Samarth. I showed support and concern over it too. She asked me suddenly, "What do you think of Samarth, now?"

"What do you mean?" I asked her.

"Do you accept him after knowing his past?" She questioned me anxiously.

"Why are you asking me this question? Do you think I will not love him after knowing the truth," I answered her confidently.

"Some people won't understand the situation of the victim. They approach negatively towards the incident. It is hard to believe that you are still here with him and I am glad you started loving him," She said it with sadness.

"I accepted him a long time ago for the man he is; not because of what happened to him in his childhood," I told her clearing the point.

"Why then you were in such a hurry to know it and forced me to fix the meeting between you and my Parents that he never wants to encounter," she angrily asked me.

"I don't know. Probably it is the impulsive nature of mine that wanted to know the reason behind his loathing," I answered her calmly.

"Basically, he doesn't hate them after all. He just needs time to overcome his anger or else he would not help them when they were broke," She told me enticing me to think.

"Broke, what do you mean by that?" I asked her.

"Our Parents were facing Bankruptcy six years ago due to bad management skills, other competitive companies were taking over the customers which lead them to be unable to pay financial obligations to the creditors in London. It was Samarth who saved them from the dishonor of the name of the company they have spent their time and struggle with by avoiding us. After that, they closed their branch in London and started doing it from the beginning as they did when I was a kid. I would have never done that if I was him. He has a good heart despite they never cared for us," she explained.

"How much did he pay them?" I was curious.

"He paid them approximately 2.5 crores Rupees," she replied.

"Wow, you are right he has a great heart. Did he have that much money at that time?" she smiled slightly when I asked it. I could not believe what Samarth did to his parents.

"No, he saved about 1.40 crore through business, I sold some jewelry, and the rest he applied for a loan from the bank," she said.

"Has the loan been cleared?" I was anxious to know.

"No. He still has to pay back around 15 lakhs including interest which will be over within this year and the next year will be prosperous for him as he will start saving again," she said it in a cheerful tone.

"I am glad to hear it. It is good to know you both helped your parents in times of crisis. You too have a great heart," I appreciated her.

"I never helped my Parents, it was my brother who was concerned about it. And I don't want him to take the burden himself," She made the point.

"Don't underestimate yourself. I am pleased that he has a sister like you," I valued her now more than before.

"Thank you. He is silent, keeps grudge but he has a soft corner in his heart, and always will be there for him. All I want is the day when he and our Parents reconcile each other," she said gloomily.

"That day will surely come soon," I said after drinking the tea. I continued, "I want to ask one more thing as a friend, not as a sister-in-law," I told her.

"What is it, dear?" she asked me.

"Did Samarth love her friend, Ragini?" This question was bugging me for a whole week. She hesitated to answer me back.

"It is not necessary to know the past," she replied after a minute.

"I need to know and I will not judge anybody about it. Please tell me," I pleaded.

"Alright, he liked Ragini. They were friends together from School to College. He trusted her and wanted to marry her. It was the first time; he opened himself to Ragini about his childhood past. She supported him despite never understanding the sensitivity of the matter. What she did wrong was trust her brother by enclosing all the secrets of Samarth to him. He became powerless when Ragini's brother met him to show support. It was not a simple topic to discuss with others and Samarth requested and made her promise to keep it to herself. Eventually, she broke her promise," She stopped.

"You are right, Friends always keep secrets. Now, she felt guilty to lose her friend. I too feel responsible for compelling you to break your promise," I told her sadly.

"Don't worry about it. We will bury the matter forever, act as if you don't know," she convinced me.

"I will try. But still, I feel guilty for being rash toward our relationship, guilty for not understanding him, guilty for lying to him. While he supported my every request," I told her.

"Please don't be harsh on yourself. All you have to concentrate on is to love him dearly, and make him trust you; so he can tell his secrets all by himself. Please leave these guilty feelings from your heart," She advised me.

"Okay," I said it. When I first met him all he expected is 'I want my wife to understand me' and he never troubled me after we married. He is a genuine man I have ever met besides Uncle Rakesh and Mayank. Madhavi distracted me by asking about my school and college days, my best memories, etc. She knows how to comfort people. We talked until after her children came from the school exam. I left the house after meeting them. Mr. Ranjan was busy with his hotel work and I will meet him next time I visit here along with Samarth.

My thoughts were only about Samarth, he gave and gave everything to me. During dinner, Samarth caught the diversion occurring in my behavior. He asked what is bothering me.

I lied that I miss my parents. He convinced me that we will visit them again. That night, he never approached me for sex instead he talked about his feelings toward me and I am thankful he did that. I listened to him till I passed out.

The next day, he was romancing me before leaving for work. It felt good when you have a loving husband. I was feeling lonely after he left, and I decided to call Roohee over the phone. She informed me that her exam got over yesterday except for her sister as she still has two papers to complete. She told me that she will visit my house this afternoon.

I would have visited Mr. & Mrs. Kaushik if Roohee refused to meet me today. She looked depressed when she entered the house. I asked her about it while drinking tea. She said that she is worried about her sister, Fahima.

"I wanted to talk about her to you for the past month. I didn't dare to say it to you. First, I want you to be broad-minded about what I am going to tell you and promise me you will not tell anybody," She asked for my approval.

"I promise I won't tell anybody," I replied.

"I have never thought that I will tell you about my brother; though I have no one to talk to besides you. You might have heard gossip about him through other people. As a friend, I want you to listen to the exact truth. We three were studying in the same school, Mohsin was in the eleventh class and I was in the twelfth class while Fahima was in the tenth class. Fahima was closer to him than me and he too reciprocated the same, told her everything. There is one thing he never revealed to her about consuming drugs. His friends are not good as we have; his best friend gave him the addiction. His name is Ejaz Mirza and he too was taking drugs. My brother's fault was consuming and started selling to other students in his class. He got caught as one of his classmates informed his parents about it. His parents called the police to enquire about the school premises. The drug he sold to his classmates gave witnesses. That day was a bad day for Mohsin and all of us. The police came to our house to arrest Mohsin. It literally broke our Father's heart and we could not do anything about it. On the way to the Police station, Mohsin got panicked and got out of the jeep to run away. He grabbed Pistol from the Inspector to scare them. It was not in his intention to shoot it, though he did shoot two Officers while they tried to stop him. After that, he ran away and our name got spoiled due to him.

The Police officer tried to find him but could not do it. We too were worried about his whereabouts. It gave us a shock when my Father and I found out that Fahima was hiding him in the Cabin while Police suddenly checked our backyard. My Father took the blame for hiding him to save Fahima. Police took him again and this time my brother died. It is not intentional but the police had no choice but to stop him. They shot him in the shoulder and carried him to the hospital. He died due to excessive bleeding.

The Judge showed mercy and jailed my father for 10 days for defending a criminal. From that day onward, many people started avoiding us. Our Customer stopped buying from our showroom. And the worst is; two deceased police officers' wives and children came to our house to curse my father. Father kept quiet as it was his son's fault to make them widows and children orphans. Father could not bear it though he stayed strong for us. Still, he never talked to Fahima for 5 months. He blamed her for his death; in Jail, he would be alive. Fahima and Mohsin never understood the situation they put our father in. She blamed the officers for killing Mohsin and still believed in it. It was our fate to happen and we must accept it. It is not like we don't mourn Mohsin's death. We miss him every day and Fahima doesn't believe that either," I listened to her without interrupting.

She continued, "She got detached from us and rarely talk to our father. She even got annoyed when our father planned to sell the house and showroom and shift to Hyderabad the next year. Our father's sister is in Hyderabad and she suggested it as we won't find a Groom over here after detecting our past. I reluctantly agreed with him though Fahima is still in debate. She loved this house more than anything in the world. I agree with her as our memories with Mother are stuck in this place." Her tears were coming out continuously and I gave her the tissue to wipe them.

"I am sorry for your loss, dear," I showed condolences. She wiped her tears and blew her nose until she is ready to carry on.

"Now, she became so stubborn by dating a person who is the root of all the problems," she said.

"Who?" I questioned her.

"Ejaz Mirza, the boy who spoiled my brother by giving him drugs," she replied.

"How do you know it was him who gave drugs?" I inquired her.

"My friend's cousin brother who was in Mohsin's class told me everything and he was one of the witnesses. His name is Samuel Scott. He regrets giving Police information as it was Ejas Mirza's fault. He confronted Ejas after Mohsin's death. He pleaded with him that he doesn't want to sell drugs but to consume them. It was Mohsin who wanted to make money. He kept quiet as he doesn't want to ruin Ejas's life but told me everything about it when he found out that Fahima is dating him behind my back. I thanked the boy's concern over us," she explained.

"Did you tell her about Ejas' involvement in her brother's demise?" I asked her.

"No, I haven't told her but I stopped her from dating him. Even if I tell her, she won't trust me as she is blind to love. I don't know what to do," she blew her nose again.

"It is better to inform her than the situation go out of your hands," I told her.

"How? Will you help me?" she requested me.

"I will help you. Please wait for her exam to get over, then we will take the stand," I replied.

She carried on by telling it will break her father's heart if he knows about it. It is a complicated situation to tackle. After she left, I was planning to handle it smoothly for all of us. That night, I could not sleep while Samarth slept soundly. I waited for two days for the exam.

Before that, I called Roohee to execute the plan and she did what I said. On the last day of the exam, Fahima will surely meet Ejas. We shall confront him with the help of Samuel Scott. I think I heard this boy's name before, but I don't remember where? We talked over the phone to Samuel to accompany us on this topic; he is willing to support us.

Roohee and I went to the College campus to meet Samuel and it was crowded. When I saw him, it triggered me that I have met him at my Reception Day along with his parents. He is the grandson of Lincy Marie Scott as Samarth introduced him and he recognized me too. We talked for a few minutes to discuss the matter of how to proceed. He got cleared what I told him and went to hide from the spot we were standing.

Roohee and I waited for Fahima to meet Ejas and she did. We were ten yards away from them oblivious to see us. They met and were holding each other's hands and left the place to the College garden. We followed them as a spy and Samuel followed us. They were sitting on a metal garden Furniture chatting.

I gestured for Roohee to call out her name. Fahima and Ejas got up from the seat facing us. They both were shocked to see us. We went near them and Roohee said to Ejas to leave her sister or she will reveal the truth about him. Fahima was unwilling to listen to her sister; so she started yelling at her. I have never seen Roohee angry like that before. Roohee revealed everything to her and still didn't believe her. I advised Fahima that she is telling the truth; she was not willing to listen to me too. So, I turned towards Ejas, requesting him to tell her or Roohee will go to his Parents to tell them that he is consuming drugs and was responsible for Mohsin's death.

Ejas didn't say a word and I cannot see any regret on his face. So, I called out Samuel's name that was hiding behind the tree near us. Ejas became nervous after seeing him.

"Ejas. When I confronted you, you said it is not your fault for selling drugs and I understand that. But have you told Fahima that you are accountable for giving drugs to Mohsin that lead him to die like a criminal," he said in a threatening way.

Still, no word came out from Ejas, Samuel continued facing Fahima, "Fahima, did he tell you that he takes drugs?"

"No. He didn't; is it true, Ejas?" Fahima turned towards Ejas. Ejas kept quiet like the cat got his tongue.

"If you don't tell her then I will send the video of you and Mohsin taking drugs to the Police. Do you want me to do?" Samuel lied.

"What? Please don't. I will tell her the truth. Whatever he is saying is true, Fahima. I am the one who gave him drug addiction but I never thought that Mohsin will do such a thing. Please forgive me," he said sadly, with slight tears in his eyes. It is heartbreaking to see a boy cry like that, though I kept my composure the same.

"For the past month, you were hiding from me. How could you do that? My brother was the only person whom I can rely upon and because of your drugs, completely ruined his life and ours. I trusted you more than anyone else. I thought my brother did a terrible crime when he panicked but you are worse than him. You were aware of and influenced him to take drugs by destroying him. Don't talk to me again," Fahima was furious at him.

"Please don't do that. I really like you," Ejas was pleading to her.

"I can't meet you again. I am sorry. My brother trusted you, and treated you like a best friend and yet you got away from getting caught. I don't want to end up like my brother if I believe you again," she was clear and strong in her words. I can feel Fahima dying on the inside after knowing the truth.

"I am sorry. Please trust me. I should have told you," He started crying a lot this time.

"Please leave her, Ejas. I beg you. I don't want you to enter our life again," Roohee pleaded for the sake of her sister. This time he didn't say a word and cried profusely.

I thought it is best to advise him before leaving, "Look Ejas, I know you like her. I would suggest you leave her forever and concentrate on your future and please get rid of drugs as soon as possible or else nobody will help you, not even your Parents. Do you understand that?" I told him. He was still crying.

"As a sister, I advise you to keep your mind on your studies and make your parents proud. Do you want to break their hearts as Mohsin did?" I asked him.

"No," He said wiping the tears with his hands.

"Then you have to go your separate ways if you care for them and never meet her again. Is it clear?" I asked again.

"Okay, I will do as you all request me to do. I am sorry, Fahima. I will not meet you again," Finally, he said and left us strolling toward the road. I hope he doesn't keep a grudge against us.

After he left, Fahima started crying profusely. We calmed her down one by one. She apologized to her sister for not believing her, and me too. We took her to the college Cafeteria to relax her. Samuel bought tea for all of us. As I handed him the money, he refused to take it. He behaved like a mature boy and I appreciate it.

Chapter 18

PROCREATION

Samuel accompanied us to Roohee's house. We both left their house when Fahima became stable. While walking toward my house, Samuel said that he used to come to my house when he was a kid. His Grandmother Lincy Marie Scott is a best friend of Samarth's Grandmother Maanika Karthik used to visit her in this house along with him. Though Maanika Karthik has 12 years age difference from his Grandmother, she never behaved like an old lady and his Grandmother loved her character and companionship. She often tells him about her friendship with Maanika which is still in her memory. Now, she could not come here as she is getting sick in between as she is 74 years old.

I felt relaxed when he told me about his Grandmother's history. He even appreciated me for giving him the idea of a false video story to stop Ejas. I invited him inside the house to drink tea though he declined and will soon visit along with his Grandmother. Instead, he offered to me to get along with his Grandmother. I accepted his offer and will meet after a few weeks after Fahima's problem get over.

He left me at the gate spot and I went inside to prepare dinner. After half an hour, I called Roohee over the phone to check on Fahima. She said that she is calm now but still worried about her. I requested her to discuss this matter with my husband as he is a secret keeper. She accepted without arguing and I am glad about it. Before hanging up, she said that Samarth and Madhavi's family are the only ones who have not avoided them during their difficulty.

I don't understand what did she mean by that? So I asked her to elaborate. She said that after five days after her brother's funeral, Samarth visited their house again and told them that if they need any help, please don't hesitate to ask. He rarely talked to them but showed condolences. Samarth is a regular customer and still is buying clothes in their showroom. He picked his navy blue silk kurta suit for engagement from her father's showroom. This is the first time, she appreciated my husband and through her, I am fond of him more.

That night, I told Samarth everything that happened today. After I completed, he did complain to me to inform him before taking any decision as Ejas may turn out to be suicidal or may harm one of us out of vengeance. I consoled him that the topic is closed and ensured he will go his separate ways.

Samarth was still not convinced with me and made me promise to inform him in the future and I agreed with him. It is been a week since Fahima has not come out of her house. Roohee said that she is repenting for what she did for the past years. Yesterday, she asked forgiveness from her father for being rude and her father accepted and comforted her, though Roohee never reveals to her father the exact reason for her apologetic behavior and dated Ejas.

A week has turned into a month, and Fahima begin meeting me in the Garden. I am glad she is coping with her grief by playing outdoor sports with us. The warm weather over here is making me love the environment and I prayed it to stay the same and never change it. I know it is impossible to ask such things; it is better to enjoy before the Monsoon Season begins.

At the end of May month, Samarth planned to take me on the honeymoon next month and I happily accepted. He discussed going far away in North India especially cold places like Shimla, Darjeeling, etc. I declined his idea as we are already settled in a chilly place. I recommended going to warm places like Hyderabad, and Mumbai, or something to do on the beach. After a brief discussion, we planned on visiting Goa. I have never visited Goa in my life as my mother thinks it is an erotic place for youngsters and dismissed the idea while Samarth went with his friends including Raghav after College days as it is safe for all people and he loved to go again with me.

The date has set to go to Goa and it was the middle week of June 2019. Samarth never booked a train or flight ticket instead he planned to travel by car as he did with his friends and the experience was phenomenal. He suggested that it will take approximately 15 hours to reach there from here and he got a partner to drive. We will switch if we feel tired while driving or stop in a hotel for a few hours to rest on the way. I thought it is a good idea but there is one thing I am worried about the bathroom break. He also got the solution for that matter as we will take a tea break in between restaurants to use the bathroom.

At last, tomorrow at 6.30 am, we will leave from here to Goa. We informed Madhavi, My Parents, and our neighbors after we fixed the date. Samarth advised me to pack a few clothes in our baggage as it has so much to shop for over there, so literally, we both packed our tiny two suitcases. This time I planned on shopping a lot as I can carry easily by car.

I am both excited and anxious to go to a place I have never seen. Excited because I was eager to go and planned on it six years before but friends and family resigned to the idea. I am nervous because as it is a long trip and we traveling by car we may face some hurdles on the way driving on Highways is a dangerous feeling for me and he wants me to drive for a few hours. I have no idea what I will do.

I got up at 5.45 am and Samarth got up before me. I heard he is in the bathroom taking shower. It is June month and cold is lurking over here as if it is winter. We got ready before 6.20 am and Samarth was keeping the suitcase one by one inside the car. We locked and checked the doors and windows before leaving. He switched on the heater of the car after starting the engine, though he and I wore jackets to stay warm. After descending from the mountains, we both removed our jackets.

At 9 am, I was feeling hungry and I needed a bathroom break too. He parked our car near the vegetarian restaurant to eat to keep our stomachs free from vomiting. We bought snacks before leaving the placc. Aftcr thc brcakfast, I fccl likc throwing up but didn't. I informed him to park sideways if I feel like vomiting. He informed me to take it out a small brown cover from the snack bag. Inside the brown cover, there were a bunch of medical tablets to stop vomit, fever, etc, and a few lemons. He bought it after having breakfast and surprised me more now with his thoughtfulness.

I couldn't hold my thoughts about his perfection; It is better that I ask him.

"How could you be so spontaneously perfect in everything?" I asked him sensibly.

"What do you mean?" He questioned me. His expression formed V between his eyebrows which look good on his face.

"I mean I have never met any person who does not have flaws. It is like you are perfect in every work you do or did now," I was

"Why do you think I don't have flaws; everybody has flaws. If you ask me one example about my physical body, I have a very big nose which has become a joke in my college days," He said.

"Like what?" I questioned him.

"Well, one of my classmates made a Joke like, 'Where can you see a nose of two men together in one man's nose?' and many more."

I chuckled at his innocent comment about his nose, "I was not talking about your nose or other body parts of your face; besides your nose is absolutely fine for me. I don't know about others' views," I explained.

"So, why are you telling me I am perfect?" He asked me finally.

"How do you know I might feel sick on the way and bought these medicines for me?" I asked him.

"It just a guess you might need it and I have learned from Madhavi about these things and she learned it from our Grandmother. She used to pack medicines while we travel and it shows how much they cared for us. If you love a person, you should be kind toward them," he explained.

"You are right, dear," I said and watched him in between. His words were making me feel how much he cared for me. I feel like I want to kiss him now, make love to him. Now, it is not the right time to do it as he is driving fast. So, I waited to do things for him after we reach Goa. We reached Madikeri at 1.30 pm and there we had Lunch. It is my turn to drive from Madikeri after lunch. I became nervous but he encouraged me to have confidence and inform him if I doesn't want to drive.

He kept his eyes open after I drove 5 km from Madikeri. Later on, he closed his eyes when I gained enough faith. After a few hours, we reached Mangalore and I was exhausted from driving. I woke him up to take the driving seat. He told me to stop the car on the narrow edge of the road. He will be back after a few minutes as his bladder is full. I watched him go near the tree to take a leak. Sometimes, I feel disgusted as men pee wherever they want and never wash their hands. I took the water bottle from the back seat and got out of the car waiting for him to return.

He gestured while walking why I was outside the car. I showed him the water bottle. He washed his hands diligently. At 5.30 pm, we reached Udupi, Karnataka and there it was raining heavily. Samarth told me to check the weather on the way to Goa which is in the Western Ghats. I checked the weather app on my mobile and it shows huge rainfall on the way. He planned on making a stop in Udupi as it is risky to drive at night on unknown roads during rainfall. He took me to one of the five stars hotels to spend the night and the next day, we planned to leave at 6.30 am again. We checked in and took some rest in the room. He ordered food as we both were hungry. After dinner, I asked Samarth whether he is exhausted from the drive. He said that he is not at all tired. He laid down on the bed watching the news on T.V. and I planned on making love to him. He became nervous when I got out of the bathroom wearing only the revealing top on my body. I seduced him by kissing him passionately. He got excited and started removing his clothes. We slept soundly after making love.

In the morning, he reluctantly got up from the bed as he want to stay here more and I understood his feelings to mate here again. We left the hotel at 7.30 am from Udupi. At 2 pm, we checked into the hotel of Goa. There we had so much fun especially on the beach, riding a Jetski, Parasailing, etc. We celebrated my birthday on Yacht and it was a splendid one for me. I shopped and shopped till Samarth got tired of it. It is been a pleasant week for me in Goa and I never had enjoyed it in my entire life. I understand now why a Honeymoon is necessary.

After staying a whole week in Goa, we planned to return to Ooty. We never took a stop in between as the climate was warm and clear while we returned. We reached the house at 11.30 pm that night. The next day, I distributed the gifts I bought to all. Madhavi could see the glow in his brother's face and I noticed it as she is happy about it.

In the middle month of July, my period was late. I bought a Pregnancy test and it showed Positive. I informed Samarth about it, and I have not seen him too much excited. I suggested booking an appointment with the doctor to confirm it. The next day, we went to the hospital and the doctor said I am Pregnant. My due date is the first week of March 2020. I got relaxed as it is very good news for him and me. I advised Samarth to wait for a few weeks to inform Madhavi as it has passed only fifty days and he unwillingly agreed with me. On the sixty five days of Pregnancy, we informed everyone.

Madhavi and her family were so pleased with the news. My Parents were proud of it to have a Grandchild. Roohee and Fahima wanted to stitch clothes for me as I will be huge in a couple of months and I accepted it. Samarth started caring more and hovering wherever I go and even he tried to shift our room to his Grandparents so I must not climb the stairs. I got annoyed with his behavior and stopped him.

I told him I will be alright as Madhu, Roohee, and Fahima often visit me every day and Madhavi and Rashmika two or three times a week. Mr. Ranjan and his boys visit me every three or four times a month. I am glad about it. At the end of September, My Parents visited me for a week and suggested taking me home. Samarth never agreed with it as it has passed only four months. He is willing to send me when I am six months pregnant and I supported him.

When I look in the mirror, I see a lady with a fat belly. I still don't believe that I am six months pregnant. Samarth got busy with his work as the season started, though he reached home before 6 pm. He stocked the kitchen with food, fruits, etc once a week; so I should not feel hungry and he paid extra money to Madhu to cook for me.

It is the first week of December, and the Cold over here is growing day by day. I always request Madhu to start the Chimney fire after lunch as I cannot bear cold. I sat on the sofa chair next to the chimney with a book in my hand. I am reading one of Samarth's book collections, Robert Frost's poems. He has a good taste in books so does his Grandmother. When I read it, it depicts my personality and my experience over the years.

The cold is growing on me, like this place. In my city, there was only heat like my anger. I craved rain and a cool breeze always over there; though could not find it. Here, this town is only cold which is soothing my raging heart softly. I am searching the hot rays; my fury is diminished by Samarth's caring, loving, and deep emotion.

I understand now the poem by Robert Frost – Fire and Ice. The poem describes the fire as human desires and ice represents the hatred among people. However, I like to think as Samarth is Ice and I am the fire. Only he can perish the hatred of mine. The fire melts the ice though here I will melt by his love.

I slept on the sofa after reading it. Samarth came home at the usual time. I know he is always tired though he never shows it. I requested him to bring food as Madhu won't cook dinner tonight as she has personal work to do today and I accepted it. After dinner, I was watching TV and Samarth was taking a shower. I planned on watching a movie as I don't feel sleepy. I heard a loud noise while closing the bedroom door. It was Samarth who did it. He was walking down the stairs slowly. When I looked at him, he looked furious and was carrying my handbag. When he came near me, he showed me his right hand holding the gold bangles his Mother gave me.

He looked into my eyes asking for an explanation, "Where did you get this?"

"I.... I......," I have no words.

"It belongs to my Mother. My Grandmother gave it to her and it is her favorite. Did you meet her?" He asked me in a calm voice though his eyes are infuriated. I switched off the TV and got up from the sofa facing him.

"No. My mother gave me this," I lied.

"Don't lie to me; it has my Great-Grandfather's mark on it. He created this bangle for my Grandmother. So, tell me the truth," He asked again. I could not say anything as I was mortified by my lies.

"Why, Leena? Why did you meet them? You know I don't like them?" He asked again firmly.

"I am sorry for lying to you. I just want to know the truth you are hiding from me," My voice quavered.

"How did you meet them? Please tell me the truth," He intensely asked me.

"I compelled Madhavi to talk with them and met them in Pondicherry," I told him in a low voice.

"When did you meet them?" he asked.

"When you surprised me at my Parent's house; the day we first mated," I replied hesitatingly.

"So, you went to Pondicherry instead of Mahabalipuram. You lied to your parents?" he questioned.

"Yes," I shook my head up and down.

"Why?" he inquired.

"I don't want to make matters worse by telling my parents about your family. So, I planned on meeting them alone," I explained.

"What my parents told you?" his tone became from serene to loud.

"Everything," I felt like crying. He sat down on the sofa chair near the chimney fire covering his head with his both hands. I don't know how he will respond; I stayed strong for his reaction. I could not stand anymore carrying my belly; so, I sat on the sofa waiting. He didn't say a word; I know he is furious with me for lying and hiding the truth. I could not bear this silence from him.

"Samarth, Please talk to me," I am ready to handle his yelling at me than his stillness.

After a minute, he said, "It is hurting to know that you didn't trust me after what I have done to you. Didn't I give you what you asked for? I could have told you all of it if you have waited a few months. Why are you so eager and impulsive, Leena?" He annoyingly questioned me.

"I am sorry, Samarth. Please don't say I don't trust you," I begged him.

"You don't trust me or else you would have waited. I asked you one thing when we first met 'to understand me and I might take time to explain' but you didn't," he looked straight into my eyes which is making me cry. He was right all along, he didn't expect anything from me except Patience and Trust which I have not provided him completely.

"I am sorry if you think like that. I tried to understand you but I didn't. I don't want my husband to hide anything from me, and I can't sleep until I find what it is you are hiding from me," I explained.

"Now, you know about me. What do you think of me?" he questioned.

"You are a good person and I love you," This is the first time I said 'love' word to him.

"Really. Do you love me or is it a pity that you married me?" Anger was oozing out from his mouth and I could not hold back my tears.

"Why are you saying that? Please trust me," I pleaded.

"Tell me, Leena. Was it love or sympathy towards me when we first mated?" he questioned.

"It is love, dear. Believe me, it was not Pity sex," I explained.

"Why do I feel like you don't love me? You can tell me the truth, Leena," he asked again.

"I love you, Samarth. Please don't doubt my love for you," I told the truth.

"I am sorry, Leena. I just don't trust you and I am going out as I feel like suffocating over here," He took his jacket and Car keys and left me hanging there on the spot where I sat.

"Suffocating," I whispered. I can't imagine he said that word makes me feel angry about myself.

I cried and cried till I passed out on the sofa waiting for Samarth. As I got up from my nap, I saw the clock ticking at 10.15 pm. It is been more than an hour since he left and I planned on waiting for him in the living room till he return.

I heard the car noise approach, it was Samarth. He entered the room and saw me on the sofa. I can see his eyeball look red, his appearance drowsy. I bet he is drunk. He was about to fall but he managed to stand. I went near him to hold him but he stopped me from coming near.

"Why have you not slept?" he questioned me.

"I was waiting for you," I told him.

"You don't have to wait for me if you don't mean it," he said making me annoyed.

"I will wait for you and I mean it whether you trust me or not," I told the truth.

"Well, you will be disappointed to gain my trust as I hold a grudge for many years," he stared into my eyes.

"We can talk about that later. First, come to bed," I insisted.

"No, I won't come. I will sleep here on the sofa," He removed his shoes, and went to the sofa to sleep. I could not say anything as he is already sleeping soundly. I went to our room to sleep and waited the next day to come.

The next day, I woke up late at 8.30 am. I went downstairs to check on him; he was not there. I called his mobile, but he didn't pick up my call. So, I called Raghav about his whereabouts. He said that Samarth is in the cabin. Obviously, he went to the factory to work. Madhu came late, so I prepared breakfast for myself. Mother called me to remind me to stay in her house as I am six months pregnant. I said I refused to come as I am planning to stay and deliver the baby here. She tried to convince me but I decline. I know it is risky to take a hasty decision despite being Pregnant; However, I have to tackle the problem that aroused here between me and Samarth.

He came late that night and I sat at the dining table waiting to have dinner with him. He saw me, then went upstairs to change clothes without saying a word. I waited for him to return and he did with a blanket and a pillow. Is he gonna sleep on the sofa every day until I gain his trust? What is this stubbornness he is holding, for how long?

Moving away from my thoughts, I requested him to have dinner with me. He said he already ate and informed me that I don't have to hang on for him for dinner. I didn't say anything as he is still angry with me.

The next night, he informed me that my Parents called him to send me to their house so they can take care of me during delivery time. I informed him as I already refused to go. He became tense when I told him that I planned on staying here all alone. He never expected that I will take such a decision. He never argued about it though he asked Madhavi to stay with me the whole day every day. I refused that help as well as I want him to take care of me, not Madhavi. She comes two or three times a week which is enough. When I told her that Samarth has found out about the gold bangles her mother gave me, Madhavi became tense. I told her all that happened between us. After a few minutes, she gave me the courage that he will be fine once the baby comes. Even if he doesn't change his attitude, then she will take a stand against him for being rude to me. I smiled at her support for me.

Roohee became busy with her diploma course in design but she used to visit me and bring some dessert in the evening. She and Fahima gave me a few pregnancy clothes and I am pleased to wear them. Fahima concentrated on her studies most of the time. Mrs. Kaushik brought a pound cake and healthy food sometimes whenever she comes to see me. I pass the rest of the time reading and sleeping.

It is been a month since the incident happened and I am seven months pregnant. Samarth is still angry with me. I insisted many times to sleep with me, not on the sofa, but he refused. He took care of me in every way; though refused to talk and share the bed. One night, he returned home early. I told him to come near me to touch my belly as the baby started kicking. He was reluctant at first, but could not resist his child kick. I saw his face cheerful after so many days after he felt the baby kick.

Day by day, he comes near me to feel the baby kick and he somewhat loosens his irritation towards me. I hope for the day that he becomes himself again, the man I married.

In the last week of December, I could feel the pain has started growing in my back. I took out the muscle pain relief cream and tablets the doctor advised me to take if I have back pain. I tried to apply the cream to the exact spot the pain was occurring; my hands could not reach it. I called Samarth through mobile to come upstairs to apply the cream. He obeyed as I requested.

I wore only my nightgown as it shows all shapes of my body. I never minded as he already saw my body. He sat on the edge of the bed at my back and put his hands with cream on my back. His hands were gentle, just as they had been when he touched me the first time. The pain was coming out as he started massaging me and I felt relieved. I said thanks after the massage and he was about to leave me. I stopped him mid-way to stay with me as the delivery date is 9 weeks away and I don't want to sleep alone. I reminded him that the doctor told us to be careful starting the week of seven months as the baby may face complications.

He agreed and went downstairs to bring the blanket and a pillow back to the bedroom as he doesn't want Madhu or anybody to know that he is sleeping separately. He always brings back the blanket and a pillow after he wakes up.

I stretched myself and hugged him when he slept next to me. I asked him if it is ok to hug him for support instead of a pillow. He didn't mind rather he hugged me back.

From that night, he started sleeping with me and it felt good. After a few days, I was getting close to him, brushing and stroking his hair with my hand. He asked me suddenly one night in the bedroom.

"Do you think I am a bad person for being rude to you even when you are pregnant?"

"No, you are not a bad person. You are just angry with me and I know one day it will go away," I replied calmly.

"Do you think it is my fault for what happened to me?" he asked again.

I don't know how to respond, "It's not your fault. Whatever happened to you, it's not your fault. That man should be ashamed of what he did to you. Honestly, I don't know how you feel but I do know that you are a strong person to keep this behind your past and move on. I am glad you did it."

"Please tell me honestly, was it love or pity when we first mated," he repeated the question he asked me before.

"Honestly, I don't want to mate that night as I was feeling insecure cause I don't want my Parents to hear us moan; though I could not resist your touch. I gave up and withdrawn my rules for not mating at my parents' home. I was ready to mate before that day especially when I saw you dancing at Raghav's daughter's birthday party and you looked cute. However, it didn't happen and we fought that night. Do you remember?" I explained looking into his eyes.

"Yes, I remember," He replied.

"One thing I pity is your parents for losing you and Madhavi," I said stroking his hair.

"Do you love me?" He asked.

"Yes, I love you," I kissed him after saying those words. I can feel he is hard when I went near him. I started removing his shirt and my nightgown.

"Are you sure, do you want to mate?" He hesitatingly asked me.

"Yes, Just be gentle" I replied.

"Okay," he replied. It is been two months since we mated and after two weeks we can't make love as my baby becomes fully grown, and might come out anytime.

The next day it was Sunday, Samarth stayed quiet the whole morning. He spoke to me only when I needed anything, I think he still sticks to that topic. It is better if I begin a conversation with him.

"Are you still mad at me?" I asked him carefully.

"No," He replied.

"I feel like you are still angry with me?" I asked again. He came close sitting beside me.

"No, I am not mad at you. What I worry about is I don't want people to judge me and that I have abandoned my parents. However, it has happened quite the opposite to me and Madhavi. When I saw you, I thought you will comprehend and stand by me. It hurts me when you went behind my back. I am not saying you are wrong, you have the right to know. It's just that you have not given me space about sharing my deepest dark secret," he explained.

"I didn't mean to hurt you. I want to assure myself that I have taken the right decision to marry you. I don't want to get betrayed as it happened to my mother. That's it," I explained the exact problem with impulsive actions.

"What do you mean?" He was curious.

"My mother loved father dearly and blindly gave him everything. But he didn't respond the way she expected from him. He didn't give anything to her except me and he is not happy about it. He wanted a son, not a daughter. He behaved rashly, and irresponsibly with both my mother and me. I don't know what father love is except for my Uncle Rakesh who treated me like a daughter. Sometimes, I envy Abhi for having such a Great Father," he listened to my words silently.

"My curiosity began when I found that you have cut all ties with your Father and Mother while we are always clingy to them when we all were children. Now, my father talks to me many times since I got married. It felt good as we both miss each other. We both started regretting what we said awful things to each other. He never shows but he loves me and My Mother who is great," I said.

"I am pleased he came to his senses for evading you for many years," he replied.

"Yes, you are right. Even your parents," I replied.

"Please don't compare your father with my parents. Your father is ten times better than mine," he replied without a commotion.

"Why are you angry even when you love them," I asked him seriously.

"I don't love them. That I am sure about it," he replied.

“Really? Why then you have paid money for their bankruptcy?”I asked him.

“How do you know? Did Madhavi tell you that?” He questioned.

“Yes. Don’t you dare be mad with her too. If you want me to be loyal, then I am being loyal,” I said annoyingly. He kept calm when I threatened him.

“So, tell me why did you pay them?” I asked him.

“I want to help them as a charity,” he replied slowly.

“I am not dumb. You still love them. People hesitate to pay the coins Rupees as a charity. And yet you paid them Crores of Rupees without interest or anything in return. Isn’t it love for your parents or what?” I pressed him.

“The truth is I don’t want to see them homeless and the money belongs to my Grandparents, not mine. I helped my Grandparent's children, that’s it,” he got irritated for being pressurized.

“Why do you despise them so much? Why don’t you forgive them? Please be honest with me this time so I don’t have to ask others” I asked him calmly.

“Do you want to know why I hate them? It is because of my dead brother. I have forgiven them after what happened to me. They got back to their routine and I have not complained about it. When he got sick, it was difficult to see him calling Our Parents' names every day, expecting their nurture, expecting their touch, he became a lovesick child and he deserve that as he was just 7 years old. Madhavi and our Grandparents took care of him but still needed a mother’s touch, and a father’s love. Madhavi told them beforehand and Grandparents constantly called them to return from London. Though they didn’t, they were on the brink of opening a branch and thought it was more important than their children,” His eyes were glistening with tears and I stroked his back to calm him.

It is complex to see him cry and one thing I know is that there is a smooth heart behind his hard-hearted face.

He continued, “All he wants to do is laugh, play, and cuddle with us. When he got sick, he stopped doing all those things. What he needed is his parents around him. He missed them as if he is going to die. He did die. If you have seen his face, you would not advise me to forgive them. It was not Pneumonia that killed him, it was our Parent's abandonment,” I could not help myself to stop crying.

I don’t know how to cope with this matter, but it made me cry if you think about a child who is breathing the last breath of his life. I have not seen anybody die; though I know the feeling of losing our beloved ones. I better stop this topic from now onwards as I confirm that he will not reunite with his parents for a while.

“I am sorry, dear. It is hard to see you have to go through a lot when you were a kid. I promise you that I will not advise or ask you about your parents anymore until you are willing to forgive and rejoin them by yourself,” I replied.

“Thank you, dear. I am sorry for being rude to you. All we have to think about is bringing our child into this world safe and healthy. And you need to eat a lot of fiber food,” he became calm again.

“Okay,” I said. He wiped his tears and mine too. He kissed me and left me to cook lunch for us.

I have no glitch in saying that he is right. As the circumstance goes on which he will value them one day by recognizing the regret of their emptiness. It moves away from my thoughts, I have a New Year's Day celebration to do after the next two days. It is our first New Year's Day, I’ll better concentrate on that thing.

Chapter 19

At Last, the Meeting

It was February 24, 2020, the day I had labor pain, the day I had my baby on my arm. I had early labor as my due date was the first week of March. It was crucial to go through that pain and I never imagined that I will give birth to my son normally. I planned on taking C-section delivery, though God planned something else for me. I planned on not marrying anybody, and staying a spinster forever, though it happens according to God's will. Samarth made me relaxed as possible as he could during the entire process of giving birth. I am relieved to have him by my side.

My Parents stayed with me for a month before and after delivery. It irritated my mother as I was stubborn enough to give birth here in Ooty, not in her residence place; though she understood the situation as I have become a changed woman. I have a loving husband, my loving, caring irritating parents, supportive relatives, and friendly neighbors who have visited me in the hospital and now I have a beautiful son. They all were mesmerized by looking at the baby boy and I thought he is some kind of smooth baby toy lying in my arms. I assume I am content in my life now by seeing his innocent cute face. All that pain I have gone through delivery has vanished by looking at his face.

It is been ten days since I gave birth. My parents left us as they think I am all set to take care of my son. Samarth has planned on naming him Aayush, and we all loved it, especially me. We declined to have a naming ceremony as the World Population is facing this Corona Virus that is spreading rapidly.

In the Afternoon, the following third week of March, we all faced a brutal blow by being under lockdown from March 25. Tea Production activities have come to a halt for a few days. However, the Government said to continue to work as usual by taking precautionary measures for people around by providing safety equipment. Most of the workers stayed at their houses, and only a few were attending to the factory. Restarting the work at this time means nothing for a few people but others think it is like inviting risk to the Communities by spreading the virus.

Samarth did his best to gather workers to pluck leaves, run machines, distribute tea to agents, and maintained payment to working and non-working employees. Samarth has to go to work in between to check the production and took showers two times a day as we have a toddler to care for it. I advised Madhu to stop working and stay inside her house by promising to pay her regular salary from us. My parents, Madhavi's family, and I called in between to check on all of us. As per neighbors, we all called for the necessary help provided in the meantime.

Samarth counseled me to stay away from people especially our neighbors though he doesn't need to advise as people already want to have distance from each other. It is important to prioritize our close-knit family and become selfish to save our own lives. But I believe this is the time to check our humanity towards each other and to care for others in need.

Neighbors in our lane never got affected by it, though others were continuously dying especially old and young people, people with less immunity, etc. All we watch is the news on the television screen and I encouraged him to call his parents to know their well-being.

Samarth is having double thoughts about his parents and whether to call them or not. I pressured him many times to keep aside his ego, grudge, and whatever it is in his heart to start a new bond with them. He just kept quiet and concentrated on his son. I even gave an example what if our son never forgives us if we do something wrong unintentionally? He assured me that it won't come to that level of disappointment for our son as we will keep him happy, provide time and protect him from vile people.

It is hard for me to change his mind but one day at end of June month he got worried about his parents as our neighbor Mr. Kaushik was affected by the virus and died suddenly leaving his wife behind to survive. We were so petrified by this news and could not visit them as the ambulance surveillance people ordered us not to enter the house or touch anybody. Even Mrs. Kaushik is affected by the virus and admitted to the hospital to recover. All we could do is call their family to give them the news. It is depressing to see a genuine man die such a horrible death and we could not do or offer help to them.

I thought Samarth will be relentless forever against his parents but he took the courage to call them after returning to our house.

"Hi," he said.

"Hi, Mom. How are you? How is Dad?" he asked again. It was his Mother who took the call and I could not hear what she was saying.

He continued, "I am good here, Leena and Aayush are also fine. I am sorry for taking so long to call. Please forgive me. I never meant to hurt you .... Is it not the virus? Okay, Mom. Can I talk to Dad?

Dad, I am sorry. How is your health now? .... We all are fine here. Please don't go outside. Just stay inside .... Yeah, She is here. I'll put her on the line," he seriously handed me his mobile to talk to his father.

"Hi, Uncle. Is everything alright?" I asked him.

"Yes, dear. We are fine here. I just got a fever one week before and it is nothing serious," he replied.

"Oh, now you are fine, right?" I asked again.

"Yes, I am fine. My fever has gone two days before. How is my Grandson, Aayush?" he asked. Madhavi has surely informed them about our son as she told me that she contacts them two or three times a month after she got married which is a good thing.

"He is good; he is started sitting now at his baby desk as he completed 4 months," I replied.

"Can we see him through video call?" he requested.

"Of Course, Uncle," I said. I cut the line to video call him to show his Grandson who is sleeping now.

They both watched our son taking a nap and Aunt started crying to see him as he looked like Abhinav, their Late son. They congratulated me to give a beautiful Grandson and always remember this day. I cut the line after a few minutes. Samarth said nothing to them on video call after their brief conversation as he felt awkward reconciling. I don't judge him as I too feel like him if I were him.

However, it was a good feeling for us as I prayed for this day to come. Perhaps, I guessed it might happen one day for sure.

We both called each other in between to check and to have a conversation. Samarth never became talkative to them and kept his conversation small and short. It is enough as I don't want to stress him as he agreed to meet them once the Virus spreading is reduced or over.

Roohee and Fahima told me that they are postponing their shift to Hyderabad may be for a year. Their father Mr. Aasif khan could not risk of starting a new showroom as it will affect his financial asset in the future. So, he continued to stay here once he is ready to transfer. Roohee probably will learn a Practical diploma course in design after they relocate to Hyderabad. Fahima was busy completing her fifth semester by taking online classes and we talk six feet apart from each other in the garden. I took my baby outside to meet our neighbors. They were so desperate to hold him but could not as they wanted to maintain distance still afraid of the Virus spreading and I understand their behavior.

Mrs. Kaushik recovered from the fever and returned to her house though she regretted every day that she could not say a final goodbye to her husband. It is not her fault; circumstances had made her stay apart. One afternoon the following September she met us and Mr. Khan and his daughters before leaving to settle in Bangalore to live with her son. She gave us blessings and to keep in contact whenever we feel like calling her or else she will call us for sure. It is sweet of her to meet us and I appreciate she stayed strong after her husband's death. I met her son for the first time when he came to pick her up. We both said goodbye to her and it is hard to see her leaving us. This lane now has become from three to two families home. I have only one neighbor left that is Roohee and Fahima khan along with her father.

I will become lonely if they too leave me to settle in Hyderabad. I don't know how I cope with that moment after they leave. Madhavi's family and ours visited each other in between post the lockdown by taking precautions all the time.

In October, we planned on visiting Pondicherry with Samarth's Parents. I never thought that we and all my loved ones survived this Pandemic. All roads, railways, and other transportation facility curfews have been lifted except the entertaining part like movie theatres, Malls, etc. And it is enough.

Today is the day; Samarth, me, and my son are traveling by car to Pondicherry. It is safe to travel by car during these times. My son is eight months old and we have him given necessary vaccination before departing.

Samarth was calm as usual driving his car and my baby covered with sweaters and a red winter knit cap taking a nap in his special baby seat on the back. He looks adorable in his dress presented by Madhavi. I was watching the beautiful view on the way as it felt like you have not seen it for years.

Samarth looked at me in between and I looked at him back. I know he wants to say something, so I asked him instead, "What is it, dear?"

"What?" he replied.

"Do you want to talk about anything?" I asked him politely.

"Like what?" he asked.

"I feel like you have something in your mind. Please say it if it is bothering you," I replied. He looked at me for a few seconds.

"Leena, I have to make you clear that we will maintain distance from my parents even after I reconciled with them," He kept his eyes on the road.

"What do you mean?" I asked.

"We will stay there only for a few hours and we leave to stay at a hotel," he replied.

"Why? I thought we will stay there for a few days," I asked.

"I know. But I feel uncomfortable after many years of being apart from each other and I don't want us to become clingy toward them suddenly. I want slowly to take a step one by one towards them as I don't want to get disappointed again," he explained.

"No. You won't and they will never let down you again and I am sure about it," I advised him.

"I believe you. It's just that I still need space and I am not saying we won't go there the next day. It is awkward to spend the night, you know what I mean," he told me.

"I understand, dear. We will stay there for a few hours as you insist and it is enough for now," I agreed with him as he took the courage to come face to face.

"Thank you. So, it is a deal, right," he asked.

"Yes, deal," I smiled at him.

"Will you support me if they insist us stay there?" he asked.

"Yes. I will follow you wherever you lead me," I assured him.

"No. We will lead and follow each other as husband and wife," he reminded me.

"It's good you have said that or else I will smack you if you insisted to chase you all the time," I replied. He laughed when I said it.

"Well, I am not scared of your punch," he replied.

"Really," I slightly hit his left shoulder with my right fist.

"Ouch. It hurts," he teased me.

"Liar. I didn't hit you hard," I told him.

"I know dear. I am just kidding," he smiled at me.

We were having fun on our way, and our son didn't bother to wake up by the continuous talk we were having. He wakes up only when he is hungry or his diaper is wet. My heart is filled with abundant joy to have a life like this.

People used to Say, 'When love passes by your way, you must grab it and stick to it or else you are not smart enough when you don't recognize it.' I was cynical about it, and now I don't want my happiness to end but last forever.

I am not saying I will be a housewife for my entire life, though I could not leave my son behind for sake of my career. When he gets a year older, I am planning on selling organic food like Orange jams, Pomegranate, etc prepared by me or maybe winter clothes through an online portal in the name of my mother which is a great idea nowadays. I know Samarth won't object for being independent by doing business at home.

We reached Pondicherry at 5.30 pm and it was a 10 hours journey. We checked into the hotel with our suitcases. We rested that night after a long trip, especially for Samarth who needed it as he drove many miles.

The next day, we left early after breakfast to reach the house. He parked in the same spot as the driver did when I first came here to meet my in-laws. Samarth stayed inside and I waited for him to make the first move to get out of the car but he didn't. He took a long sigh and my son is cooing and giggling when I looked at him playfully.

At last, he got out of the car and I followed him with our baby in my arms. He opened the front gate slowly; looking at the house he has been to when he was a kid. I stood next to him near the Large Main door.

He asked me, "Please stay with me by my side and guide me when I am wrong. We will stay here for a few hours. Okay."

"Of course, dear," I replied with a smile.

He took a deep sigh, "Here we go," he pressed the doorbell.

And we waited for them to open the door.

Characters

Leena Kumar is a 28 years old Female Protagonist who lives in Chennai and is the Wife of Samarth Karthik, Daughter of Harini Kumar and Rajesh Kumar. She is impulsive, and cynical about Marriage; she is protective and caring towards her loved ones. She is a justifiable woman.

Samarth Karthik is a 32 years old Male Protagonist who owns a Tea Factory in Ooty, Husband of Leena Kumar, brother of Madhavi Rao, and Brother-in-law of Ranjan Rao. He is a quiet man, who understands and motivates others, especially his loved ones.

Madhavi Rao is the wife of Ranjan Rao, Sister of Samarth Karthik, and Mother of Rashmika, Siddharth, and Vinay. She is calm and selfless in nature; she is worried about her brother more than herself.

Ranjan Rao is the husband of Madhavi Rao, Brother-in-law of Samarth Karthik, and Father of Rashmika, Siddharth, and Vinay. He is a free-spirited man. He is one to think about Leena as the perfect match for his brother-in-law Samarth.

Harini Kumar is the mother of Leena Kumar, Wife of Rajesh Kumar. She is a loving, Optimistic and dedicated mother who is after her daughter to get married.

Rajesh Kumar is the father of Leena Kumar, Husband of Harini Kumar. He is sarcastic, selfish, and rude to others and his family, especially his wife and daughter.

Rashmika Rao is a 16-year-old daughter of Madhavi Rao and Ranjan Rao, the elder sister of Siddharth and Vinay Rao. She is a humble, quick thinker, and sweet girl who idolizes Leena's fashion sense.

Siddharth Rao is a 9 years old son of Madhavi Rao and Ranjan Rao, younger brother of Rashmika and elder brother of Vinay. He is a free-spirited boy like his father and speaks little in front of guests.

Vinay Rao is a 7-year-old son of Madhavi Rao and Ranjan Rao, the Younger brother of Rashmika and Siddharth. He is a naughty, chatty boy.

Rakesh Kumar is a paternal Uncle of Leena Kumar, elder brother of Rajesh Kumar, Father of Abhi Kumar Sanu, and Aakash Kumar, a friend of Ranjan Rao. He is a calm, clever man and acts as a father figure for Leena Kumar.

Tejaswini Kumar is a wife of Rakesh Kumar, Mother of Abhi Kumar Sanu and Aaakash Kumar. She is selfish and furious with Leena, her father, and her mother always.

Abhi Kumar Sanu is a 26-year-old cousin of Leena Kumar, Daughter of Rakesh and Tejaswini Kumar, Married to Mr. Sanu. She is a sweet and clever woman who Leena adores always.

Aakash Kumar is a 19 years old cousin of Leena Kumar, Son of Rakesh and Tejaswini Kumar. He is uncaring around people and spends his time with friends.

Fahima Khan is a 19 years old neighbor and friend of Leena Kumar, the Younger sister of Roohee Khan. She believes in love and is passionate about falling into it.

Roohee Khan is a 21 years old neighbor and friend of Leena Kumar, Elder sister of Fahima Khan. She is calm and independent and passionate to become a Fashion designer with her talent.

Aasif Khan is the father of Roohee, Fahima, and Mohsin Khan, a Neighbor of Samarth Karthik and Leena Kumar. He is a hard-working, emotional, and selfless father toward his daughters.

Ejas Mirza is the love interest of Fahima Khan, a Friend of the Late Mohsin Khan. He is an irresponsible person that caused the tragedy in Mr. Aasif khan's family.

Lincy Marie Scott is a 74-year-old woman, Best friend of the deceased Maanika Karthik.

Samuel Scott is a 20-year-old boy, the Grandson of Lincy Marie Scott. He is a school Classmate of Mohsin khan, studying in the same college as Roohee and Fahima.

Ragini Desai is a school and college friend of Samarth Karthik. She is a beautiful, smart, and caring person who befriends Leena Kumar.

Suresh Desai is the husband of Ragini Desai. He is a sociable person who likes to talk about his business.

Bhavana Karthik is the mother of Samarth Karthik, Madhavi Rao, and Abhinav Karthik, wife of Sundar Karthik. She is ambitious like her husband and wants to live a luxurious life.

Sundar Karthik is the Father of Samarth Karthik, Madhavi Rao, and Abhinav Karthik, Husband of Bhavana Karthik. He is ambitious, hard-working, and practical.

Mr. Raghav is the manager and friend of Samarth working in the tea factory, both are school and college buddies. He acts as a strong adviser to Samarth Business and works as a Manager.

Mayank is a school friend of Leena Kumar. He is broad-minded and has a pleasing Personality. He teases his friends all the time.

Abhinav Karthik is the deceased Younger brother of Samarth Karthik and Madhavi Rao.

Vijay Karthik is the deceased Paternal grandfather of Samarth Karthik and Madhavi Rao

Maanika Karthik is the deceased paternal grandmother of Samarth Karthik and Madhavi Rao.

Mohsin Khan is the deceased brother of Roohee and Fahima Khan, Son of Aasif Khan.

www.ingramcontent.com/pod-product-compliance
Lightning Source LLC
LaVergne TN
LVHW041019150826
845672LV00001B/141

* 9 7 9 8 8 9 0 2 6 4 3 5 0 *